unexpectedly YOURS

from *USA Today* bestselling author

REBECCA SHEA

unexpectedly
YOURS

from *USA Today* bestselling author
REBECCA SHEA

COPYRIGHT

Cover design by: Letitia Hasser, RBA Designs
Edited by: Megan Hand - Story Girl Editing and
Beth Lynne - Hercules Editing

ONE

Gracie

My eyes snap open when I feel the soft puffs of warm air against the back of my neck. That same warm air causes a shiver to roll through me just before shame sets in. I curl into myself as the guilt of last night's events flash through my memory, when a hand suddenly palms the curve of my hip, trapping me in this bed. I'm spooning a stranger. Technically, a stranger is spooning me. A handsome stranger as I recall, one I willingly had sex with last night, but a stranger nonetheless.

Drew.

He said his name was Drew.

I can feel his bare legs curving into the back of my knees, and his hard as hell washboard abs pressing against my back. But it's his rock hard— "Jesus," I hiss when my phone buzzes on the nightstand, startling me. It's the buzzing phone that steals my attention from his long, thick member pressed against my bottom. I reach for the phone carefully, pulling away from all the body parts this man has pressed against me. The phone continues to buzz as I strain for it, and my heart rate kicks into high gear when Drew shifts behind me, pulling me even tighter to him.

Please don't wake up. Please don't wake up...

My fingers nudge the phone to the edge of the nightstand where I can finally get my full hand around it and pull it to me. Pressing my thumb against the home button, I launch the phone to life and instantly notice the crazy amount of text messages I've missed, all of them—except for one—from Jamie. My best friend and co-worker who got me into the shenanigans that led me here...in Drew's bed, at a swanky Midtown Manhattan hotel. I should be home in my shitty Brooklyn apartment.

1:07am: Jamie – *Don't do anything I wouldn't do... which means DO IT. He's hot and I'm 99% sure he's not a serial killer.*

1:15am: Jamie – *Use protection though. I'm not worried that he's going to kill you, but I am worried he might give you herpes...or a kid.*

1:23am: Jamie – *I also want details tomorrow. Specific. Details. Comprende?*

5:30am: Jamie – *You didn't text me that you made it home. Are you alive?*

5:31am: Jamie – *Gracie. Answer me.*

5:32 am: Jamie – *Oh, god. He killed you.*

5:33am: Jamie – *There better be a good reason you're not answering me. Are you having morning sex?*

5:35am: Jamie – *Gracie. This is bad, isn't it? TEXT ME BACK.*

6:23am: Jamie – *Shit. Marisol just called. Urgent work meeting at 8:30. Text me ASAP.*

7:01am: Mom – *Happy birthday to my best girl. I hope you had a wonderful night with Jamie. I'm so*

thankful you have such a great friend. I miss you and love you dearly.

I glance at the clock, 7:03am. Guilt continues to roll through me thinking of my mom texting me birthday wishes while I lie with a naked, albeit hot-as-fuck stranger wrapped around me. Happy birthday to me. I pinch my eyes closed, trying to remember last night's events in specific detail. One drink. Then two. Then a shot. Then another drink. Laughing, a whole ton of flirting, and then sex. A lot of sex.

I type out a quick text to Jamie: *I'm alive. Just woke up. I'll be at the office in 45 minutes.*

Glancing at the alarm clock on the nightstand, I do my best to wiggle out of Drew's grasp. His breathing is heavy, telling me he's sound asleep, and I'm thankful for that. My toes dig into the plush carpet as I gently slide out of the bed and hustle across the room to the bathroom, picking up my undergarments and purse as I go. Quietly sliding the large pocket door closed, I make quick work of my hair, wrapping the long, dark tresses into a bun on top of my head. I step into the shower and take the fastest one I've ever taken in hopes I can wash away any hints of sweat, sex, cologne, and booze still lingering on me.

Patting myself dry, I wrap a large towel around myself and spot Drew's toothbrush and toothpaste on the counter. My hands shake as I hesitate for half a second before squeezing a generous string of toothpaste onto the bristles and scrub my teeth clean.

This is a new low for me, using the toothbrush of my one-night stand.

Silently, I praise myself for keeping some make-up samples in my oversized purse. Brushing my cheeks with blush and my eyelashes with a heavy coat of mascara, I finish with a quick dab of red lipstick and give myself an approving smile in the mirror. I can't believe I've almost pulled off a look that doesn't give the appearance that I just crawled out of a stranger's hotel bed in Manhattan.

Sliding into my panties and fastening my bra, I leave the towel in a pile on the bathroom floor. I wiggle into the same black pencil skirt I wore yesterday and glance at the red silk blouse sitting wrinkled on the floor, a reminder of last night's adventures. I can't help but sigh. How the hell am I going to pull off wearing the exact same outfit I wore to the office yesterday? Then, out of the corner of my eye, I see a crisp white dress shirt hanging on the back of the bathroom door still in the thin plastic bag, which tells me it was recently laundered and pressed.

I rip the bag from the shirt and wince at the noise the plastic makes. Sliding the starched fabric off the hanger, I pull it over my arms and button the oversized shirt, tucking the long length into my black skirt. I roll the sleeves carefully and decide to leave the top three buttons undone, giving the appearance the shirt is supposed to be wide-collared and feminine. I smile at myself in the mirror, not believing I was able to pull this off.

Sliding the bathroom door open, I pause, taking in the sight of Drew, last name unknown, sleeping peacefully with a white sheet twisted around his waist. His tan skin and dark hair are a stark contrast to the white sheet, comforter, and pillows he's encased in. My heart races and I'm relieved he's still sleeping. I've never had a one-night stand before, and I'm not prepared to have an awkward morning-after conversation. What do people say anyway? *Thanks for last night? See ya around?* No thanks.

This morning will just be me high-tailing my embarrassed ass out of this hotel room, thankful I'll never have to see him again.

I tiptoe quietly across the room to the door, twisting the handle slowly to avoid any sounds or chance of waking the hunk of a man in the bed. Swallowing back my regret, I remember our deal: "One night, no strings attached." I remember that sexy smirk of his when I said that. With one last glance over my shoulder, I take in the sight of the sexiest mistake I've ever made.

TWO

Gracie

It's just after eight in the morning when I slide into my office chair and power up my computer. I kick off my black heels and open my desk drawer, pulling out a pair of nude heels, and slip into those. I've never been more grateful that I always keep spare accessories and shoes at work for last-minute client meetings or after-work drinks. It's amazing what a change of jewelry and shoes can do to change up an outfit.

It's hard not to notice Jamie coming down the hall, with her oversized Louis Vuitton bag hanging from her shoulder while she balances a cup of coffee in each hand, a giant smirk on her face.

I ignore her and punch my password into my computer, launching the home screen. I know Jamie is about to grill me on the details of last night, and I groan inwardly, just wanting to forget last evening's indiscretion. I click on the envelope icon and my email springs to life, filling my inbox with unread emails. A cardboard cup suddenly appears in front of my face just as Jamie drops her designer bag to the floor and slides her butt across my desk, crossing her legs. She rolls her perfectly manicured fingernails on my desk but doesn't say anything. She doesn't need to. Her face says it all. It screams, "Tell me every last detail and don't leave anything out."

I pretend to ignore her and the dangling cup of coffee, but there is no ignoring Jamie McQuiston. She's over the top, in your face, and a presence that takes up all of a room. She's personable, beautiful, a force that cannot be ignored. Plus, that coffee smells delicious.

I swivel in my desk chair and sit back, my shoulders slouching. She pushes the cup of coffee toward me and I take it.

"Details. All of them. The Cliff Notes version. We have to be in the conference room in twenty minutes." She looks at the watch on her wrist, that I guarantee cost more than my entire college education, before scanning the nearby desks around us. Our nosy co-workers would get off on the gossip of last night's escapades, especially because it is one-hundred percent not like me to do what I did. I don't do casual. I don't do one-night stands with strangers in hotel rooms, or even shitty New York apartments. I do relationships. At least, that was what I did until last night. She whispers, "Tell me everything."

Blushing, I take a sip of my coffee, cradling the cup in both hands before I look up at her. What do I tell her, the truth? He rocked my world. He was kind and considerate and the ultimate gentleman. A man I could see myself falling in love with. I swallow down the emotion I feel rising from the pit of my belly, and I hesitate, choosing my words carefully. "He was nice."

"Nice?" she whisper-yells.

I shrug. "Yes. Nice. He was a gentleman."

She rolls her eyes and lets out an exaggerated sigh. "I don't want nice. I want wild. I want raucous. Did he twist his fists in your hair and spank you—"

"Jamie!" I look around the office to see if anyone is listening and hold up a hand to stop her right there.

"Tell me you at least—"

"Yes," I shush her. "We did. It was great—"

"And much needed. You look like a new woman." She rawrs at me and giggles.

I roll my eyes at her. "Yes, it was needed; he fulfilled a need." He actually broke an eighteen-month dry spell, thank the good Lord. "He scratched an itch, and I'll never see him again. Thank God," I mumble under my breath, not sure if it's relief or guilt I'm feeling.

Jamie smiles widely. "Was it worth it? I mean, I know you were hesitant..."

Was it? I've asked myself the same question over and over this morning.

"I don't know," I answer honestly, turning back to my keyboard. Part of me is proud I let go of my inhibitions, and another part of me is ashamed I was so careless to go home with a stranger.

"Don't beat yourself up, Gracie," Jamie says, sliding off my desk. She knows exactly where my mind is. "You deserve to let loose and have a little fun." She picks up her purse and takes a drink of her coffee. "You're the most serious person I know—"

"Because I have to be," I interject, reminding her of my reality.

She smiles compassionately, my pathetic life a total conversation downer. "I know. But it's also okay to have some fun once in a while. You're the best person I know, and if enjoying a romp in the sheets with the hottest guy I've ever seen is the worst thing you do, consider yourself Mother Teresa."

I close my eyes and choke down the sudden lump growing in my throat. Guilt hits me like a brick wall and shame fills me. For one night, it was nice to forget my money problems or the fact that I can't get a guy to even go on a date with me. Every man wants something I'll never be: pussy he can hit when it's convenient for him, a cover model, or a wealthy Hampton's girl like Jamie that they can marry and proudly display as arm candy. None of those are me.

I nod my head, unable to speak.

Jamie pauses, seeing my mood shift. "Don't beat yourself up," she nudges me with her shoulder, "but fix your hair. That bun isn't working." She winks at me, trying to lighten the suddenly somber mood before she saunters away, giving me time to collect my thoughts.

"You clean up good, kid," Jamie says, sliding into the chair next to me. I'm sitting along the long side of the giant conference room table, and I have my notebook, pen, and coffee placed right in front of me. Everything perfectly in its place. It's how I operate. I'm timely, efficient, and the most Type A person you'll find east of the Mississippi. Everything has a place and a purpose. Routine is what keeps me sane. I run my hands over my dark hair, which I untangled from its bun fifteen minutes ago in the bathroom. It now hangs in long, perfect waves just past my shoulders. I also touched up my makeup and suddenly felt more put together.

"Thanks." I roll my eyes at her and she lets out a little laugh.

She hands me a small box and I look at her funny. "You didn't think I'd forget your birthday, did you, bestie?" I thought that that was what we were celebrating last night, but obviously, that wasn't enough. A couple of other co-workers filter into the room, and having overheard Jamie, offer up their own birthday wishes, so I thank them. I open the box to find a pair of gold filigree hoop earrings and a matching bracelet. Classic and beautiful.

"Thank you," I tell her, choking back another growing lump in my throat. I can't remember the last time I got a birthday gift.

The best my mom could do for me was a homemade vanilla cake, and that stopped when I turned ten. "It's beautiful."

Jamie reaches over and squeezes my hand when she sees me get emotional.

A man clears his throat behind me, and suddenly, the room falls silent. Jamie's eyes grow wide like she's seen a ghost, and she turns away from me, folding her hands in her lap. Just as I'm about to turn around, a familiar voice cuts through the silence.

"What do we have here?" A hand reaches over my shoulder and picks up the box. I'd recognize those long, perfectly manicured masculine fingers anywhere—because they've been everywhere—on me, in me, holding me.

Drew.

My heartrate spikes and I can feel my entire face burn with embarrassment, or maybe lust, or perhaps a combination of both. Whatever it is, I can feel that burn crawl from my face to my chest, and suddenly, my lungs constrict. What in the hell is he doing here?

He's bent over my shoulder, holding the box Jamie gave me, his hot breath hitting my ear as he whispers, "Nice shirt."

I sit up taller as I remember that I'm wearing the shirt I stole from his bathroom this morning. "It's Gracie's birthday," Jeff from accounting says from across the table as Drew stands back up, the box still in his hand.

"Gracie." Drew says my name like it's the first time he's ever heard it.

"Grace." Slowly, I turn in my chair to face him. "You can call me Grace. Only my friends call me Gracie." I do my best to still my voice and calm my racing heart. What in the actual hell is he doing here?

Our eyes meet. His smoldering blue to my green hazel. Eyes I spent all of last night peering into. Eyes that have seen every part of me. I shake the thought away and notice the vein in his neck pulse before he swallows and his head tilts ever so slightly. His eyes narrow and his lips tighten in what looks like a mischievous smile that he's trying to hold back. I'm thankful I'm sitting down, because my entire body is shaking from the intensity of his smoldering stare.

"Grace," he corrects, reaching out to shake my hand as if he's meeting me for the first time. Clearly, a show for the audience in the room. "Happy birthday." He holds out the box and I take it back from him as I spin around in my chair, away from him, and face the conference room table. My stomach churns violently. I want to barf. I chance a glance at Jamie, who meets my gaze and shrugs at the unasked question she sees in my eyes. *What is Drew doing here?*

"Breathe," Jamie hisses quietly, reaching out and placing her hand over my shaking forearm. She squeezes it gently and I try to pull large breaths deep down into my lungs. The room is bustling as the rest of the agency's employees filter in. Hushed conversations and small bouts of laughter fill the space as everyone settles into the remaining chairs around the conference room table. I focus on Jamie's hand on my arm and continue to breathe steadily.

"Everyone!" Mr. Williams—the owner of Williams Global Advertising, the company I work for—announces as he comes bounding into the room, holding a small stack of papers. "I want you to meet Andrew McPherson, owner and CEO of AM Advertising who, as of this morning, procured Williams Global Advertising."

Drew moves from behind me and walks over to the head of the table where the now former owner of our advertising agency, Kevin Williams, stands, a sad look in his eyes.

"Holy shit," Jamie mumbles next to me. "Mr. McPherson purchased Williams Global. . ."

I don't even hear what Mr. Williams says after that. All I

know is that Drew—Andrew McPherson—is the man I slept with last night…and the man I slept with last night is now my new boss.

I stab my salad aggressively with the metal fork before I shake the lettuce I just stabbed off of my fork and back into the bowl. "Why don't places that serve salads cut the lettuce up into smaller, bite-sized pieces? It's annoying," I question before finally shoving the bowl aside. I don't have an appetite anyway, let alone the desire to try to shove giant pieces of lettuce into my mouth.

Jamie takes a bite of her sandwich and sits back in her chair, dabbing the corners of her lips with a napkin before she speaks. "Because bigger pieces of lettuce make the bowl look fuller. That's how they cheap out on their salads."

I don't know why, but I laugh. A loud belly laugh.

"It's why I eat sandwiches. More bang for my buck." She smiles and winks at me. How she can eat a sandwich and not mess up her lipstick is a damn mystery and a beauty trick she needs to trademark. Also, the fact she can eat bread and not gain an ounce of weight is almost as annoying as the big lettuce chunks in my salad. She's tall and lean, and I'm tall and curvy, a size ten to her four. She's got boobs and I have hips. She's blonde and I'm brunette. We're polar opposites on almost every possible level, but she's my person and I'm so thankful for her.

After the meeting this morning, I all but ran from the conference room to my desk, where I thankfully had a deluge of voicemails and emails waiting for me to return. News spread fast in the advertising world about the sale of the East Coast's smallest, but most premier, advertising and marketing firm to the West Coast's largest and most premier firm. It was a sale that was kept so quiet, no one in the industry knew it was happening, and everyone is still reeling with the news.

"So Jeff said after lunch we're having another meeting where Mr. McPherson is going to share the go-forward organizational structure. Guess we'll find out if we still have jobs then," Jamie says, tossing her napkin on her empty plate.

The thought of losing my job makes me nauseous. I pinch my eyes closed. I cannot lose my job. My mom depends on the small amount I'm able to send her each month.

Jaime senses my mood and reaches across the table and squeezes my shaking hand. "Hey, don't stress. If anything happens, we'll land on our feet at another agency. People salivate over Williams Global employees."

She's right. Mr. Williams runs—or, ran—a top-notch, professional, and highly-profitable advertising agency. He built this agency from scratch and employs only the best. He pays us decently, treats us well, and the clients we bring in are a direct result of his employees and his no-nonsense approach of not having the biggest agency in New York City, but the best.

It's just the stress of knowing one missed paycheck could utterly destroy me. Student loans, credit card debt, and the cost of living in New York City, even in a small, shitty, gross Brooklyn apartment takes every last cent I earn. And the guilt of not being able to help my mom brings tears to my eyes.

"We're going to be fine," Jamie reassures me, and I try to calm my inner hysteria. "We have to get back. Meeting starts in fifteen minutes." She pushes herself up from the small metal table of the café that Jamie eats at nearly every day. I join her when I have an extra few dollars, which isn't that often.

"Thank you for my birthday lunch." I look down at the uneaten salad and feel guilty I didn't eat it. I'm not really in the position to turn down meals, but I'm so anxious from Drew's appearance this morning, the thought of food in my belly makes me want to vomit.

"You're welcome." Jamie reaches out and laces her arm through mine as we walk down the crowded Manhattan street and back toward our office.

THREE

Drew

I rub the heels of my palms over my eyes, trying to shove back the headache I can feel coming on. Forty-eight hours ago, Kevin Williams asked me to buy his company, Williams Global Advertising. He had recently been diagnosed with terminal cancer, a diagnosis no one knows about except for me and our team of lawyers, and the call to purchase his company came at a bittersweet price.

Mr. Williams wanted someone with integrity and a good reputation to take over his company, while allowing his wife to be financially stable after his passing. His request was unmistakably hard, but a sense of peace in his tone made the decision easy. He was asking me for a favor, a favor I could help him with. My father worked for Kevin Williams twenty or more years ago, and Mr. Williams taught him everything he needed to know about marketing, advertising, and public relations, which he then passed down to me. To say Mr. Williams has been a trailblazer in this industry would be an understatement.

Williams Global and AM Advertising have always been friendly competitors, but I was honored that, of all the qualified people in this business, he asked me to purchase his agency...his legacy. I've been wanting to expand to the East Coast and this was the perfect opportunity to purchase a company that is not only profitable, but is also a perfect fit culturally with AM Advertising. He's basically handing me millions of dollars in profitable clients and one of the strongest employee bases in the industry.

Within twenty-four hours of that phone call, our lawyers had worked up the purchase agreement and the funds were wired. Twelve hours later, I was on a cross-country flight headed to New York. The next few hours were a blur of quiet celebration, meetings, and subsequently bedding the most beautiful girl I've ever met. Grace.

Tall and curvy, with hazel eyes that are more green than brown, and a smile that literally made my knees weak. It's rare that I pick up women in a bar. Hell, it's rare I pick up women at all, but something about her called to me. I needed her, and somehow, I felt like she needed me as well. Two consenting adults who needed to get lost in each other for one night. That was the deal, until I saw her this morning.

Now I want more. Need more.

It was supposed to be one night where I freed myself of the expectations I consistently put on myself. The long hours, the pressure to keep my business successful, a leader in the industry, while keeping my reputation squeaky clean. She wasn't the typical "bar bitch" trying to get in my wallet through my pants. The only thing she asked of me was my first name. Not what my career was, not where I was from, or what my parents' names were. She wasn't trying to forge a connection through one of those as a means to my money, and *that* I fucking appreciated more than anything. She's honest and humble and...gorgeous to boot.

Over a few drinks, we exchanged first names and that was it.

The conversation was just like her. Simple. Casual. Beautiful. I didn't expect her to be gone when I woke this morning, and I sure as hell didn't expect her to work for Williams Global. The look on her face when she saw me this morning was a cross between shock and utter disbelief. I'll never forget the way her lips fell apart like she was going to say something, but the words were caught in her throat.

I didn't miss her dig at me about her name. Gracie. Only her friends call her Gracie. She wants me to call her Grace, because that would mean our relationship is strictly professional. Only *Gracie* doesn't realize we'll never be professional because I've seen every part of her. I've seen her fall apart in my arms and underneath me. I've felt every inch of her—and now I want more. I've felt every inch of her, every fucking soft curve, every hard peak, and I want it all over again.

I run a hand through my hair and stand, yanking up the laptop with the presentation I've prepared from my desk, and carry it to the conference room. Meeting number two for the day. I hope this eases the fears I saw splayed across the faces of the Williams Global employees this morning, as I lay out the direction for our new combined company.

The conference room is unnervingly quiet and the tension in the air is palpable. Everyone sits quietly, and hushed conversations suddenly stop when they notice I've entered the room. Grace sits in the same chair she was in this morning, her fingers laced tightly, all balled up in her lap. She won't make eye contact with me, and something about that makes me smile. She's affected by me. Something about that excites me and also calms me; however, the other faces around the conference room table display anxiety and stress. I should have gone over the details with the staff this morning, but I wanted to be one-hundred percent prepared and have a game plan that made sense. My company is nothing if my people aren't happy.

"Good afternoon," I say, clearing my throat and unbuttoning my suit jacket. I shrug it off and roll up the sleeves of my black dress shirt. The same shirt I wore yesterday because Gracie stole the one I intended to wear today, and she looks hot as fuck in it.

She pulled it off, I'll give her that. The buttons she left undone at the top tease me as I barely make out the tops of her round, full breasts. Pulling my attention away from *Gracie*, I launch the PowerPoint presentation that projects brightly onto the large screen just off to my side.

"I first want to apologize for not going over all of the details with you this morning. I know the news of this acquisition came as a surprise to all of you, and that's not normally how I operate." I wiggle my necktie, loosening it. "Honestly, it was just as much of a surprise to me."

Mr. Williams sits in the back of the conference room, not at the table, but in a chair behind everyone. He looks grateful, yet somber. I can't imagine what he's feeling right now, and my gut twists when I think about why I'm here. "First, I want you to know how honored I am to be acquiring Williams Global. The vision and values of Williams Global align perfectly with AM Advertising, and I just know we're going to be the leading force in advertising, marketing, and public relations both coast-to-coast and internationally.

"Second, there will be no displacements." You can actually hear the sighs of relief when I say that. "There is a place for everyone in this acquisition. The work isn't going anywhere and we won't be doing any consolidating. In fact, I presume we'll end up needing to hire additional personnel. Typically, when two great companies come together, we see an uptick in client acquisition."

I do my best to not focus my attention on Gracie. She sits straight and tall, her hands still locked together. Her long, dark hair falls over the front of her shoulder, resting right above her breasts, which draws my attention back to the open collar of the shirt she's wearing, my shirt. I catch her gaze and her eyes dart away.

I clear my throat and continue. "As you may know, AM Advertising is headquartered in San Francisco and we have a public relations branch in Los Angeles. Nothing will change with those two locations. New York City will still operate out of this same Midtown office. We're updating leases today, and we expect no change in physical real estate here.

"Our new company name will be AM Global. It made sense that in blending two powerhouse companies, a piece of each name was appropriate to maintain. This will take some time to change legally, but I'd like you to use that name immediately on all customer correspondence, including email signatures."

I see a sea of heads nodding and taking notes, except for Gracie, who watches me carefully. Studying me. Looking at me and through me. I hold her gaze before she finally looks away, a blush spreading across her face. I continue to go through each slide, showing the layout and structure of our new combined company, and a sense of excitement builds inside me.

My plan was to be bi-coastal—splitting my time between New York and San Francisco—until I find someone, or, I determine who will manage the New York office," I announce with a smirk. "But I've decided that I'll mostly be in New York until we get everything fully operational, so get used to seeing me around. San Francisco is a machine at this point. That office basically runs itself, so I believe I should be here in New York, with all of you." I smile and see heads nodding again. At this comment, I see Grace's shoulders rise and she inhales sharply, sharing a quick look with her friend who sits next to her.

That's right. I'm fucking staying. Get used to me.

I continue, "There will be an opportunity for anyone in New York who would like to relocate to San Francisco to do so, and vice versa. I'd just ask that requests be emailed to me so that we can address real estate needs and/or limitations in each office."

Everyone sits with looks of disbelief on their faces and it makes me smile. I'm not the asshole they expected me to be. "Los Angeles will continue to be our public relations hub, and since Williams Global did not staff publicists, nothing will change at that location, including management. Aaron Maxwell, who many of you may be familiar with, will continue to manage the L.A. office." A low chuckle rolls through the room and I pause, thinking of the public relations office and Aaron, who is consistently in the tabloids managing all the shit his clients get him into. He can continue managing that office and keep his dick wet with all the L.A pussy he wants, but Gracie and New York are mine. Aaron has a name and a very public reputation for being a Hollywood playboy in the PR world...as long as he stays in L.A. and away from us, everything will be just fine. If Aaron took one look at Gracie, I know he'd try to bed her. Fuck that. Not this time; she's mine. "As needs arise, we'll add more publicists, but only in L.A." Thank God, Gracie isn't a publicist and won't request a position in L.A.

I stifle back a small laugh when I remember Kevin Williams telling me he didn't play in the public relations game, that he had no desire to clean up other people's shit all day long. No truer statement has ever been made; however, we have celebrity clientele, some of Hollywood's A-list actors and actresses, athletes, and some of the music industry's biggest names as our clients. There's a need for good publicists; it's an extremely profitable business, and I have the best publicists in the country, including Aaron, so for me, it makes sense to keep the public relations arm of my business operating as is.

I close my laptop, which ends the presentation, and I take a deep breath, finally relaxing as I sense a new energy in the room. "A press release should be in your email as soon as this meeting is over. You are free to share that with your clients. Everything is status quo. Nothing changes. Meetings stand. Also, creatively, absolutely nothing changes. Keep your clients happy. Allow them to ask questions and answer them honestly. We expect zero impact to clients as we merge these companies, other than the name on the check they write to us."

I get a small bit of laughter from that comment and the tension in the room seems to have dissipated. "As far as I'm concerned, it's business as usual. I expect you all to continue to deliver the same quality work you always have: on-time, on-budget, and with superior attention to detail. My reputation is only as good as the people who work for me, which is why I agreed to this deal. You're the best of the best." I peer around the room at the happy faces and my eyes land on Gracie's before she looks away.

The room hums with excitement and any nervousness I had about this deal begins to vanish. "I look forward to building an even better combined company with AM Global. Thank you for allowing me to lead you. I won't take any more of your time, but know that I have an open-door policy. Any questions you have, please come to me and ask. If I'm unavailable in person, please email me."

With that, the room bustles with people gathering their things and preparing to leave. I clear my throat and make one more announcement. "Grace Morgan, if you could stay, I'd like to speak with you separately." I grin at my own brazenness.

Gracie freezes in place before offering me a quick nod. The room clears, but she doesn't move a muscle. She makes no attempt to move closer to me, so I make the move, sauntering across the room to her. Gracie was so very wrong when she thought last night was going to be a one-time deal. I plan to have many more nights like last night, starting with tonight.

FOUR

Gracie

I finally get the courage to stand up. I won't have him standing over me as I sit in a chair; I won't give him that power. As I hear the conference room door shut, Drew stalks across the room toward me. A lion hunting his prey. Prey that is too scared to even try to flee its predator. The glass-encased conference room makes it easy for everyone to watch us, and I can feel their penetrating gazes.

My legs shake underneath me and I will myself to breathe. Three deep breaths from me and four long strides from Drew before he's standing mere inches in front of me. Too close. So close, I can smell his sweet, familiar cologne and I see his full upper lip twitch as he holds back a smirk. I swallow hard and my heart beats wildly against my ribcage when he takes another small step forward, close enough I can feel the heat from his body. A power play. I've seen this shit before.

"Everyone can see us, and yes, they're watching," I manage to muster through my dry mouth.

Drew nods, and then slides both of his hands into the pockets of his suit pants and rocks back on his heels, allowing a small of amount of space between us. A decent, professional distance, but not too much. His head turns and he looks out the glass conference room windows at all of the people pretending not to watch us. In an effort to appear casual, he takes another step back before pulling a hand out of his pocket and gesturing for me to sit.

"Grace." He says my name with almost a growl. The same way he said my name over and over last night in my ear. The same way he said my name in between kisses and nips . . . and oh, my god, just the mere presence of this man makes my panties wet. I clench my thighs and he smirks. He knows what he does to me. The simple act of saying my name has me damn near ovulating.

I finally sit down in the chair next to him and cross my legs. Tightly. I do my best to think about anything except the throbbing between my legs. He runs his tongue over his bottom lip and rakes a hand over his face. Before he gets a chance to speak, I jump in.

"Last night," I start, before looking out the glass-lined conference room wall to check again who's watching us. Jamie looks up briefly from her desk, but when my eyes meet hers, she drops her head and goes back to work. "You said your name was Drew."

He smacks his lips and tilts his head. "It is. Andrew. I go by Drew."

I do my best to keep my voice steady and swallow down my anxiety. "You said you were in town for one night to buy a company."

"And I bought Williams Global." He says it so matter-of-factly. A confident air to his statement. His crystal blue eyes hold mine, unwavering. He doesn't look around. He looks only at me, not caring who's watching us now or what they're thinking. He's confident and direct and he owns it. Just like he did in bed last night. Leaning back in the conference room chair, he props a foot on the knee of his opposite leg.

With one hand resting on the large wood table and the other on the arm of the leather chair he's in, he is a dead ringer for Matt Bomer. Perfectly combed dark hair with just a hint of a wave in it, a chiseled jawline with a sprinkling of rough, dark hair, and those eyes...as blue as the Caribbean ocean. And the package he is carrying between his legs still has me wonderfully sore from our marathon last night.

"I don't understand what the problem is, Gracie. I've told you the truth about who I am and why I was in town." He smirks, knowing I don't want him to call me that. He's taunting me, trying to get a rise out of me, and I do my best to seem unaffected.

I take a deep breath and exhale slowly, trying to calm myself, but he's right. It's not him I'm mad at, it's me. I'm mad at myself for jumping into bed with the sexiest man I've ever met after knowing him for only a couple of hours. I'm mad at how he affects me—*still*.

I clear my throat and sit up straighter. "We weren't supposed to see each other again."

"Who said?" he challenges me. "I don't remember any agreement, just that there were no strings attached—"

"There was no actual agreement," I snap at him, hating that he can fluster me so easily. "But last night was just what it was... one night—"

"You liked last night." He grins at me, clearly amused. "You liked what we did together...when I ran my hand—"

"Stop," I mutter and shake my head, cutting him off, but he can see right through me. I loved last night. I loved letting go of my inhibitions and the crap that weighs me down for a couple of hours. I loved sharing my body with a man I didn't expect to see again, yet here we are, seeing each other, *again*, and I'm turned on all over again.

He exhales before speaking. "Listen, I was just as surprised to see you as you were to see me. But the way your nipples tightened underneath my shirt when you turned around and saw me. . ." I gasp at his brazen observation and he smirks before he leans in and looks me dead in the eyes. "I want them in my mouth again." I don't know if I'm more appalled at how direct he is or completely turned on. I cross my legs tighter, hoping to drown out the growing ache. Rolling his fingers on the wood conference room table, he clears his throat. "We had a good time, Grace...and I'd like to do it again. More than just again." His eyes burn holes right through me.

My face flushes at his words, and I don't know what the sound that comes out of me is, but I liken it to a cough-snort. "Absolutely not."

"Why not?" There's that damn smirk again. He rubs his chin and I narrow my eyes at him.

"Because. One. Night. Stand. Means just that. One night." I enunciate each word, quietly, discreetly. Hoping that anyone watching us through the glass isn't good at reading lips. "That's all last night was. Plus, you're my boss. Please don't make this weird—"

"You're the one who said just one night and I'm not your boss," he points out, all too pleased with his response. "You report to that senior account manager...what's his name?"

"Eddie."

"Ah yes, Eddie." He pauses for a moment. "Grace...you know I'm a man who gets what I want, don't you?" His eyes hold mine, no sense of humor in them. He's serious. He means business.

I actually roll my eyes at him, not even trying to hide my disgust at that statement. It's so barbaric. "I'm not available."

He cocks an eyebrow at me. "Not available? So you have a boyfriend and you're a cheater? That's not what this says." He grabs a manila folder that's on the table and opens it. He pulls two pieces of paper out and looks back and forth between both of them. "Grace Morgan," he reads off the sheet. "Twenty-five years old from Antelope Hills, Montana. *Single*," he emphasizes that word, "graduate of the University of Montana with a degree in Marketing, emphasis in Advertising. Moved to New York City in twenty-eighteen. Only known relative is Jennifer Morgan, mother. Lives in Red Hook, Brooklyn." He pauses, his eyes looking at me for confirmation of what he's just read, only I'm too shocked to respond. "Red Hook isn't safe," he says disapprovingly, shoving the papers back in the folder.

I blink at him several times, shocked at his boldness. Who does he think he is, just reading my file like that? "Where did you get that information, and what are you trying to prove?" I ask, my voice laced with annoyance. How does someone get that kind of information?

One side of his mouth tips up. "I'm showing you I can find out anything about you. I know you're available, Gracie. And I'd like to see you again." His voice softens and he sits back in his chair, his shoulders falling comfortably as he laces his hands together.

I do my best to temper my voice, but my anxiety has changed to anger. "Why? So we can fuck like rabbits, and risk the chance I might get attached to you just in time for you to turn around and move back to San Francisco? No, thank you. That's why last night will only be a one-night stand."

His eyes seem to widen at my sharp tone and foul language, or perhaps it's because I told him I might get attached. I blink hard to keep from squeezing my eyes shut. God, I'm such an idiot. I'm not good at casual sex and how it's supposed to work. Sex has always been about love and caring and, yes, attachment for me...until last night.

Drew clears his throat and leans forward. "If I recall last night correctly, we had a great time...fucking, if that's what you'd like to call it. And I'd like to do it again. We're grown-ups here, Grace. We'll set boundaries, and we won't cross them. We both mutually benefit from our time together—"

"Not going to happen," I cut him off and push myself up from the chair. Who the hell does this guy think he is? "As I said before, it was one night. Please don't make this awkward for us, and please don't ever bring it up again." My voice shakes and I hate that he knows he can get to me.

He throws himself back in his chair and laces his hands behind his head with that damn smirk still plastered across his face. "I like it when you're bossy."

"And I like it when you don't talk to me. So please leave me alone." I grab my notebook off the table and march toward the door, my stomach twisting and turning the entire way.

"Never going to happen, Gracie," I hear him say with a chuckle as the door shuts behind me.

When I finally hang up my phone from fielding client inquiries regarding today's acquisition developments, I realize I'm the last one left in the office—except for Drew.

The automatic office lights have begun to dim or turn off completely and the sparkling Manhattan skyline is on full display outside my office window. This is why I'm here. The dazzling lights of New York City. Those lights represent opportunity. Opportunity for me to grow in the greatest city in the world. Opportunity to change my circumstances...change my mom's circumstances. Through hard work and perseverance, I hope to change both of our lives. Growing up in abject poverty has shaped me. I've seen the worst of the worst and survived on literally nothing. I'm living the American dream and trying to do better for myself—for my mom. This is why I'm here. This is why I won't ruin this opportunity by bedding Drew again.

Shoving those thoughts away, I decide to call it a night. I'm thankful that it's Friday and I can spend the weekend forgetting about Drew and last night. Only, I don't know that I'll ever be able to forget about Drew and the night we shared.

The clock on the office wall tells me it's after eight in the evening and my stomach growls in hunger. I pull a long sweater out of my cabinet and change out of my heels into a pair of ballet flats—much more comfortable for commuting in.

After powering down my computer, I shove my phone in my handbag and head toward the elevator. Sliding through the open double doors, I step to the back corner of the elevator car and let out a long sigh. I'm ready for this whole weird, stressful day to be over. As the two metal doors are just about to meet, a hand reaches in and stops them. Two bright blue eyes peer at me as the doors part. Drew. My stomach sinks at the same time my heart flutters. Why do I have such a traitorous heart?

Wearing dark grey suit pants and a black dress shirt, he carries the matching grey suit jacket over his shoulder. In his left hand is a black, sleek leather briefcase and he looks every bit the GQ model I thought he was when I met him at the bar last night.

"Late night, Miss Morgan?" he questions, sliding right next to me. His shoulder brushes mine and I step as far as I can to get away from him, but this puts me up against the wall. When he takes two steps sideways, I'm pinned between Drew and the cold elevator wall. My nipples harden, and I cross my arms over my chest to cover the firm peaks his white shirt that I stole does little to hide.

I hear a snicker from Drew, but I ignore him and close my eyes as I feel the elevator descend. I don't like elevators and I don't like that my body betrays me every time Drew is within eleven feet of me.

I hear a click and the elevator stops abruptly. My eyes snap open as a loud gasp escapes me. Drew stands with his finger on the emergency stop button, that damn smirk he's had all day still plastered across his face.

"What are you doing?" I hiss and swat at his hand, trying to get to the button and reengage the elevator.

"This." He drops his briefcase to the floor and quickly backs me into the corner, pushing his entire body into mine. Every hard inch of him is pressed against me, allowing me to feel every ripple of muscle from his arms, chest, stomach, and thighs. But it's the long, firm erection nudging at me that makes me weak. The same one that made me come three times last night.

"You can deny this all you want," he says, pressing his lips to the edge of my jaw and placing a gentle kiss against it. "But you feel it..." His lips move slowly to the soft spot on my neck just behind my ear where he kisses me again, this time sucking the flesh into his mouth ever so lightly. "And I feel it." He thrusts his hips gently against me, every pronounced inch of his dick rubbing against me.

My hands grip his muscular arms and my head falls backwards as my body reacts to his. I hiss out a "Jesus," when his fingers find one of my nipples through my shirt and he pinches it—hard. A jolt of electricity trails right from my nipple down to my very wet core, and now it's my hips that buck against his.

"Don't deny us, Grace."

I whimper as his hand falls from my breast, down my stomach to the hem of my skirt, his fingers brushing quickly past the edge of my skirt before trailing up my thigh. My traitorous body leans back into the wall, allowing him greater access. I bite my lip...feeling the sting as I fight off the growing pleasure seeping through me with every kiss, every touch.

"Let me touch you, Gracie."

It's a simple request, but I don't need to give him permission because my body does it for me. My legs shift slightly, and his fingers move hungrily, finding the edge of my panties before pushing them aside. A single finger nudges at my opening just as his lips suck on that sensitive skin behind my ear where he nips at it gently. He circles my opening, spreading my arousal around and teasing me, all while nipping at my neck.

A single finger slides into me, and a groan escapes my lips. His thumb finds my clit and works small circles over it as his finger keeps pace inside me.

"Jesus fucking Christ, Gracie," he hisses against my neck when he suddenly stops, pulling his finger out of me. He grabs both sides of my face and slams his lips to mine. This kiss is needy and aggressive, and his tongue swirls passionately against mine. Pulling away from me, he groans, readjusts his erection in his pants, and smacks the red emergency button causing the elevator to suddenly fall.

My chest heaves as I pull long, harsh breaths into my lungs, my body aching from his touch and the sudden absence of it.

"What the hell just happened?" I look at Drew for answers. Except he doesn't answer; he simply straightens my skirt and runs his fingers through my mussed-up hair. His face is twisted in confusion, or maybe guilt. I reach a shaky hand up, pressing my fingers against my lips, still feeling the sting from his kisses.

"I'm not doing this here," he says as the elevator chimes, alerting us that we've reached the main level. He reaches down and picks up his briefcase with one hand and grabs my wrist with the other.

"Oh, no!" I tell him as he all but drags me out of the elevator. It's not aggressive enough to look like he's kidnapping me, but more of a *he's walking fast and I can't quite keep up* kind of dragging. "Let me go!" I whisper-yell to him, trying not to cause a scene.

Cloyd, the doorman of our building, smiles at us and opens

the large glass door just as we pass through. "Good night, Mr. McPherson," he says with a nod. Cloyd gives me a strange look, and I just smile at him, hoping this doesn't look as weird as I think it does—except I know it does.

"Night, Cloyd," I wave with my free hand, and he just shakes his head at me.

The humid evening air slaps our faces when we hit the bustling Manhattan sidewalk. Drew guides us down the sidewalk and around the corner. His grip on my wrist tightens when he feels me trying to free myself. When he stops suddenly, I slam into the back of him and I yelp in surprise.

"Drew!"

He stops, his eyes rabid and hungry. Releasing my wrist, he instead laces his fingers through mine, his grip still firm. With his other hand, he pulls his phone from his pocket and glances at the screen.

"My train station is that way." I point to the right, where the green stair rail encases the steps that lead down to the subway station I use to get back to Brooklyn. Instead, he pulls me to the left and toward a waiting black Town Car, where a driver stands at the rear passenger door.

"Mr. McPherson," the driver greets us and opens the back door.

"Tony." Drew nods and pulls me in front of him, guiding me into the car. Drew slides in next to me and the door closes.

"Where are we going?" I ask, my heart beating wildly in my chest. Drew doesn't answer, but the driver gets into the car and starts the ignition, lunging the car into the still crazy Manhattan traffic. I should be afraid, but I'm not. It's Drew.

"Four Seasons, sir?" the driver asks and Drew grunts out a yes.

As the car weaves in and out of traffic and down Manhattan's side streets, Drew leans in and presses his lips to my ear. His warm breath causes my entire body to break into goosebumps.

"We're going to finish what we started in that elevator, Gracie. Do you understand?" His voice is quiet but commanding.

I should fight him. I should instruct the driver to drop me at the subway station right this second, but this time, it isn't my body that defies me; it's my brain. I close my eyes and rest my head back against the seat. I don't even fight Drew on this, because right now, I want this, my body wants this as much as he does... and once again, I hate myself for it.

FIVE

Drew

I'm a fucking asshole. Who finger fucks someone as amazing as Gracie in an elevator? She's not some whore I picked up. She deserves better than an elevator romp and a pat on the head before I send her home.

"Where are we going?" she asks.

I ignore her. What I want to say is I'm taking her back to my hotel to fuck her living brains out, in a bed instead of a trashy elevator. That I want to feel every inch of her perfect soft body underneath me all night long. That I want to wake up next to her in the morning instead of having her disappear like she did this morning. Instead, I keep quiet, hoping my silence is less intimidating.

Her head rests against the headrest in the back seat of the car as our driver zigzags across Midtown to get us to my hotel. I can see her pulse throbbing in her neck as she takes deep, slow breaths, I assume to calm herself. I want to press my lips to her neck, but I notice her black skirt is tugged up to about mid-thigh and her long, toned legs are on full display, distracting me.

My dick hardens to the point of being painful as I take in

those long legs. I can't wait to have them wrapped around me again while I fuck her, and then have them draped over my shoulders while I taste her. As Tony gets us closer to the Four Seasons, I lean over and whisper in her ear, "We're going to finish what we started in the elevator, Gracie. Do you understand?" Now it's her who doesn't acknowledge me. She's opened her eyes and now stares straight ahead, giving me a dose of my own medicine.

I check the rearview mirror and Tony keeps his eyes trained straight ahead, on the road, not looking back at us once in the backseat. He's a professional. He knows to give us privacy and do the job he was hired for—to drive.

Reaching over, I run my forefinger over that dip at the base of her throat. She gasps at my touch, her heavy eyes finding mine. God, I want all of her. Her mouth, her pussy, her ass. I want to squeeze my dick between her full tits and come all over her chest. I want her full lips wrapped around my cock, milking me.

I tap her right knee and her beautiful hazel eyes look at me in question. I tap her knee again and she narrows her eyes in confusion. Instead, I nudge her knees apart with my hand and those same beautiful eyes widen in surprise.

Leaning in to kiss her, I mumble a "shhh" against her lips as my hand slides up the inside of her warm thigh. She leans back further into the seat, sliding her ass forward, giving me better access. My hand finds her warm center, where I meet her wet panties. Instead of sliding my finger inside of them like I want to, I tease her, circling my finger over her clit through the satin panties. I can feel the warm bud grow harder with every circle I make as she purrs in the seat next to me. She's fucking beautiful when she's turned on, and her body reacts exactly as I want it to. I see her hesitation and her fear, glancing to the front seat and Tony, who keeps his eyes on the road, not even chancing a glance in the rearview mirror. From what I've learned about Grace, one-night stands and back-seat rendezvous are not her style. Only I don't give a shit right now. I need to feel her come on my hand.

"Wait until we get to my room, baby," I whisper into her ear and gently nip her neck. She sucks in a breath and rolls her hips gently against my finger, getting herself off. Her nipples are tight, and her breathing is labored, she's not even trying to suppress her arousal now. I grin. There is nothing sexier than Grace grinding against my hand—her need and want palpable.

The Town Car slows to a stop at the entrance of the Four Seasons and Grace freezes. I give her clit a hard pinch through her panties before pulling my hand out from under her skirt. She sits up straight and brushes her skirt down as I lean in and brush some stray lipstick off her bottom lip with my thumb. "Thank you," she whispers before looking at me.

Something passes between us, but I can't put my finger on it. Understanding? Loneliness? The door opens and I abandon those thoughts, stepping out into the tepid evening air. I reach in for Grace, and she grabs my hand as I pull her gently from the car. She stands on wobbly legs and I lace my fingers through hers again, this time without her resistance. This feels good...right. Her hand in mine. *Her*. With me. This is how it should be; this is what I want it to be.

She straightens her skirt and inhales sharply as we walk through the main entrance of the hotel. Her hand grips mine firmly, as if she's afraid I'm going to let go of her. The lobby is bustling with people checking in and checking out. Business men and women stand around sharing stories and drinks and enjoying their Friday evening, as I have so many times before in hotels across the country.

I steer us toward the private elevator that leads to the floor with penthouse suites, one of which I'll be staying in until I purchase a condo. When I said I planned to be bi-coastal, I really meant if things continue with Grace. I'll fucking appoint myself the permanent manager of the New York office and relocate here. Someone else can manage the San Francisco office. Regardless, I need a place in New York City.

I can feel Grace hesitate when the elevator doors open. She's second-guessing this, second-guessing us. Her brain is telling her a million reasons why she shouldn't do this again.

"Stop overthinking it," I tell her quietly, confidently, and lead her into the elevator.

She pulls her bottom lip between her teeth and nods. It should be me nibbling that full lip, and I will... in about two minutes. Before the doors close, another couple joins us in the elevator. I smile politely at them and squeeze Grace's hand, a silent gesture of support. She squeezes mine back and I pull her in closer to me, wrapping an arm around her lower back. Shit, she fits fucking perfectly into the crook of my arm, even though she's almost as tall as me. Her head leans back against my shoulder and her warm body sinks into me. I love that she's letting me comfort her in this moment. She trusts me.

The couple discuss their dinner reservation and theater plans as the elevator rises quickly. When it comes to a stop, the couple exits first and turns to the left, presumably toward one of the other penthouse suites on this floor, and we turn to the right, headed toward my room. Grace releases my hand and walks slowly next to me. But I hate the miniscule distance already. I reach around her, pressing my hand to the small of her back, guiding her to my door. I need to be touching her.

When I wave the keycard over the pad, the door unlocks, and I feel Grace tense up. Pushing through the double doors, she follows me slowly into the grand foyer. She looks around and then back to me.

"This isn't the room we were in last night," she comments, her voice soft, but her eyes still taking in the extravagant surroundings.

"No, it isn't. My trip was very last minute, and the penthouse wasn't available until today."

She runs her fingers across the base of her neck as if she's touching a necklace as she looks around, her eyes taking in the luxury before us. "Penthouse," she whispers...whether to me or herself, I don't know.

"Please, make yourself at home." I drop my briefcase on the large, round table that sits underneath a giant crystal chandelier in the foyer. Placed in the center of the table is an enormous vase of fresh roses, probably six dozen. A common staple in all the penthouse suites I rent, only I don't give a shit about flowers, but Grace does. Her eyes twinkle as she looks at them.

Grace sets her handbag on the table next to my briefcase, slips off her shoes, and we move into the living room, where there is a full-sized sectional couch, two chairs, and a large table that could double as a conference room table or a dining room table.

I should ask Grace if she's hungry or needs a drink, and I will —after I've buried myself so far inside her, she'll never forget me. Fuck first, food later.

She digs her perfectly painted toes into the plush carpet, her arms wrapped protectively around her waist. She looks vulnerable but not scared.

"Stop over-thinking this." I toe off my shoes and walk over to her.

Grace's hands fall to her sides and her bottom lip quivers. "I'm not," she whispers.

"You are." I place my hands on her biceps. She's trembling. "Grace...Trust me."

She shakes her head to silence me and drops her eyes from mine. "Can I use the restroom?" Her voice is so quiet, I can barely hear her.

"Of course." I reach for her hand and guide her through the living area of the penthouse and into the bedroom. I gesture toward the bathroom and miss her touch the moment her hand breaks free of mine.

After she disappears behind the closed door, I hang up my suit coat in the closet. Unlatching my watch, I set it on the built-in shelf in the closet next to the wallet I pulled from the pocket of my suit jacket. I run my hand over my wrist where my watch just was, noticing it's rough and dry in comparison to Grace's soft, supple skin. Skin I plan to touch, and suck, and mark—letting her know who owns her body...me. I've never wanted someone as much as I want Grace. Our connection is undeniable but maybe she's scared. Maybe I should back off, but I can't. I won't.

I'm caught by surprise when I hear Grace clear her throat and I turn around to find her standing in the doorway between the closet and the bedroom. Her hands are twisted together in front of her and she rocks slightly in place from heel to toe. But it's when I notice she's wearing nothing but my white dress shirt that my breath hitches. She's fucking stunning, her long brown hair hanging in loose waves over her shoulders.

"Grace," I hiss as my eyes fall from her beautiful face to her chest, which peeks out from the unbuttoned shirt, and then down her long, bare legs. Those tan legs peek out from that white dress shirt and my dick stiffens immediately. It takes everything inside me to not push her over to the bed and fuck her like she's never been fucked before—the kind of fucking where every fiber of her soul becomes mine. Which is a problem, because I promised her casual. Only, after one night with her, I don't want casual.

Two steps are all it takes for me reach her, my hands finding each side of her face as I pull her mouth to mine. Our kiss is soft yet intense. Needy yet caring. I feel her fingers fumbling with the buttons on my shirt as her breaths become needier.

She pulls away, breaking our kiss when she gets the last button undone. She stares at me, her eyes scanning my face, my chest, and down to the bulge on full display under my thin dress pants. She stares at all of me like she's never really seen me before. Grace reaches a shaky hand out and tugs on the shoulder of my shirt and I help her—shrugging out of it. It falls to a pile at my feet and Grace's breath hitches.

"Like what you see, Gracie?" I ask smugly. I know she does. I can see the effect I have on her...her hard nipples poking through the white dress shirt, and the way she tries to clench her thighs together to stop the throbbing between them.

"I didn't really look at you last night—" She pinches her eyes closed and pulls her bottom lip in between her teeth.

"Hey," I say softly, reaching out to her, but she pulls away and takes a deep breath. Then she looks me in the eye and her arms fall to her sides. She's beautiful and complicated, a mix of raw emotions and natural beauty and her hazel eyes speak a million unspoken words. I see her trepidation and her fear, and I also see her need and want.

"Drew," my name falls off her trembling lips, "I don't typically do what I did last night," she states and takes another step backward.

Instead of letting her put distance between us, I take a step forward and right into her, pulling her to me. If she wants to pull away, she can try, but I'm not going to let her. I'm not some monster who wants to fuck her and leave her. Her chest is pressed against mine, and even through the dress shirt, I can feel the hard peaks of her nipples, those tight little balls pressed against my chest, aching for me to suck them.

"Don't do what, Grace? *Fuck,* as you call it?" I smirk, using her word from earlier today against her.

She shakes her head and I snake an arm around her waist, not allowing her to back up any further.

"Casual sex," she says. "I don't go home with strangers."

"I'm not a stranger."

"You were last night." Her eyes fall in shame.

"Technically—"

"I don't do one-night stands. I don't go home with men from bars or restaurants, or even on first dates. I'm not that kind of girl. I've never been that girl until last night," she hisses as she tries to defend her actions, her chest rising and falling with each rapid breath.

"Then why did you go home with me?" I slide my hand from the small of her back, down and under the hem of my dress shirt that she's wearing, resting it on her ass. Her bare ass. She's not wearing any panties. My already hard dick gets even harder. I don't let her answer before I crash my mouth into hers—claiming her. It's raw and feral. One-hundred-percent pure need and lust. My hands find the collar of her shirt, and in one swift motion, I rip it open, tearing the shirt from her body and tossing it to the ground.

Now I'm the one who breaks our kiss, pulling her across the room to the bed. I guide her to the center of the bed, where I lay her down on the silk sheets and spread her legs. Her pink, wet pussy is on full display and I run a finger through her slick slit, spreading her juices. Grace gasps as I circle her clit, much like I did in the car over her panties, only now I get to feel her skin to skin. A low growl erupts from the back of my throat, and selfishly, all I want to do is slide into her and fuck her hard, but tonight, I need to taste her.

Her hips buck as I continue running circles around her hardening bud, applying pressure every few seconds. Grace's head falls back and her fingers grip the sheets with each rotation around her clit. I can see her orgasm build and I slip a finger inside her, feeling her tight walls clench around me. I withdraw my finger and bend her knees, spreading her wider. Settling between her legs, I run my tongue from clit to center, teasing her wet entrance.

"Drew!" She gasps my name and reaches for my hair. One of

her hands grips my head, the other is still wrapped tightly in the sheets as I continue my assault on her clit. She tastes like summer...sweet and salty. With one hard suck of her clit, she's falling apart beneath me. Her legs shake and she screams my name, her hips bucking under my face. Her entire body convulses and her arms fall to her sides. After she rides out her orgasm, I take position at her center, sliding into her.

"Condom!" she manages to say, but with one thrust, I'm fully seated in her. Her walls grip me as she comes down from her orgasm.

"We discussed it last night," I remind her. "We're both clean and you're on the pill."

She gasps as I begin to move and a small smile pulls at the corners of her lips. Her tight pussy grips my dick and every movement has both of us highly aroused. Her eyes close and her head falls back as I move in and out of her slowly, watching what I do to her.

"Fucking beautiful, Grace," I manage to say before pressing my lips to her neck. "All of you."

SIX

Gracie

"Fucking beautiful, Grace," he says, nipping at my neck. I whimper in pleasure as he gently stretches me with each careful thrust. I'm mesmerized by him. All of him. His mind, his body, and his ability to make me do things I never thought I'd do.

I wrap one leg around his waist, allowing him deeper inside me, and I move my hips in rhythm with his.

"Fuck, Grace!" he mutters, pressing his pubic bone against my still overly sensitive clit as I writhe underneath him. I moan, and he knows he's hit the right spot as he applies even more pressure. "That's it, baby." He pulls a nipple into his mouth and sucks...hard. He just called me baby and I didn't blink an eye. I'm so entranced by him right now, I gasp at the intensity of the pressure as I feel another orgasm building low in my stomach.

My hands instinctively find their way to his muscular ass, palming each firm globe. "Oh, god!" I cry out when he hits that spot inside me I've never felt anyone hit before...until last night. He chuckles as my fingers dig into the soft flesh of his ass when he purposely hits that spot again and again. He knows exactly what he's doing. If there is one thing this man knows how to do, it's fuck.

Every movement is careful, deliberate, and nothing short of erotic. He has found every sensitive part of my body and played it like a guitar. Slow and soft, fast and hard, a different sound erupting from me with every strum of his methodical fingers.

Bringing me to the edge of orgasm yet again, he suddenly stops. This time, he denies my pleasure and I whimper at the denial. A grin spreads across his face when he sees my disappointment and he rolls his hips slowly, bringing me to the edge once again.

"Please," I beg him as he slows, withdrawing from me completely. He hovers at my entrance and I raise my hips to draw him in again. It's a game of cat and mouse and he's winning.

"Say it again," he says. Pulling my other nipple into his mouth, he rolls it between his teeth and I scream in pleasure. He teases my entrance again with his cock, edging in slowly before he slams into me with one solid thrust. Simultaneously, he bites my nipple and a jolt of electricity shoots straight down to my core where he is stretching me. Every nerve in my body is on high alert with each heady thrust.

"Please, Drew. I need to come," I pant between ragged breaths as his movements become faster. He's now succumbing to his own needs. Where he was once gentle, he's now rough, every plunge into me harder than the last. "Drew, please," I beg him again.

Our bodies are slick with sweat, and with one swift motion, he lifts my legs over his shoulders, allowing him complete access to me. The way he looks at me with hunger, concern, and want, is enough to make me weep.

With one last deep stroke, he's the deepest he's ever been inside me and I cry out in a mix of pleasure and pain. With this last thrust, he empties himself in me and matches his ragged breaths with my own.

"Unbelievable," he mumbles as he falls on top of me, staying firmly rooted inside me. As our breathing finally returns to normal. I can feel him soften inside me as we lie together in a tangled mess of sweaty limbs. Then my eyes fall closed and I soak in the closeness of him.

I suddenly wake with a start, realizing I must've dozed off. The bedside clock reads twelve twenty in the morning. Drew still lies between my legs, his head resting on my stomach. Soft, steady breaths tell me he also fell asleep after our lovemaking. I gently coax myself out from underneath him and search for my clothes in the dark.

"What do you think you're doing?" Drew's gruff voice startles me.

"Jesus!" I jump up, trying to cover my naked body with my hands. "You scared me." I hear him shift in the bed, and suddenly, the bedside lamp turns on.

There sits Drew, in all his naked glory. Rippling abs and tan skin, not a self-conscious bone in his body. "You didn't answer my question." He swings his legs over the side of the bed and stands up, his perfectly round, muscular ass on full display. He walks around the perimeter of the bed and right over to me, a man with intention. I try to use my right arm to cover my full breasts and my left hand to hide my stomach and bottom half, but Drew reaches for both of my arms and pulls them away from me, exposing me fully.

"I think you've forgotten that I've already seen all of you." His voice is soft and caring as he rests my arms on his shoulders and pulls me into a hug, our naked bodies pressed against each other. Every rigid muscle of his meets my soft form and I melt into him.

His lips find my neck, and instinctively, my head falls back. I release a moan and can feel his lips pull into a smile against my neck, while at the same time, his dick hardens between us. That alone makes my knees weak. The control he has over my body frightens me. No one has ever been able to get to me with a single touch.

"You're not leaving," he murmurs, trailing kisses from my neck up to my lips. He pulls my bottom lip into his mouth and sucks on it gently before I break our kiss.

"I have to go."

"Not gonna happen." His hands move deftly from my sides all the way up to palm both of my breasts. He rolls my hardened nipples between his fingers before he pinches them and I yelp in surprise.

"I need to go home," I say shakily, trying to pull out of his embrace, but he spins me around and backs me to the bed. His eyes catch mine and all I see are need and want, and he damn well sees that in mine as well. His lips pull into a devilish grin and he knows he's won.

As he shakes his head, we tumble to the bed when the back of my knees hit the edge of the mattress and he has me pinned beneath him—exactly where he wants me. Drew lies between my open legs and he smirks, knowing he's got me again. He props himself up on his shoulders, and his cock nudges at my wet entrance. I bite on my bottom lip as he edges himself in.

"Feel that," he whispers, his eyes holding mine. I nod and bite my bottom lip, doing my best to not show how much he affects me. "That's how you're going to wake up tomorrow morning, Gracie. With me buried inside you. We can't do that when you're at your apartment and I'm here."

I wiggle underneath him and he slips further into me.

"Ahhh!" I gasp when he hits that spot inside me. He knows exactly where to find it and he uses it against me. I'm weak to him.

"Feels good, doesn't it, baby?" He rolls his hips and I literally lie like a wet noodle underneath him—limp and soft, soaking in the pleasure he brings me.

He laces his fingers from both of his hands through mine and places them on either side of my head. This time, our lovemaking is slow, careful, and passionate. He watches me intently, his blue eyes holding mine, telling me this is so much more than just casual sex, as his moves become more rhythmic.

His long, slow strokes ignite something deep inside me. "Drew." I manage his name on a hiss. "I'm going to come already." Since his first touch last night, my entire body has been on the cusp of a constant orgasm. He leaves me heated, on edge, and needy... for him.

His thrusts slow until he stops, still rooted deep inside me. "You're not leaving tonight," he tells me. His tone leaves no room for negotiation. "We have plans tomorrow—" he starts before I interrupt him.

"What if I already have plans?" I argue breathily.

"Cancel them." He's so direct and matter-of-fact.

"I don't have clothes," I point out. "Or my pills."

His eyes widen at that revelation. "We'll get them tomorrow."

He rolls his hips and continues his slow assault, his pelvic bone rubbing against my clit perfectly, every movement one step closer to ecstasy. Every nerve in my body is on high alert when I finally fall, my entire body trembling beneath him.

"There you go, baby," he whispers and releases my hands. As I fall apart, Drew takes his time...long, rhythmic strokes bringing him to the edge until he joins me in my fall. We both gasp for breath, but before I have time to fall back asleep, Drew is pulling me from the bed. "Come here." He guides me toward the bathroom, where he turns on the light. The bathroom is lavish and huge, almost as big as my entire apartment. There is a giant soaking tub in one corner and a shower that takes up an entire wall. Everything is white and grey marble and over-the-top exquisite.

Drew turns on the spigot of the tub and runs his hand through the water before plugging the drain. "Get in." He pulls me toward the tub. It's so large, four grown adults could bathe at the same time. "Just relax. Don't talk, don't overthink."

I quickly twist my long hair up into a bun on top of my head while Drew squirts bubble bath from a bottle into the hot water. I step into the deep tub carefully while he holds my hand since my shaky legs still have me feeling unsteady.

Once I'm in the tub, he sets two large bath towels on the counter and slides into the tub behind me. We're quiet as the rumbling water rises around us. My muscles finally relax once the hot water reaches my chest.

Drew pulls me back against him and I'm able to stretch my long legs completely. Amazing. I normally can't stretch out in a standard tub, I'm too tall. I use my foot to turn the knob and shut off the water, then I sink further down, my head resting back against Drew's shoulder. His arms wrap around my waist and his fingers draw slow circles on my stomach.

We soak in silence, the hot water relaxing our bodies until our fingers prune and the water begins to cool. Drew massages my neck and shoulders, and I'm so relaxed, I could fall asleep right here in the water.

"Let's get you to bed," he whispers in my ear and guides us up and out of the water. Drew dries me carefully, not missing a spot before wrapping my body in the oversized bath towel. I've never had anyone take care of me before and it's nice.

"My toothbrush is in that bag if you'd like to use it again." He points to the leather toiletry bag sitting on the counter.

I blush in embarrassment. "How did you know?"

"You left the lid off the toothpaste," he says with a smirk. Pulling his toothbrush and the tube of toothpaste from his bag, he hands them to me. "Maybe it's anal, but I have a system. Everything has its place. Lids always go back on. Everything is organized—"

I snort. "I'm not like that at all." Which is ironic, because being in control is my M.O., except for my bathroom. It's a disaster of epic proportions.

"Obviously. It was a dead giveaway when I went into the bathroom this morning. Towel on the floor, toothpaste open, toothbrush sitting in a puddle of water." He laughs as he describes what a mess I am. It's the first time I notice he has a dimple. I don't know why, but I reach out and press my finger to that small curve in his cheek.

He stills. The move is simple, but intimate.

"You have a dimple," I say softly. "I like it."

He snakes an arm around my waist and pulls me to him. His gaze holds mine. "And I like you."

My heart stammers in my chest and he presses his soft lips to mine. His kiss is soft and sweet and my body sinks into his.

"As much as I want to make love to you again, Gracie, we need to rest. We have a big day tomorrow."

Drew removes our towels and walks us to the king-size bed. I ease into the center, my bare skin sliding against the silk sheets. Drew slides in behind me and pulls me to him, caging me in his arms, where I close my eyes and easily fall asleep.

SEVEN

Drew

As much as I want to wake Gracie up and fuck her senseless this morning, I let her rest. It's early, still dark outside, and she's curled into herself, her face so serene and peaceful. I spend a moment listening to the soft sounds of her breathing that tell me she's sound asleep. I slip out of the bedroom and work from the living room answering emails, texting my realtor, and ordering us breakfast.

I recently reached out to a realtor to assist me in finding a small apartment, but now I've asked her to find me something a little bigger. Hopefully, the last-minute change of plans won't trip up today's real estate viewing.

Just as breakfast arrives and our room service attendant is setting up our food on the dining room table, Gracie appears all wrapped in a plush robe.

"Smells good," she says, her voice husky with sleep.

Gracie slides onto my lap and wraps her arms around my neck. I bury my face in the crook of hers and drink in the sweet smell of her warm skin. She's beautiful in the morning. Her face is make-up free and her long wavy hair is all twisted into a high bun on top of her head. Her simple beauty is what's most attractive about her.

"You smell good," I whisper and I see her visibly shiver. I love the way I affect her. My touch. My words. Her body reacts to both. I run my hand under her robe and caress her bare thigh. My fingers trail higher to the apex of her thighs, where I stop before I get to the place I love to touch. I want nothing more than to eat her for breakfast, right here on this dining room table, but we have a big day ahead of us and I need her to eat and get ready.

The room service attendant quietly leaves and Grace pushes herself up and meanders over to the table.

"You could feed an army with all this food," she says, her eyes scanning the elaborate display of eggs, bacon, sausage, fruit, toast, muffins, coffee, and juices.

"I didn't know what you liked," I remark, and join her at the table.

"Everything," she says with a small smile. She's not afraid to eat, another thing I find attractive about her. She slides into one of the chairs and reaches for a plate.

"What can I get you?" she asks me as I take the seat next to her. She wants to serve me my food and I let her.

"Some eggs, bacon, and fruit, please."

She plates up my breakfast and sets it in front of me before helping herself. You'd never know by how comfortable we are that we've known each other for less than forty-eight hours. I feel like I've known her a lifetime.

"What are we doing today?" she asks, biting into a bright red strawberry. She reaches for the cream and pours it into her coffee, turning the black liquid to a milky light brown.

"Shopping," I say, sipping some orange juice.

"Shopping? You like shopping?" Her eyes widen in surprise.

"The kind of shopping we're doing doesn't involve stores or

malls," I remark, and she sits back in her chair, her forehead wrinkling in confusion. "You'll see."

We finish our breakfast and I hand her a shopping bag. "I asked the concierge to get you an outfit until we can get to your apartment. I'm sorry if it's not your style, but I didn't think you wanted to wear my shirt again, or that skirt you've worn for the past two days."

She pulls the tissue out of the bag and I see that they sent up a pair of black yoga pants, a tank top, and jacket. Also in the bag are a pair of new tennis shoes and socks.

Her eyes widen when she sees the logo from that popular fitness store that women seem to rave about. "Thank you," she says, shoving everything back in the bag. I can't tell if she's appreciative or embarrassed that I purchased clothing for her, but her face softens as the bag of clothes dangles in her hand, so I'll take it as appreciative.

"Go get dressed. We'll go to your apartment so you can grab anything else you need." I rush her along.

She nods and slips back into the bedroom while I shut down my laptop and join her. By the time I get there, she's dressed and in the bathroom brushing her teeth with my toothbrush again. If this were anybody else, I'd have thrown that toothbrush away, but with Gracie, I could oddly care less.

She runs her fingers through her long hair and reties it up on top of her head as I slip into a pair of jeans and a long-sleeved polo shirt. I join her in the bathroom, take the toothbrush that is once again sitting in a puddle on the counter, and brush my teeth, before running some water through my short, dark hair.

"Ready?" I ask as I arrange the toiletries on the counter that Gracie has left a mess.

"Ready," she responds, sliding her hands into the pockets of her tight-fitting athletic jacket. The form-fitting fabric of her pants and jacket hug every luscious curve on her body and I can't help but get turned on. Her breasts and curvy hips are on full display and the way her ass sways when she walks damn near gives me an erection. She needs to change before we look at homes; no one else is allowed to ogle that body...just me.

We exit the hotel to the waiting Town Car, and Tony eases into Saturday morning Manhattan traffic. I reach over and pull Gracie's hand into mine as we make our way through New York City and into Brooklyn. I visibly shudder when we pull up in front of the old pre-war brick apartment building in Red Hook. I glance out the window and up and down the street that's questionable at best. Is this where she lives? I know what we pay Gracie, and while she wouldn't be living on the Upper West Side with her salary, she has to be able to afford better than this. I make a mental note to review her salary again.

She can see the disapproval written across my face. I'm horrible at masking my emotions, which is why I'd make a shitty poker player. She opens her door and slides out and I follow closely behind her. "Give us a few minutes," I tell Tony and follow Gracie.

She pulls keys from her purse and I get a better look at the area. There's a bodega at the end of the street where people are loitering. The surrounding buildings are in rough condition, and there is an abundance of dollar stores, hole-in-the-wall restaurants, and check-cashing places in every direction. A typical lower income area in New York City. I assumed she was living somewhere that was more revitalized, because that's what I would do. But I'm quickly learning that Gracie isn't me. She's her own person, with her own ideas and her own plans. While she frustrates me, it's something I appreciate about her nonetheless.

She fights with the lock on the door to enter the building. With a swift kick and a hard turn of her key, the main door swings open and we step inside. Cool, musty air fills my nostrils as we take the three flights of stairs to her apartment.

Gracie fumbles with her keys again, finally sliding the right one into the deadbolt of the shabby wood door. The white paint is chipping off the door and trim, and the numbers three-zero-one that once appeared to be black are now a faded grey. Her apartment door creaks open and we step into what has to be the smallest kitchen I've ever seen. Nothing more than a tiny fridge, a miniscule counter, and a miniature stove fill the small, outdated space. The apartment is old and dingy, but clean. Everything is dated, from the kitchen cabinets, the countertops, all the way to the old, scratched parquet wood flooring.

Gracie has a small but quaint kitchen table and two chairs that sit up against the only wall in the kitchen. Straight ahead is a nonexistent transition to the living room where a loveseat sits with a grey slipcover on it. A large, colorful throw rug rests under the loveseat and on each side are mismatched end tables with large ferns on them. Finally, there are two bookshelves that flank another wall, completing the entire living space.

"Make yourself at home," Gracie says self-consciously, tossing her purse onto the kitchen table that doubles as a catchall. She moves through the small space and into what I presume is her bedroom directly off the living room. I follow her. There's no door, just a framed opening.

The tiny room holds what looks like a full-sized bed and a small dresser. That's it. There is a tiny closet with a single door and a window off center on her bedroom wall. Everything about this apartment is small and awkward. But it's Gracie's, and because of that, even though we just met, I love it. It's different. Like her. I don't know what it is about her, or me, but this woman has me feeling like I've never felt before. An immediate connection, a sense of possessiveness, and a longing to protect her.

"Do you have a garment bag, or..." I gesture toward the too-small closet, hoping she has some type of bag she can put some clothes in.

"A garment bag?" she asks, her face twisting in confusion.

"You know, a bag that carries clothes." My tone is dripping with sarcasm and I can't help but smirk when I see her eyes widen in realization of what I want her to do. Pack an overnight bag.

"Oh, no. I'm not staying with you again tonight." She shakes her head and crosses her arms over her chest, highlighting those perfect breasts of hers.

I tilt my head and watch her argue. She's cute when she tries to be assertive. "Yes, you are. I don't know how long we'll be out today and we'll be on the Upper West Side of Manhattan. It just makes sense that you stay with me tonight instead of coming all the way back here."

She continues to shake her head, ignoring everything I'm telling her. She's defiant and tells me no and, while it drives me insane, I also love it about her. I'm used to everyone doing what I tell them to, when I tell them to, so I appreciate the challenge Gracie provides. It's become fun to watch her try to stand her ground. She shakes her head defiantly, her eyes wild. "I thought we were coming back here so I could change clothes for today and take my pills. I didn't agree to spend the entire weekend with you, Drew."

Ignoring her protest, I march over to her closet and open the small door. A large black shoulder bag hangs on a hook she's attached over the door. I grab it and hand it to her. "Get changed. Put what you'll need for the next two days in here. We've got to be back in Manhattan in forty-five minutes for an appointment."

She doesn't argue this time; instead, she sighs. Loudly. I can't help but smile knowing I've won, again, and she rolls her eyes at me. I sit on the edge of her bed, scrolling through the real estate listings my agent provided while she scurries around, shoving things in the bag.

"What are we doing today?" she asks, not turning around to look at me. Instead, she thumbs through the hangers in her closet, assessing each clothing article as she passes by them.

"Wear something comfortable," I tell her, not looking up from my phone.

"I'm in something comfortable," she mumbles under her breath. I fucking love her snark. I've never met a girl that's sassy, sweet, and snarky all rolled into one person, and she's beautiful to boot.

"Just pack what you think you'll need for the next two days," I tell her again. Honestly, she won't be needing clothes other than today when we're looking at condos. I plan to spend the rest of the weekend in bed, devouring her. No clothes needed for that.

I hear her rummaging through a cabinet in the bathroom and mumbling to herself.

"Do you always do that?" I ask, amused, shutting off my phone.

"Do what?" she growls.

"Talk to yourself."

She appears from the bathroom with a toiletry bag and shoves it on top of her black tote full of clothes.

She shrugs, unfazed. "I've always done it."

"It's cute," I tell her. There are so many things she does that I find cute, including her wittiness and ability to banter, and also the way she purses her lips when she's concentrating.

She rolls her eyes at me, and I let out a small laugh.

Walking over to her nightstand, she plucks her pack of birth control pills off the top, wiggling it in one hand before dropping them into her bag. "I'm ready," she announces, reaching for the bag before I take it from her.

"Let me get this."

She reluctantly hands over her bag, then grabs her purse and keys from the table before locking up. We make our way down the rickety old stairs and back out to the waiting car. Of course, even on a Saturday morning, Manhattan traffic is a bitch. It takes us almost an hour to get from Red Hook to the Upper West Side, where we meet my realtor. Gracie had her eyes glued out the window, taking in all of Manhattan on our way here.

My realtor is an older woman dressed in a red power suit. Her grey hair is stick straight and cut into a simple bob that hits at her jawline, and her makeup is heavy and overly done for her age. She looks every part the uppity New York City realtor I expected her to be.

"Mr. McPherson," Janet, the realtor, greets me, reaching out to shake my hand. She looks at Gracie and offers a tight smile but doesn't greet her. Strike one. "I got your email with your last-minute request." She pauses and looks at me out of the corner of her eye. "I've got six places I'd like to show you today."

She turns away from us and heads into the newly built fifty-story building we just parked in front of. I reach for Gracie's hand and she settles into my side. Janet rambles off facts for the building and apartment. "There's a gym, a pool, and a spa. This apartment has two bedrooms and three bathrooms." She continues rattling off details as we take the elevator up to the twentieth-floor apartment. She unlocks the door, and when we walk into the open and bright space, I hear Grace gasp as she takes it all in.

Everything is new and modern and enormous compared to Gracie's humble Red Hook apartment. The kitchen in this place alone is bigger than her entire apartment. The island is at least eight feet long. Janet points out the custom kitchen cabinets made from imported wood. Gracie runs her hand over the white marble counters, her pointer finger tracing the grey veins that run throughout the white stone.

We follow Janet through the condo while she points out the bedrooms, bathrooms, and a den. Janet likes to throw around all the realtor schtick—"vaulted, luxury, one-of-a-kind"—and I don't give a shit about this. I just want something comfortable and homey. Something Gracie will feel comfortable in. "Two-point five is a steal for this—"

"What else do you have?" I ask Janet, cutting her off as she tries to convince me the two and a half million-dollar price tag is a good deal for this place. "Do you have anything a little less modern, something more comfortable with some outdoor space?"

Janet looks shocked, but quickly regains her composure as she pulls the iPad from her shoulder bag. She quickly scrolls through her listings as Gracie and I step back into the kitchen.

"What do you think?" I release her hand and she leans back against the kitchen island, resting her hands on the edge of the marble counter. I mimic her and rest my back against the island, our hips touching. I don't like distance between us, but I allow it. For now.

"I think this is the nicest place I've ever seen." Her eyes fall to the travertine floors. "I also think my opinion doesn't matter. You're going to be the one living here, not me." I go to argue with her that her opinion does matter, but she continues before I have a chance, which is good, because I just met her and I don't want to scare her. "But if you really want my thoughts, I think it's pretentious and you'd fit in much better in Red Hook. Nineteen-fifties parquet wood floors are just more your style. Travertine is soooo overrated," she drawls.

I see her fighting back a grin and I can't help but laugh. Loudly. It's been a long time since a woman has had this effect on me. Her sense of humor might be my favorite thing about her. "Red Hook, huh?"

"Don't knock it until you try it," she says, nudging me with her elbow. I turn to her and pull her into my arms. It's intimate and close, natural. My hands travel up her sides and I pull her face into my hands. Her beautiful eyes meet mine and I search them...for what, I'm not sure.

"Your opinion matters to me," I tell her softly.

"It shouldn't. I've known you for what, forty hours?" Her eyes are vulnerable, guarded and I want to know what she's thinking, but this isn't the place to ask. The reality of her comment strikes me. It has only been a couple days, but it feels much longer. Our connection is undeniable, like I've known her forever. No woman has ever edged their way into my heart in a matter of hours, let alone days, weeks, or months.

"Mr. McPherson, I have a place in Chelsea I'd like to show you," Janet interrupts our moment.

Gracie shrugs out of my hold and I turn to Janet, still feeling the sting of Gracie's words.

I clear my throat and reach for her hand anyway. "Let's go."

Gracie rests her head on my shoulder the entire way to Chelsea. It's not far, but again, Manhattan's traffic is like no other cities. We finally pull up to a newer, but much smaller building and Janet once again meets us eagerly.

"Mr. McPherson," she scrolls through her iPad, "this listing was built in twenty-ten, completely gutted and remodeled this year. This home is over thirty-four hundred square feet and has three bedrooms and four baths." We walk into the main entrance and are greeted by a doorman, who calls the elevator for us.

"This unit is located on the ninth floor," Janet adds.

"How many floors are there?" I ask, noticing that it wasn't a very tall building.

"Nine." She smiles at me, seemingly knowing that was the answer I was seeking.

We exit the elevator and walk down the sleek, modern hall to the unit marked P1. We're greeted by a grand foyer with a large, modern chandelier made of wood and iron with large round globe light bulbs. The colors inside are neutral and warm, mostly whites and greys, and the beautiful large plank wood floors are impeccable.

Janet continues her sales spiel as we move from the foyer into the open concept living room and kitchen area. "You'll notice off the large living room is a formal dining area," she gestures toward the vast open space off the kitchen where another similar chandelier hangs over a long, sleek table, "and the kitchen is a chef's kitchen with custom cabinets and a ten-foot island."

Gracie releases my hand and ambles into the kitchen. I've noticed she's drawn to kitchens and this one she likes. The kitchen cabinets are white with a dark grey island. The counters are white marble just like the other condo we visited. High end appliances complete the space, from the commercial-sized refrigerator to the gas cooktop and four wall-mounted ovens. Four. If Gracie thought the other condo was excessive, this is over the top.

Janet notices Gracie checking out the kitchen and turns her attention back to me. "All of the bedrooms are oversized and the master leads out to a private terrace that is also accessible through the sliding living room doors." Janet points to the glass wall where two large glass doors open to a concrete terrace that is full of potted trees and plants.

Oversized plush outdoor furniture fills in the space and I notice a built-in barbeque and outdoor kitchen at the far end of the terrace.

"No inch was left untouched," Janet tells me, overly pleased with herself.

I nod, keeping my face blank. I don't have much to say, though. My only concern is whether Gracie will feel comfortable here. I intend for her to spend all of her time with me outside of work.

"What is the price on this one?" I ask as I follow Janet down a hallway lined with doors. "Three-point nine-nine, but I expect multiple offers on this. They priced it low to get interest. This place is worth over four and a half. It went on the market yesterday."

I glance over my shoulder to Gracie, who is still lingering in the kitchen, her arms wrapped tightly around her waist. "Gracie," I call to her and she looks up and over to me. "Please join us."

Janet lets out a soft sigh as I stop and wait for Gracie. Strike two.

"Is there a problem?" I ask, my tone laced with irritation.

Janet stands up tall, plastering on a fake smile. "Of course not."

Gracie catches up to us and I wrap my arm around her waist, pulling her in as we follow Janet to the master bedroom.

Janet is quick to point out all the extraordinary features, including the high coffered ceilings, the doors to the terrace, the oversized luxury bath with soaker tub, and views of the Hudson River from the terrace.

Gracie once again releases my hand and, without a word, strolls across the bedroom to the oversized French doors, where she pushes through them and out onto the terrace. She seems to relax outside, her shoulders falling and her long hair whipping around her face in the wind. I love when her hair is down, and I notice a small smile tug at her lips as she tips her head back and up to the sky, where her eyes slip shut.

My heart leaps in my chest as I watch her, trying to tune out Janet's grating voice. I notice the drops of water falling from the sky and that's when Gracie spins slowly. She spreads her arms out as if summoning the rain herself, and I can't fucking look away.

Everything about her mesmerizes me. The way she moves, graceful and with intent. The way she speaks, every word carrying meaningful decisiveness or laced with humor. But mostly, the way she looks at people, as if she can see into their soul. I've never noticed this about another woman, and I'm fascinated with how quickly I see all of this in Gracie.

"Excuse me for a minute," I tell Janet, hoping it'll shut her up. With three long strides, I'm across the bedroom and out the door, joining Gracie on the terrace.

Her eyes snap open when she hears the door close behind me, and her lips twist into a giant smile when she sees me walk over to her. Her face is sprinkled with rain drops and I pull her into a kiss. It's passionate and needy and telling of something so much more than I can understand, let alone explain. Her arms wrap around my neck, and I lift her and spin slowly just like she had been spinning only moments before. She giggles against my lips and I slow us to a stop before I get dizzy.

"I like dancing in the rain with you," she mumbles against my lips as the rain falls harder.

The rain soaks my hair and I brush the water from my eyes. "I like you, Gracie. I'll dance with you anytime, anywhere."

EIGHT

Gracie

"Write up an offer. Four-point-five and a five-day close." Janet's eyes just about bulge out of her head at Drew's request.

"Mr. McPherson, that's all but impossible," she starts before Drew cuts her off.

"Nothing is impossible, Janet. The place is vacant. There'll be an additional three percent bonus for you if you make it happen." I see Janet mentally doing the math and she nods. Drew continues, commanding, like he makes real estate deals every single day. "Open escrow today and I'll have the funds wired first thing Monday morning. The rest is paperwork, Janet. Don't tell me it can't be done. Tell the seller I'll be sending some people over tomorrow and they are to have full access to the unit for as long as they need."

I hold back a grin as I watch Drew bark orders at Janet. I know she doesn't like me, the way she looks down her nose at me and her disgusted looks speak volumes. She doesn't believe I'm good enough for someone like Andrew McPherson. Maybe she's right, or maybe she's wrong, but it's nice to see Drew putting her in her place.

She nods and taps frantically on her iPad.

"Anything else you need from me?" he asks, gripping my hand and all but dragging me out of the condo.

"No, I don't—"

"Good. You have my number if you need anything else." And with that, the door to the condo shuts behind us and Drew is pulling us to the elevator. He punches the down button at least ten times impatiently.

"Why are we in such a hurry?" I ask as the chime sounds and the elevator doors part.

"Because I don't like the way Janet looks at you... dismisses you." He pauses, a sympathetic look washing over his face. "I wanted to fire her the second she looked at you, but I need her to close this deal for me and fast. She's the only one who can do it." He presses the heel of his palm to his eye.

"Don't worry about it; it happens all the time," I tell him, brushing off his concern. "I'm not society, Drew. Look at me." I gesture to myself with one hand. While I'm not ugly, I'm hardly anything special.

"I am looking at you and you're fucking beautiful." He drags his knuckles across my cheek and I sink into him. "And I promise to never let anyone treat you like that again."

"She didn't do anything, Drew—"

He sighs loudly, clearly aggravated. "But she did, Gracie, I hated the way it made me feel, and you should too."

I look up at him and see the anger and the hurt all over his face. "I'll never be someone who cares about that, Drew. Appearances, titles, money...none of that matters to me." And there it is. I've laid it all out for him. If these are important to him, he's definitely barking up the wrong tree with me. I care about digging myself out of the financial mess I'm in, not what some lady I'll never see again thinks about me. My entire life, I've been looked down on by people who had more money, nicer clothes, better education, and an easier life. I've learned to keep my head down, work hard, and that the fruits of that labor will eventually pay off...I hope.

I see the muscles in his jaw tick as he contemplates what I've told him and he doesn't say anything in return. The elevator doors open and we exit into the luxurious lobby. As the doorman sees us coming, he opens the doors that lead out onto the lovely tree-lined Twenty-third Street.

The rain has stopped, but the skies are still overcast and grey. Drew leans into the car and exchanges a few words with Tony before the car pulls away from the curb and into traffic.

Drew's demeanor has shifted and he smiles, seemingly more relaxed. "Ready to explore our new neighborhood?" he asks, lacing his fingers through mine.

"Your neighborhood," I correct him.

"Our."

My heart races when he says this. While I'm flattered, this is all happening very fast and he doesn't understand the baggage I come with. If he knew the depths of the shit I'm digging myself out of, he'd go running in the opposite direction, so I correct him again. "Your."

Drew stops, turning to me. "Stop arguing with me, Gracie. If you think for one second that I'm letting you go back to Red Hook—"

"Whoa!" I stop on the sidewalk and press my palm to his chest. "Stop right there." I shake my head and take a deep breath. "My apartment is *my* apartment. I've worked hard to get that place and everything that's in it—"

"But—"

"But nothing," I cut him off. "I'll visit you here at your place." The corner of my lips twist into a coy smile.

He sighs, exasperated with me. I don't know why; he's the one who's being so unreasonable. I'm flattered but also concerned with how quickly this is moving. "Gracie, I know you feel what I feel. What we have is undeniable." He swallows hard. "Never in my life have I met someone and felt an instant connection. I've never met a woman like you before—"

My heart races as he confesses this.

He must see my hesitation, my fears. "I'm not asking you to move in with me...yet," he smiles, "but I would like you to stay with me." He brushes a piece of my hair back and tucks it behind my ear. "I like spending time with you," he whispers and wraps his arms around my waist, pulling me in tightly to him.

I can feel a grin tugging at the corners of my mouth. "Maybe just a couple of days a week...but Brooklyn is my home." Brooklyn is the first place I laid roots in New York City. While it's not Chelsea or the Upper West Side, it's home to me.

"Five days a week," he bargains, and I almost want to laugh. I can't believe we just met two days ago—not even—and he's negotiating how many days I'll stay with him in his enormous, gorgeous condo.

I bite my lip, having fun with this. "Three," I counter.

"Six," he tosses back. A smile begins to crawl across his face, highlighting that adorable dimple in his cheek.

I sigh, but I'm still amused. "Four."

"Five, Gracie." He smirks at me. He always fucking smirks at me when he knows he's got me. I fight back a grin and look away from him.

"You don't even know me," I whisper. "What if I'm crazy?"

"Oh, you're crazy all right." He laughs darkly and places his hands on either side of my face. "Crazy for me."

I chuckle and roll my eyes just as he leans in and kisses me. "Four days and maybe sometimes five," I tell him between kisses as I loop my arm through his and head toward Tenth Avenue. An excitement grows in my belly with the realization that I've just agreed to spend most of my days with this deliciously beautiful man I just met. I'm never impulsive and this may just be my biggest regret yet, but there's only one way to find out.

Drew and I spend the next two hours walking the streets of Chelsea. We take in the local shops and restaurants and stop for the best Mexican street tacos I've ever had. We stroll along the High Line, which is half a block from Drew's new condo and is an elevated walking trail built over an old railroad track. Today was perfect; it was easy and simple. And I loved it. Maybe too much. Unease grows inside me as I find myself getting comfortable with this... *us.*

Throughout the day, I found myself slipping easily into the space in my mind where I could see us creating a routine. Walking the High Line. Dinner at nearby restaurants. Grocery shopping at the local market, and I can't let myself do that. My life is a far cry from Drew's, and the sooner he realizes that and we go back to being nothing more than co-workers, the easier it'll be for both of us.

"What are you thinking about?" he asks as his driver appears at the corner.

"Nothing," I lie to him.

He side-eyes me and I know I've been caught. I shake my head and look out the window. "You're going to love it here," I say quietly, my throat tightening with growing emotion.

"*We're* going to love it here," he corrects me. How can this man be so certain about us?

I'm not in the mood to argue, so I let him finish with that, but the silence in the car is suffocating. He pulls me closer and I resist.

"Grace." He says my given name, not Gracie. This is how I know he's serious. "Talk to me."

I give my head another little shake and he takes my cue and lets it go, but not before reaching out and pulling my hand into his.

When we pull up to the Four Seasons and exit the car, Drew all but drags me through the bustling lobby to the private elevator for the suites. The tension in the air around us is thick and heavy. We step off the elevator and he taps the card reader on the door. Pulling me inside, he pushes me to the wall and slams his mouth into mine, stealing my breath, and my worries momentarily vanish.

His touch is intoxicating, and when his fingers pinch my nipples through my shirt, I instantly feel the heat pooling between my legs. I moan as he drags his lips across my neck and bites that sensitive spot behind my ear.

"Get out of your head, Gracie," he whispers as he slips his hand into the front of my pants and right into my center. His fingers slide between my slick folds and he groans as he inserts a finger, spreading my wetness around my opening. He removes his hand and pulls me toward the bedroom, and I don't resist. I can never resist his touch.

Just inside the bedroom, Drew pulls my shirt over my head and slides my pants down my legs. While I kick them off my feet, he removes his jeans and shirt and guides me to the bed.

My entire body trembles when he lays me down on the bed and settles between my legs. His gaze holds mine as he slides into me with one firm thrust. He never breaks eyes contact with me and I gasp as my body stretches to accommodate him. A moan falls from me as he slowly moves in and out of me.

His movements are slow and methodical, careful and telling. This isn't him owning my body; this is him owning my heart. His body is telling me what he won't say because he knows it'll scare me. He's telling me this is more than one night, this was never one night. It's so much more. I close my eyes and accept what he's giving, even if it's just for tonight. I wrap my legs around his waist, pulling him deeper into me and allowing him greater access, both physically and emotionally, to my body and to my heart. As much as I fight it, I can feel my walls slowly begin to crumble.

Drew takes his time making love to me. This isn't sex. This isn't fucking. This is emotional and deep. He lets his body speak to me without ever muttering a single word. His hands and his lips explore every cavern, every peak, and every curve of my body while he devours me gradually, claiming ownership of me.

We lie wrapped in each other, a tangle of arms and legs, and also my silent fears. I need to keep my focus and not lose myself or my career over Drew. My body shakes beneath his as he brings me to orgasm, and he finishes at the same time, spilling himself into me. We lie, staring at the ceiling as we both catch our breath and come down from our climaxes.

"Tell me what's bothering you," he murmurs against my ear, brushing my long, tangled hair away from my face and tucking it behind my ear. I tense and he feels it, but he pulls me closer to him anyway. "Don't pull away from me. Talk to me, Grace."

What do I tell him? I can't fall in love with you? Because that'd be a lie. I'm already falling for him. Every smirk, every touch, every kiss draws me into him, and I fear once I fall completely, I won't be able to let him go.

Do I tell him that I have so much crap to deal with that adding a relationship to the heaping pile of shit that is my life will literally break me? That my focus has to be on my career, my mom, and paying off the loans that are literally robbing me of any happiness.

I wiggle out of his arms and push myself up. Drew grabs the

bedsheet I've wrapped around me and pulls me back down next to him. "Don't walk away, Grace. Talk to me."

"I can't." I choke out the words, my throat closing around them. Tears sting the backs of my eyes and I feel the anxiety building. "Let me go!" I cry out and he releases his grip on the sheet.

I haul the sheet and my body across the dark room to the bathroom, where I close the door and throw myself down next to the toilet. The dry heaves come as they always do. My body does its best to expel the stress and anxiety I do my best to hide on a daily basis. Physically, I can't continue with this much longer; my body won't allow it.

With every heave, my stomach tightens into a ball of knots, and the tears I've managed to keep at bay until now fall in streams as I sob quietly. I'm angry. Angry at the life I was given. Angry at the circumstances I can't seem to escape. Angry that people like Drew have so much money, life-changing money, and they can walk into a building and drop four and a half million dollars on a house like it's a five-dollar bill in their wallet. I'm angry that life is so cruel, and the divide between the rich and the poor is so very, very unfair.

From behind me, I hear the water faucet turn on and then off before a wet washcloth is handed to me over my shoulder.

I take it with a shaky hand and clear my throat. "Can you give me a minute?" I ask without turning around. I can't look at him right now because I'll want him to scoop me up and tell me everything's going to be okay when it's not. It'll never be okay, because I will never get on top of everything. I have to get myself out of the mess I'm in without dragging anyone else into it. Even Jamie doesn't know the extent of the shit I'm knee deep in.

I hear the door close quietly and I lean against the bathroom wall, my back pressed to the cold tile. I adjust the long sheet around my body and tip my head up, blinking my eyes rapidly in hopes the tears will stop.

I do my best to focus on the breathing techniques I've been taught from a therapist to keep my anxiety at bay. Slowly inhale, hold that breath, and then slowly exhale. Repeat ten times. Focus on something happy. The beauty of a Montana snow-covered mountain or the summer sun warming my face. I place the cool washcloth over my eyes and let the cool fabric absorb my hot tears.

I don't know how long I sit here, but after a while, my pulse finally slows and my stomach releases the knot of muscles I had when I entered the bathroom. Finally, I push myself up and take a deep breath. I catch a glimpse of my reflection in the mirror and I'm horrified: wild hair and a splotchy red face. I'm a mess. I actually laugh because of the irony. My outward appearance actually matches the disaster my life is and I don't even bother trying to fix it or hide it anymore.

I open the door slowly and there stands Drew in a pair of boxer briefs, pacing the bedroom. He spins around when he hears the door open and he hesitantly moves toward me. With one hand, I hold the sheet around me, and with the other, I stop him. "Don't," I tell him when he tries to shove my hand aside and pull me into his arms.

"What the fuck is going on, Grace?" His normally calm and cool demeanor is now short but still concerned.

"I need to go," I tell him quietly and move around him as I collect my clothes from the floor.

His eyes narrow and his tone is sharp, full of anger or hurt. "So that's it? You're not going to tell me what's going on? You're just going to run away and pretend we haven't spent the last two nights together? You're going to deny the connection we have?" He grips my upper arms, stopping me. "What happened? Please talk to me."

And it's those words that break me. Tears form and fall in a split second. My voice shakes, my body trembles, and I feel my bottom lip quivering. "Yes, Drew. I'm going to run away. Because that's what I do best. Except my problems are too big to run away from." I'm a runner, not literally, but figuratively. I run from men. I can't tell you the last relationship I've had because I don't let men close to me. I also ran from my mother, thinking I could solve our money problems by moving as far away from her as possible. Running is what I do when I'm scared, and I'm so afraid of letting Drew in and hurting him, that to protect him I'll run from him too.

"What problems?" His face twists in anger.

My voice is weak, full of shame. "Problems I have to fix. On my own. I don't have time to get into—" I look away from him. "— whatever this is."

He lets go of me and staggers back a step. His jaw is tight with hurt. "Whatever this is."

I have no more fight in me as the tears fall. I simply sob and break down. I no longer have the strength to hold it in.

He closes the gap between us, his hand clasping my forearm in concern. "Gracie, let me help you, please."

And as much as I didn't want to hear those words, I needed to. I crumble into his arms and allow him to hold me tightly. He allows me to break and fall and let go, all while holding me up. Slowly, he guides us over to the bed and carefully eases us under the comforter. As afraid as I am to let him in, something inside me wants to trust him. I allow him to comfort me and we lie in bed for hours while I cry in his arms until sometime in the middle of the night, I finally cave to my exhaustion and succumb to sleep.

The room is pitch black when I finally crack my eyes open. I can see a sliver of light peek through the edge of the curtains telling me it's morning. I'm congested from the hours of crying, my burning eyes the proof. I reach across the mattress for Drew, but he's not there. All I find is a cold spot on the sheets where he was lying last night. The bedside alarm clock reads almost noon and I groan when I feel how sore my body is. I must have slept all tensed up and curled into a ball. My muscles ache as I stretch. I reach for the lamp and turn it on, then I swing my weary legs over the side of the bed and slide out, traipsing across the plush carpet and into the bathroom. The huge soaker tub is calling my name, so I draw a hot bath and brush my teeth while the tub is filling.

Dark circles have taken hold under my eyes and the whites of my eyes are still bloodshot from last night's episode. It's been a long time since I've had a breakdown of that magnitude and I know it's because I have a decision to make—a decision that hurts my heart, but I have to end whatever this is with Drew. Because I'm falling, hard and fast. He's what I've always dreamed of, but I can't lose focus on my goals, and that has to be my top priority.

I ease into the scalding hot water. While it hurts, it also feels amazing on my sore body. I rest my head against the back edge of the tub and close my eyes while my body slowly begins to relax and feel normal again.

The dull squeak of the door hinges startles me when Drew pokes his head inside the bathroom.

"Hey," he says quietly. "Can I come in?"

"Yeah," I answer, my voice hoarse from sleep and crying.

He pushes through and I notice the large Starbucks cup in his hand. He's dressed casually in a grey t-shirt and a pair of black joggers. His hair is mussed up, but he still looks every bit as handsome as the night I met him. This man looks like he could walk off a runaway even in gym clothes. "Uber Eats," he says, handing it to me with a small but concerned smile. I return the same smile, grateful for the coffee and that he thought of me. "It's been sitting for a bit. Hopefully, it's still warm."

I pull the plastic lid to my lips and the warm liquid spills into my mouth and hits my tongue. I moan in pleasure, knowing the coffee will also help bring me back to life along with this hot bath. Drew sits on the edge of the tub and watches me.

"Thank you," I start, and set the coffee on the ledge next to him. "For everything." My eyes meet his and he watches me carefully, his face full of concern.

"What happened last night, Gracie?" he asks. His voice is uneasy, yet full of concern.

"The culmination of every bad decision I've made in my life finally coming to a head," I tell him. My heart hurts as I tell him this. Drew is everything I've ever wanted in a partner.

"Wow." His face is contorted with hurt.

"Not you," I tell him. "Except that, in a way, it all ends with you." Silence fills the space between us for a moment.

He sighs. "I guess I don't understand."

"I can't get involved with you, Drew. I can't pull you into the mess that is my life. I have to keep my focus and you're a distraction." I pause and take another sip of coffee. "This ends today," I finally say, my voice breaking.

I pull my knees to my chest, feeling vulnerable under the weight of his stare. His eyes are impenetrable, a brick wall.

He takes a deep breath and reaches for my hand, pulling it into both of his. "This doesn't end today." His voice is quiet but firm, confident. "We're a team, Gracie. I know all of this is new for both of us, but two are stronger than one. I believe in us. Whether it's at work with our clients or out of the office. Whatever it is you need to work on, I'll be by your side to help you through it. I've never met anyone like you and I'm not ready to let you go, whatever it is, we'll figure it out—together." He pulls my hand to his mouth and presses a gentle kiss to my palm. "So you take all the time you need in this tub. Soak your worries away, relax your mind, but when you get out, you're going to tell me what *we're* up against and we're going to make a plan."

And in this moment, I fall a little more in love with Andrew McPherson.

NINE

Drew

I pace the living room floor in the suite as I wait for Gracie to finish her bath. She's been in there for an hour. I've never been good at patience. While I want to give her privacy, I'm anxious as hell to find out what had her on the verge of a goddamn nervous breakdown last night. My mind is running wild with possible reasons. I don't understand what has her wound so tightly and afraid of getting close to me.

She sure as hell isn't walking away from me without a really good explanation, and there is basically nothing that I can't fix. So it's settled, in my mind at least. She's not going anywhere. It was only three days ago that I met her and now I can't imagine not having her in my life.

I shake off those thoughts when Gracie finally emerges from the bedroom a few minutes later. She's wrapped in an oversized plush robe and her long, wet hair hangs down over her shoulders. Her cheeks are flushed pink from the hot bath, but she looks remarkably calmer than I expected.

She sits down in the corner of the sectional, tucking her long legs underneath her and then she pulls a throw pillow into her lap. It's a defense mechanism, a barrier between us, a safety net.

I sit down right next to her and pull her hand into mine before she takes a deep breath and looks at me. Her eyes carry so much pain yet so much strength. Whatever she tells me, we'll figure this out. I refuse to abandon her.

"This is a long story, so bear with me, okay?"

I nod my head and give her my undivided attention.

Her eyes drop from mine to the pillow in her lap. "I have to go way back to give you a better understanding of where some of this started." She tugs at a loose thread on the pillow in her lap, twirling it around the tip of her finger. She's nervous and I can't help but notice the slight hitch in her voice. "My dad died in a car accident with his parents, my grandparents, when I was only a few months old. My parents were high school sweethearts, only eighteen when I was born."

She stops, clears her throat, and I give her hand a small, encouraging squeeze, urging her to continue. I tell myself I will refrain from commenting or asking questions until she's done.

She looks away from me and out the large window of the hotel room. "My mom grew up in the foster care system from the time she was very young. She doesn't remember her parents or if she had any siblings. Her foster parents were decent people— they fed her, clothed her, but's that's about all they did. She was a paycheck to them. When she turned eighteen, she aged out of the system and she was no longer of any use to them.

"My dad was the only person my mother ever trusted, and they were head over heels in love with each other. They were high school sweethearts, starting dating their sophomore year of high school and totally in love by their senior year when she found out she was pregnant. By the time she realized she was pregnant, she had already phased out of the foster program and was on her own. She had no one other than my father, who was only eighteen years old himself. They graduated high school, then she and my dad got a small apartment together. My dad worked as a ranch hand to make money while my mom took some classes at the community college and worked at a grocery store."

She pulls her hand from mine and rubs her temples. I can see this is painful for her to talk about. "As you can imagine, they were young, working awful jobs just trying to pay their rent and survive. When I was born, my mom didn't work. They couldn't afford childcare and that left the burden of financial responsibilities on my father. From what my mom tells me, he was a good man, but still a kid. He worked hard and loved both of us, but times were hard for them. His parents had wanted him to go away to college. They said that my mom and I could live with them and they'd help us while he went to college and got a degree. He was adamant he wouldn't leave us, but even my mom felt that it might be the best thing for all of us, for the long term. She knew they'd end up working dead end jobs for the rest of their lives and this was a good opportunity for my dad to get a leg up. She was willing to sacrifice having him with us, so that he could do better for us."

Gracie pauses and takes a deep breath. I can tell this is extremely hard for her to talk about. Her voice is soft as she continues to tell their story. "She convinced him to go, so he left for college that next fall. He told my mom he wanted to get a degree in accounting, work for a few years to get experience, then open a small firm in Antelope Hills where he was born and raised. When he left for school, we moved in with my grandparents and they helped take care of me so my mom could still work a few days to help pay for diapers and formula. They gave us a free roof over our heads and watched me a couple of days a week. I don't think they were particularly happy with the situation, but they did their best to support my mom and dad in the ways they could or would."

She hesitates for a moment and takes a deep breath. I see her chin quiver as she begins and I know this is where things take a turn. "All was fine until my grandparents left to get my dad for Christmas break. On the way back from Missoula, they hit a patch of black ice on the interstate and their car rolled six or seven times, killing all of them."

I stroke the top of her hand with my thumb as I struggle with the weight of what she's just told me. Tears that have built in her eyes slowly fall as she continues.

"Obviously, I was a baby, so I had no idea any of this happened, but that night set off a series of unfortunate events for me and my mom. We were suddenly on our own. We jumped from apartment to apartment. She worked odd jobs to keep a roof over our heads and food on the table. My mom and dad weren't married, so she wasn't entitled to anything financially, and honestly, they didn't have much anyway. Suddenly, we had no one. From that day on, it's always been just me and my mom."

Until now, I think to myself. She'll always have me.

Gracie takes a deep breath and forges on. "There were times we couldn't make ends meet and my mom would run up credit card debt. It always seemed insignificant, but we could barely afford the minimum payment on those cards over the years, yet we always managed, or so I thought."

Gracie pauses, her voice thickening with emotion. "Then, when I was in high school, my mom got cancer. I was covered with insurance through the state because I was a minor, but she had no medical coverage. There were some medical grants she applied for and received but not enough. I put myself through college with student loans and a handful of scholarships. After I graduated, I consolidated all of our debt and I swore I'd repay everything so that my mom didn't have to worry for one more day. She's spent her entire life worrying about money, and in my gut, I feel that was ultimately responsible for her cancer. Her worry and stress manifested itself physically in her body, and I wanted her focus to be on getting better and nothing else."

I nod slowly, taking it all in. Now Grace is the one worrying about money. She's the one manifesting the stress onto herself. I'm also confused about how much debt she has since people do debt consolidation loans all the time. This usually helps them focus on repaying their debt faster with one loan versus a handful of loans. My mind is racing, but I continue to remain silent and let her finish.

She exhales heavily. "When I finally consolidated everything, it was almost three hundred thousand dollars, most of it medical bills."

I almost choke at the amount. She didn't just consolidate her student loans; she consolidated everything into one giant loan. I swallow hard, realizing the trouble she's gotten herself into financially.

She looks at me warily. "I know that doesn't sound like much to you, but for us, that's a big deal. Even with my job, the payments are hard to stay on top of and I found myself in the same position as before. Every month, I make the minimum payment, and it barely covers the interest. I just feel like I can never get ahead. My paychecks barely cover my rent, a small amount I send to my mom, and the payment on the loan."

This is where I stop her. "Where is your loan through?" She better tell me it's a legitimate bank or I'm going to lose my fucking mind.

She shrugs. "Some financial company I found online. They're the only ones that would help me," she says, her face defeated. "I was just a kid right out of college and had no credit."

I nod my head and feel the anger bubbling inside me. I know exactly what she did.

"First of all, financially, this burden should not be yours to bear alone." This really pisses me off. I get that Grace loves her mother, but she shouldn't have to bear the burden of all this debt. "And we'll get back to that, but it sounds to me like you've gotten wrapped up with a predatory lender. They're all over the place. Those payday loan places you see on every corner in poor neighborhoods are exactly that. They prey on those who need help. They hike up interest rates in return for quick cash. It's awful and many states are cracking down with laws regarding them."

Her eyes mist with tears and her face reddens in embarrassment.

"Let me help you—" I begin and she cuts me off, her head shaking from side to side.

"No! I don't want any help and I also don't have the time to get involved with anyone. I need to focus and work my ass off—"

"Grace!" I stop her, reaching out to cup her cheek. I lift her chin so her eyes meet mine. "You *can* do this alone, but I can help you. Let me help you get this loan refinanced—"

"Stop trying to save me," she snaps. "I don't need to be rescued."

There's the stubborn woman I've fallen in love with. I sigh, leaning forward on the couch, and rake my hands over my face. I want to help her, but how will I get through to her? "I'm not trying to save you," I try again, my voice even. "Just let me help you figure this out. Let me help you with a plan."

Her head falls forward and her eyes are downcast as she picks at her thumbnail in silence.

"Please," I urge her.

"I can't get involved with you," she says quietly. "I can't afford to lose my job over this relationship."

"You're not going to lose your job, Grace. We've already been over this."

"Then I can't afford the distraction. I need to focus on my clients—"

I shake my head and cut her off. "Give me one week to prove I won't be a distraction in your life." What in the actual hell am I doing? Am I negotiating myself? I have never begged a woman for anything, let alone to give me a chance at proving myself. Anyone else, and I would have packed her bag myself and had the bellhop up here escorting her out. But not Gracie. What in the hell is she doing to me?

What feels like ten minutes is more like fifteen seconds, but she finally lifts her head, her eyes meeting mine. "One week?" she asks.

"One week," I confirm, feeling hopeful. I can see the wheels in her head turning. "Then this is done?" Her voice shakes.

I swallow hard at how easily she says that. "If that's what you want, then yes, after one week, this is done."

She's pondering my proposal. "Do you promise to not be all weird at work?" She sits up a little straighter and I know she's considering this.

I chuckle softly at her remark. "I'm not weird, Gracie."

She tilts her head. "You know what I mean. You're not going to use this against me at work, are you?"

"Our relationship is separate from work," I tell her, not even disturbed for using the word relationship.

"What am I doing?" she mumbles to herself and buries her hands in her face before rubbing her temples. "This is a really bad idea."

It's not a bad idea. It's the best idea. I will do anything in the next week to prove to her that we belong together.

I send off an email to the same private investigator I used to get information on Gracie the first time, when I walked into that conference room and found out she worked at Williams Global. I asked for a complete report on her, her mother, and any known relatives, including credit reports, addresses, and any last detail to find out more about her. I know the right thing to do would be to ask her, but she's convinced that she's done with me in one week, so I don't know that'd she'd share any more than she already has, and I will do anything it takes to keep her. *Anything.* In a matter of days, this woman has changed me, softened my hardened heart. Gracie makes me want a future, something I gave up on when I found my ex-fiancée in bed with my brother.

We spend the afternoon binge-watching HGTV, and I order lunch in. Even though Gracie doesn't say it, I know she's exhausted and needs some time to simply rest her mind. She's cautious with her space on the couch next to me, but I pull her closer anyway and she doesn't fight it.

She sets a pillow in my lap and rests her head on it, her body facing the television in front of us. I take this opportunity to run my fingers through her silky hair and she lets out a little moan when my fingers graze the back of her neck.

Damn. What is she doing to me?

I could spend every weekend like this. Gracie curled lazily around me, spending our time together exploring New York City, or simply watching TV. Just having her next to me. I've always been a workaholic, and I'm learning to love and appreciate these simple, carefree moments with her.

Gracie dozes off and I send a text message to the concierge to make a dinner reservation for us. Less than five minutes later, he confirms our reservation for eight thirty at La Mesa de Abuela, the newest and most chic Mexican restaurant in Manhattan.

With plenty of time left to get ready, I enjoy the quiet comfort of having Gracie snuggled up next to me. Watching her sleep stirs something inside me. Something possessive and needy, something I don't want to let go of. Never in my wildest dreams did I think a one-night stand would turn into me falling for this woman resting in my lap. But then I remember, she only guaranteed me one week. I have seven days to convince her that she needs me as much as I need her.

"Please tell me this is not a fancy restaurant," Gracie hollers through the closed bathroom door where she's getting ready.

"Not fancy!" I respond, stepping into a pair of blue jeans. Gracie steps out of the bathroom in a pair of skin tight skinny jeans that are cut off just above her ankle and a lacy black top with a high neck. Perfect for where we're going.

"Ugh," she says with discomfort, tugging at the high neckline of the shirt.

"You look beautiful," I tell her as she slides her arms into a black leather jacket before stepping into a pair of heels.

Fuck. Me...

"Twenty dollars," she says, unplugging her cell phone from the charging cord where it was charging on the nightstand.

"Twenty dollars?" I repeat, shaking out of my thoughts.

She smirks. "Yep. Twenty dollars. This entire outfit cost twenty dollars." Her eyes fall to her feet. "Except for the shoes. Jamie gifted these to me. Some designer that she loves. She claims to have bought them for herself, and they didn't fit. But her feet are two sizes bigger than mine, so it was no accident. Then she had the nerve to lie to me and tell me she couldn't return them," she says, sliding her hands into the pocket of her leather jacket. "But everything else was twenty dollars. Thrift store shopping at its best."

"I'm impressed," I tell her sincerely. I spend more than twenty dollars on a damn pair of socks, and that's not something I should be proud of.

"Me too." She laughs. "Growing up poor used to be so

embarrassing. Now thrift store shopping is the chic thing to do. Like being poor is trendy." She rolls her eyes.

"You're not poor." I don't know why I tell her that, but I do.

She snorts in response. If I have anything to say about her life, she'll never struggle for another dollar, but I can't tell her that. I have seven days to make her mine, and then she won't have a choice.

"Ah, I beg to differ." She props a hand on her hip and purses her lips.

"Let's talk about this over dinner." I reach out and grab her hand, pulling it into mine. "If we don't leave now, we'll be late, and I'm starving."

"You're not starving; you don't know starving," she mumbles under her breath, and sadly, she's right. That was a bad analogy.

"Drew." Gracie hisses my name as the hostess directs us to our table. "This place is gorgeous!" Gracie is right. This restaurant is hip and trendy and full of rustic Mexican décor with a modern flair. It's casual but swanky. "And I freaking love Mexican food," she says as I pull out her chair for her to take a seat.

Our waitress recommends margaritas and table-side guacamole, and we decide to share an order of steak fajitas.

She takes a long sip of her margarita before setting it down. "Tell me about you," she says, picking up a tortilla chip and taking a small bite off one of the corners.

"What do you want know?" I ask, hoping she doesn't ask about my family. That is territory I don't like to cover.

"Everything." She shrugs. "Tell me about your family." I inwardly cringe when she says that, but she continues. "What were you like in high school? Where did you go to college? Have you ever been married?" She smirks and raises her eyebrows.

I let out a laugh and shake my head. "No, Gracie. I've never been married."

"I'm shocked." She feigns surprise and places her hand over her heart. "You seem like such a catch. I'm just surprised someone hasn't snatched you up yet."

"A catch?" I laugh again.

"Well, you know what I mean." She takes another sip of her margarita. "You're successful, you own a company, and you're clearly not hurting in the looks department." She winks at me and I can't help but smile at her as she continues. "Okay, you've never been married...I get that, you're still young. When was your last relationship?"

I take a sharp breath and call our server over. "Shot of tequila. Don Julio, please."

Gracie laughs and sits back in her chair, rubbing her hands together. "If you need a shot, I can only imagine this is going to be a really good story."

I wince. "Not sure 'good' is the word I'd use to describe it, but it was interesting." I sit up a little straighter and take a deep breath before starting. "I dated a girl named Melissa all through college. We met when we were freshman at Berkley and hit it off immediately. She was getting a degree in political science and wanted to go to law school, and I knew I'd be taking over my father's advertising business, so I majored in business with an emphasis in advertising."

I pause, taking a moment to remember, something I rarely let myself do. "We got engaged our senior year of college. We were that couple all our friends envied, seemingly perfect by all outward appearances. We both had our futures all planned out and we were fully supportive of each other, but still very independent. I used to think that's why our relationship was so easy."

I stop when our server delivers the shot of tequila, only I

don't shoot the tequila; I sip it. Don Julio is an experience. It's smooth and the burn is minimal as it slides across my tongue and settles in my throat before I swallow it, allowing the slow burn to warm me.

"But it wasn't easy," I continue, deep-seated anger finding its way to the surface. "Somewhere along the way, she fell for someone else, and by fall, I mean fell into his bed while we were in the middle of planning our wedding...that someone else being my brother." Reliving this memory burns worse than the damn tequila.

Grace audibly gasps and her eyes bulge. "Your brother?"

My throat tightens as I remember finding Melissa and my brother fucking in my bed when I returned home early from a business trip where my father was introducing me to peers and partners in the advertising industry. I nod my head, wincing again. "And after all that, it didn't even last between them. Six months later, they were done, but it drove a huge wedge between me and my brother and we've never fully recovered from it."

"Jesus," she mutters and picks up her margarita, taking a long, thoughtful drink.

I clear my throat, taking another sip of Don to numb the memory. "Yeah, it was tough. But I buried myself in my work and forgot all about her. It was my goal to build up AM Advertising to be the West Coast's top agency, and I did just that. I'm not sure my focus or dedication would have been fully on the company if Melissa had been in the picture."

"There's more to life than work," Gracie says quietly.

"I realize that now," I respond, holding her gaze. What she doesn't know is that she has made me realize that and I want her to know how serious I am about it. I take a moment, folding my arms on the table and continue to hold her gaze. "You've taught me that."

She blinks twice at the intensity passing between us. "How?

You've only known me for a couple of days." When the intensity is too much, her eyes drop to her margarita, where her pointer finger runs around the rim of the glass.

"Because for the first time in years, I enjoy something other than work. I find myself obsessed with something other than landing the next big client." I swallow hard at my admission. I realize this could scare her off, but I'm laying all my cards on the table.

She takes another bite of her tortilla chip and swallows hard. "Don't get too comfortable with this newfound enjoyment," she says softly, winking at me, trying to lighten the mood. But I know the weight those words bear. She clears her throat and turns the conversation away from us. "So things are still not good with you and your brother?"

I shake my head and swallow hard. "Not really. We manage to be civil to each other, but that's about it. Holidays with my mom are always interesting. She's been trying for years to painstakingly rebuild the burnt bridge between us, and we manage to let her think it's happening, but honestly, I'm not sure the damage can be repaired. I never expected my brother was capable of this kind of betrayal."

"Maybe someday you two will be able to mend your relationship," she responds thoughtfully, pulling me out of my thoughts.

I shrug halfheartedly. "Maybe."

"What's that saying?" She taps a finger over her pursed lips and tips her head back. "Everything happens for a reason? Or something like that."

I nod, trying not to let my smile be bitter. Thankfully, her smile is enough to warm me and make me forget how fucking awful that time in my life was.

"That's what I always tell myself," she says. "There has to be some reward in all of the misery life throws at us. Like, after all the pain, the heartache, and the challenges we face, there is some grand reward that will suddenly appear." Now she shrugs. "I know that sounds stupid, but life can't always suck, right?"

I let out a small laugh. "The amazing moments far outweigh the shitty ones, I most definitely believe that."

"I like it," she smiles, "and I want to believe it too."

I reach across the table and pull her hand into mine. "Then let's both believe."

The rest of the evening is filled with laughter and getting to know each other. Favorite colors, movies, animals, restaurants, and guilty pleasures.

"*Pretty Woman.*" She smiles widely. "There is no greater love story than Edward and Vivian." She sighs, shoving a piece of fajita steak into her mouth.

My eyes widen in horror. "She was a hooker, Gracie! It was the most unrealistic love story there is!"

She gasps exaggeratedly and sets her fork down. "You obviously know nothing about love. True love conquers all of the crap life hands us, even for hookers, Drew." She runs her hands over the cloth napkin in her lap and leans back in her chair.

I can't help but smile. Leaning in, I rest my forearms on the edge of the table. "Say it again."

"What?" She wrinkles her forehead in confusion.

"What you just said. Repeat it."

"True love conquers all the crap life hands us—"

I grin, gloating just a little. "Stop right there. Say it one more time."

She swallows hard, knowing what she's said and what I'm implying.

Her lips close and her face shifts from playful to somber.

I urge her, "Say it again."

She stubbornly shakes her head.

I'm not letting this go. "Say it."

"Drew, that's only in the movies."

Now I shake my head in response. "But it's not, Gracie. Go ahead, say it."

She inhales deeply. "True love conquers all the crap life hands us." Her words are barely above a whisper and her eyes fall from mine to her lap.

"Look at me," I tell her.

She lifts her head and pulls her lips between her teeth.

"Remember those words, Gracie. True love conquers all the crap life hands us." I plan to use her own words as leverage against her when I need to, and she knows it.

TEN

Gracie

I find Drew sitting at the office desk in the hotel suite, his face buried in his laptop. He once again insisted that I spend the night with him, and after we both unloaded some heavy personal information yesterday, I didn't argue. I feel like we now have a better understanding of each other. He understands why my focus is on my career so that I can concentrate on paying down my debt, and I better understand his possessiveness and his need to want me nearby.

"Morning," I say quietly behind him, doing my best not to startle him. He turns around quickly, the office chair spinning in my direction.

"Morning," he says, a large smile spreading across his face.

"Busy?" I ask him, nodding toward the laptop.

"Not really. Just coordinating a few things," he says, "and wanted to let you sleep without disturbing you."

Twice now I've woken up and he hasn't been in the bed. Selfishly, I hate waking up and not having him there. My days are limited with Drew and waking up without him next to me hurts a little.

"You don't sleep much, do you?" I tighten the belt of the robe around my waist as he watches me intently.

"Some nights I don't sleep much, other nights I do. Just depends what I have going on in my head," he says matter-of-factly.

"Since I've been here, you haven't slept much. I stress you out—"

He shakes his head. "Stop. You don't stress me out." His eyes fall from mine, trailing down my body, taking me in. The short silk robe that appeared in the closet, replacing the large, soft robe I used the other day had to be his doing. He stands quickly, taking three large steps across the suite to stand directly in front of me.

He reaches for me, his hands gently grasping my upper arms. Leaning down, he presses a soft kiss to my mouth before trailing his lips to my jaw, where he places another soft kiss before burying his face against the base of my throat. When he pulls away, both of his hands now cup my cheeks, and his possessive blue eyes hold my gaze.

"I need you, Gracie." His thumb slides across my lower lip, those words holding so much meaning. Yesterday morning, I was prepared to run; today, I want to tell him I need him too. He backs me toward the large dining table until my bottom hits the edge, stopping us. His firm hands fall from my arms to cup my bottom, and he carefully lifts me, setting me on the edge of the table. Nudging my legs open, he slides his body into the vacant space, his hard length pressing against my bare core through his gym shorts.

My breathing hitches as his fingers fumble with the tie of my robe until the knot is undone and the silk robe falls from my shoulders, exposing all of me.

"Fucking beautiful," he mumbles against my breast before pulling one of my taut nipples into his mouth. His gentle sucking shoots pleasure straight to my core just as a traitorous moan slips from my lips.

"Jesus," I hiss as another bolt of electricity rips through me.

Drew guides me down, my back pressed to the hardwood table as he trails kisses from my breasts down to the soft curve of my stomach. His hands run along the long line of flesh from my knees up to the apex of my thighs, where I yearn for his touch.

His thumbs get there first, separating my wet flesh, while his mouth trails lower until his tongue meets my clit.

"Oh, god!" I scream when he sucks the soft, throbbing bud into his mouth, my hips bucking gently against his face. My fingers clench the edges of the table, my fingernails clawing into the smooth, hard wood.

Edging a finger into my core, he works it in and out in perfect rhythm with the swirl of his tongue around my clit. My body is on high alert, my nipples taut and my thighs shaking with every thrust and every lick. I am powerless to his touch.

"I need all of you, Gracie. Always," he confesses as he fucks me with his mouth and fingers. He's shown me the greatest pleasure, support, and trust these last three days, and my heart breaks at his words.

Tears build in my eyes and I pinch them closed. He is everything I need, yet something inside me wants to protect him from my baggage. He deserves someone whose focus is on him... solely. "You have me for six days."

Thankfully, today is a holiday and the office is closed. It's nice to have a three-day weekend, especially with how fast and furious things have been going for Drew and me. I find my way into the shower, allowing the hot water to steam up the glass-encased space. I press my back to the cool glass and breathe in deeply.

Drew made love to me on the dining room table. He devoured me slowly, lovingly, and carefully, every inch of me. He made sure to worship my body, but it's my heart and soul that are hurting. Tears sting my eyes as I think of saying goodbye to him, to this, to us. Our connection is undeniable, and as much as I try to convince myself it's only physical, it's not. He's worked his way into my heart and damn if it doesn't hurt.

I quickly shampoo my hair and wash my body before drying off and getting ready for the day. Drew wanted to finish some emails before taking me out to run errands. He's always secretive about what we're doing and that keeps me on my toes, but it also doesn't allow me to plan ahead and that drives me crazy.

I slip into a pair of black skinny jeans that are ripped at the knees, and a chunky cream off-the-shoulder sweater. I wear my hair down in long beachy waves and grab my old black Chucks. They've seen better days, but I'm not ready to part with them. These were the one thing I bought new for myself and I've walked hundreds of miles in these shoes and I'm damn proud of that.

I brush some taupe eye shadow on my lids and line my eyes with a thin line of black eyeliner. It makes the green in my hazel eyes pop. Two swipes of mascara and I'm done just as Drew steps up behind me and wraps his arms around my waist.

"You ready?" he asks, nuzzling his face into the side of my neck.

"I am now." I lean back into his embrace, sighing.

"Good, because if we don't leave now, I'm going to reconsider our plans and we're going for round two on the dining table." He growls against the side of my neck and my legs weaken.

"Then we better get out of here," I manage as his lips suck at that spot just below my ear that drives me wild. My heart stammers and my core warms. Damn him.

"Come on," he says reluctantly, pulling away from me. I

internally praise everything holy because I would have laid down on this bathroom floor and let him have his way with me.

"Are you going to tell me what we're doing?" I ask as he drags me out of the bathroom.

He grabs my purse off the table in the foyer and pulls me right out the door of the suite.

"Not yet." He smirks and laces his fingers through mine, pulling me possessively to his side as he hits the elevator call button with his other hand. The bell chimes and the doors slide open as we step in.

Drew is dressed casually in worn jeans and a long-sleeved t-shirt, but his watch and shoes tell anyone looking that his casual appearance is anything but inexpensive. He's designer from head to toe. I could buy jeans like that for three dollars at my thrift store, and my guess is he paid hundreds for his.

Sadness twitches inside me as I'm reminded of the difference between us. I don't fit in his world, and he doesn't understand mine.

Tony waits for us just outside the doors of the Four Seasons. Drew hands him a sheet of paper and, with nothing more than a curt nod, Tony closes the door behind us after we slide into the back seat.

The overcast New York City skies don't damper the excitement I have every time I travel the streets of Manhattan. I live for this city. It holds all of my dreams, every bit of my excitement, and hopefully, the opportunity to dig myself and my mom out of the debt that has been crippling us for years.

A relatively painless few minutes pass when we pull up in the back-alley of a nondescript building in SoHo. I look at Drew, who's pounding away on his phone but quits when he realizes the car has stopped.

"What is this place?" I ask, scanning the semi-scary-looking building with no signage and what looks like a warehouse where the mob might hide dead bodies. However, it's SoHo, and knowing Drew, it has to be something chic.

"You'll see," he says as Tony opens the back door and Drew slides out, reaching inside for my hand. He helps me from the car and we walk to a set of steel double doors where Drew raps his knuckles on the heavy metal.

Before I have time to ask any further questions, one of the back-alley doors opens and a woman greets us with a giant smile.

"You must be Andrew," she says with a soft voice. "And Grace, correct?" She reaches for my hand and shakes it first before reaching for Drew's. "I'm Shannon and I will be helping you today."

From what I can see, there are floor-to-ceiling rolls of fabric and the sound of loud machines coming from an area beyond the fabric.

Drew clears his throat and his eyes scan the enormous space. "Thank you for meeting with us on such short notice."

She glances down at her tablet and nods. "We have a lot of ground to cover," she says and taps her finger on the tablet. "I received your list of wants, and while your timeline is tight, we should be able to cover it." She looks up and smiles brightly at both of us. "My team will have access to the property starting today, correct?"

Drew reaches for my hand and pulls it into his. "Yes. We're here to pick colors and fabrics and I'll entrust the rest to you. You came highly recommended."

Shannon blushes, pleased, and waves us to follow her. "What were you thinking in terms of an overall palette?" We follow her through a narrow walkway between giant rolls of fabric in all colors and textures.

"Grace?" Drew nudges me to answer her.

"Um," I stutter, not sure what to answer. This isn't my house and my style is most definitely not Drew's, or at least I assume it's not. I haven't known him long enough to make that assumption. "I don't know."

Shannon leads us to a wall of neutral fabrics, all in varying shades of grey. "Grey is a great color to use for emphasis. We have light grey, dark grey, and charcoal. It's easy to use this for your statement pieces, then add a pop of color with accent pillows, accessories and art."

Shannon pushes a button and the giant rolls of fabric begin to move. She stops at one in the lighter end of the color spectrum that has some soft texture to it. "I'd recommend this for a large sectional."

Instinctively, I reach out and run my hand over the soft fabric. It's durable but still has a soft feel to it.

"What do you think?" Drew asks, also running his long fingers over the fabric. In another life, I'd enjoy picking out fabrics and furniture with a potential boyfriend. In this life, I have to keep him at a distance. It's not fair to him to be this involved in the process of decorating his place, and that makes me sad.

"It's beautiful. I think it'll complement the grey in the kitchen," I tell him while looking at Shannon, who's taking notes in her tablet. I don't want him to think I want an opinion on his furnishings.

"We like it," Drew says, and Shannon takes a picture of the fabric with her tablet.

"Excellent; this gives me what I need. Do you have a preference on accent colors?" she asks as we walk toward another wall. The wall is covered in darker-colored fabrics: dark navy, rich greens, deep reds.

"I like the navy," Drew says, looking at me, waiting for my response.

"Me too," I answer quietly, feeling awkward. I just said I didn't want an opinion, yet here I am offering one. I want Drew to be happy, and I know that participating and supporting him with these decisions will make him happy, so I go along with it.

Shannon seems pleased with Drew's decisions, and she smiles as she taps away at her tablet. "Excellent. How do you feel about gold as an accessory color? We can do some modern furniture with gold metal legs; brushed gold is really popular right now."

"That sounds great," Drew answers.

"One more thing," Shannon begins, walking us through the walls of fabric and down another corridor toward the room where the loud machinery is. We stop before two double doors and she turns toward us. "It's going to be loud. This is where the furniture is manufactured. Everything is custom, made to specification for your space. However, there are many samples, so you can see the style of furniture you might like. If there's something you want to add or tweak, we can do that too. Just ask and I'll let you know if it's possible."

She pushes open both doors and the room is bright and full of activity. Men and women are working at constructing and upholstering large pieces of furniture. I can see giant sectionals, modern couches, small accent chairs, dining chairs, and headboards. I had no idea a place like this existed. I knew of chain furniture stores and, of course, Goodwill, but this blows my mind. I can't even imagine the cost of having your own furniture made.

I follow behind Drew and Shannon, taking in the enormous space. It must take up an entire city block. When we finally reach the area with samples, I'm shocked at the different styles of couches. Plush and comfy to stiff and modern, tufted with buttons to clean and sleek.

I lean in to Drew and whisper to him, "I'm not helping you choose this. This is for your place—"

"What do you think of this?" Drew cuts me off, pointing to a large sectional. The cushions are deep and full, but with clean lines. Nothing uncomfortable-looking but still stylish and modern. I swallow hard and look at him, squeezing his hand hard in a gesture of defiance.

"You can sit on it," Shannon offers as she continues tapping away on her tablet.

Drew pulls me to the giant couch and we sit in the middle of the sectional. I sink into his side and he wraps his arm around my shoulder, pulling me into him. The embrace is comforting, and for a flash of a second, I imagine myself curled into him at his new place, wrapped in a blanket, watching TV. I push that thought aside just as I feel his chin on top of my head and his arm pulls me even closer to him.

"I think this will be perfect," he tells Shannon. "Make sure there is a matching ottoman," he adds. "A big one."

"Sure thing," she responds and looks at us with a kind smile. "I think that's all I need from you. Now that we have colors and the style selected, I can fill in the rest. My team will be at your new place later today for measurements and we'll have this delivered by the date you requested. Will there be any contractors we need to work around?"

"No. It was remodeled right before it was placed on the market. A cleaning crew will be coming in too, but that won't interfere with delivery. If there is anything, please reach out to me immediately. Nothing aggravates me more than lack of communication," Drew answers.

"My team will be there to accept delivery and ensure everything is ready for you, Mr. McPherson. Thank you for entrusting me to decorate your home." She smiles sincerely at him before looking at me. "And, Grace, it was a pleasure meeting you. I hope you and Mr. McPherson love your new home."

My throat tightens at those words. Words I won't correct, but my heart falls as she says them. Drew pulls me tighter to his side and I muster out a simple, "Thank you."

"We are going to love our new house," Drew adds, smirking at me.

I mouth to him, "Six days," and he rolls his eyes before mouthing back to me with a wink.

"That's what you think."

ELEVEN

Drew

"Six days." I hear those two fucking words on repeat like a broken record as I drag Gracie out of the furniture store. Fuck that. I'll let her believe she has six days left, and I'll make those six days the best of her life, so phenomenal, she won't want to walk away.

Our car waits for us in the alley right where he left us, and Tony walks over to meets us at the rear passenger door. "Were you able to get what I requested?" I ask him discreetly.

He grins with a curt nod. "Yes, sir. Everything is secured."

"Thank you." I shake his hand.

Tony knows he'll be rewarded handsomely with a generous tip at the end of the day. I provided him a detailed list of what I wanted, and for him to pull it off in the hour Gracie and I were in the furniture warehouse is actually quite impressive, considering traffic alone probably accounted for more than half of his time.

Gracie and I settle in to the backseat of the car as we head out of SoHo and back toward the Upper West Side of Manhattan.

"Thank you for your help," I say softly, resting my hand on Gracie's thigh.

She turns and looks at me but doesn't respond. I see her

trepidation, her fears, her concern. This was too personal for her. She thinks she's leaving in six days and picking out furniture for our home—or, to her, *my* home—was too much for her. "Your opinion matters to me." I give her thigh a gentle squeeze.

"I don't know why," she answers quietly in return. There isn't that edge of sarcasm or snark in her tone that's normally there; her voice actually sounds pained. "This is for *your* home, Drew, not mine."

I swallow hard, ignoring her statement, but I can't ignore the emotion in her eyes and how they suddenly turn pink and misty.

"You matter to me," I respond to her, holding her gaze. "You're important to me." I need her to know I'm not going to let her go easily. I've never fallen for anyone as quickly and as intensely, and I plan to show her just how much she means to me. As her emotions build and become even more visible, I whisper, "Talk to me." I run my hand up her thigh until I reach her hand before sliding her fingers into mine and holding them tightly.

She shakes her head slowly from side-to-side and I see her swallow hard.

"Please, Gracie." I try to be patient, to be who she needs me to be in the moment, but I want her so fucking badly to know she can count on me. Maybe she couldn't count on other people in her past, other men, but dammit if I won't use every last breath in my body convincing her that she can count on me.

In defiance, and without a word, she shifts away from me and looks out her window, but I won't release her hand. She can try to pull away from me all she wants, but I won't let her go. An uneasy silence fills the car and we sit in the uneasiness until Tony announces our arrival at our destination.

"Mr. McPherson," he says, pulling me out of my thoughts. "We're here."

Gracie's gaze snaps from her window to mine. Plush, green grass and tall trees shadow the entrance to Central Park. Our driver pulled over just past Columbus Circle where there's an entrance to the park. Gracie looks at me, confused, but I slide out of my door and offer her my hand to help her out. She accepts and slides out next to me.

Tony pops the trunk and hands me two large brown paper bags with handles. Gracie looks at the bags, then at me, her confusion sinking deeper.

"Ready?" I ask her.

She takes a deep breath, her shoulders rising with tension. "What's that?" she asks, glancing at the bags.

"You'll see." I wink at her.

Her shoulders fall and she sighs. "Everything is a surprise with you, isn't it?"

"I like surprises." I pause. "And I like you. I like surprising you."

She drops her head and I see her fighting back a smile, a pleasant change from her emotional state in the car.

"Come on." I nudge her gently with my shoulder and we walk into Central Park. I carry both bags with my left hand and she holds my right as we wander further into the park. We find a nice grassy area under a large tree and I set the bags down. To our right, two men throw a Frisbee back and forth. Other people are congregated on the thick grass, enjoying an overcast New York City afternoon.

In one of the bags, I find a large plaid blanket and spread it out on the grass before I unpack the other bag. I requested two salads, two sandwiches, a bottle of wine, and bottles of water. Tony went above and beyond, throwing in a dessert and a pasta salad. He's good. Even remembered glasses and utensils.

"What is this?" Gracie squeals, clasping her hands together in front of her chest.

"What does it look like?" I ask, setting up everything on the blanket. I smile at the sound of excitement in her voice. Nothing makes me happier than seeing Gracie smile, to know that I might make her day a little brighter. Her happiness is my happiness.

"A picnic! I haven't done this since I was a kid," she exclaims.

"Then you'd be correct." I grin. "Sit down." I gesture to the blanket, where she sits and crosses her legs.

Birds chirp in the tree above us and the sounds of laughter in the park has put me at ease. This is how I want our time to be spent. Relaxing and basking in each other's company—comfortable and happy.

"Pick a salad," I tell her. "There's shrimp Caesar and a chicken quinoa. There's also a chicken salad sandwich or BLT."

The plastic containers are stacked in front of her and I can see her mind going a million miles an hour as she tries to decide. Thankfully, the wine has a twist-off top and I unscrew the cap and pour us each a glass of Pinot Grigio. I take a sip and do my best to hide my wince. It's not Napa Pinot Grigio, but it's also not the worst I've tasted. Just a little bitter.

I hand her a glass of wine and she sets it in the grass, balancing it carefully in the long blades next to her just as she reaches for the Caesar salad and the BLT sandwich.

"This is too much food," she says, popping the plastic lid open that holds her sandwich. "But who can turn down bacon?" She shrugs, taking a bite of her sandwich, and I can't help but laugh. "I tried to be a vegetarian once," she mentions around a mouth full of food. "Then I remembered that I couldn't eat bacon." She covers her mouth with her hand before swallowing. "I was technically a vegetarian for four hours. Bacon ruined it for me."

I tip my head back and laugh, trying to picture it.

"You can take anything away from me but bacon," she says around a grin. "I just couldn't live without it."

That's how I feel about her. She's my bacon. I laugh, shaking my head at that thought.

"What's so funny?" she asks.

"Nothing."

"Tell me."

"That's how I feel about you." It's rare I'm so honest, but with Gracie, I can't help myself. "You're my bacon."

She sets her sandwich down and reaches for her glass of wine. "Drew," she says quietly.

"Gracie, listen," I begin, cutting her off. "I'm not asking you for forever." Not right now anyway. I can see myself spending every day for the rest of my life with her, but it's too soon to tell her that. "Just give me more than six days. Give me a chance. Lean on me. Let me help you. We're better as a team."

Her eyes are full of doubt. "How do you know?"

"Because I can feel it here." I pound my chest just over my heart. "I just know we are."

She traces the rim of the plastic wine glass with her finger and drops her eyes from mine to her hand.

I clear my throat, angry at myself for feeling choked up. I wanted this to be lighthearted—this picnic, us here, together. "I know we've known each other for only a couple of days, but this is... different." That's the only word I can use in hopes of not scaring her away. It is different. It's comfortable...and safe, and I haven't felt like this about anyone in a long time, especially someone I've just met.

She drops her head and sighs. "I need to figure out my mess on my own."

My jaw tightens. "No, you don't."

"Drew—"

"Stop!" I cut her off again, my voice louder than I anticipated. I inhale and exhale, giving myself a moment. "I'm not going to take over and fix this for you, but let me help you figure out how *you* can fix this."

She bites her bottom lip and balls her fists in her lap. Before she has the opportunity to say no, I continue.

"Just don't limit our time together, Gracie. No end date. Let's just take this day by day, okay? No expectations except that we'll support each other. No pressure for more."

Her shoulders fall in defeat and I fight back a grin, not because she feels defeated, not because I won, but because I've gotten her to give us a chance.

"Let's enjoy our lunch and this weather," I tell her, reaching for my glass of wine.

She looks at me, and something crosses her face. Relief? Happiness? Both? She smiles and also reaches for her glass of wine.

"To no end dates," I tell her and hold my glass out toward her to toast our new arrangement.

"To day by day," she says in response and taps the rim of her glass to mine.

It's not exactly what I wanted, but I'll fucking take it if it means Gracie will be by my side while we figure this out. Now it's her smiling, and fuck if my heart doesn't beat wildly in my chest in return.

Over the next hour, we finish lunch, polishing off the wine. Then we lie on the blanket, her head on my chest as we look up at the sky. The sprinkling of clouds cleared and we're left with a beautiful sunny New York City day. Warm enough to enjoy being outside, but cool enough to not be miserable.

"I could do this every day," she says quietly, running her hands gently over the blades of grass.

"Me too," I answer her, running my fingers through her long, soft hair. She turns her head to look at me and I can't help but stare into her beautiful hazel eyes.

"Thank you." Her lips turn up at the corners slightly and I

love that it's close to a smile. It's nice to see her at ease and not a bundle of stress.

"For what?"

"This."

I take it she means the relaxing afternoon. I push myself up to sitting, keeping her head resting in my lap. I bend over and lightly brush my lips over hers.

"You're welcome," I say against her lips.

We spend the rest of the afternoon walking through the park, renting a boat and floating through the lake. The view of New York City from a small row boat in the center of a lake in Central Park is something everyone needs to experience. I've never seen Gracie's smile so large and so genuine. I may have snapped an unsuspecting picture of her while she took in the views.

Back at the Four Seasons, I see Gracie grab her large bag from the closet.

"What are you doing?" I ask as she pulls clothes from the hangers and folds them carefully before putting them in her bag.

"It's Monday night and I'm going home. I have to work tomorrow." She looks up at me and smiles that mischievous smile I've become all too familiar with.

I let out a long sigh. "It's Monday night, we're going to have dinner here before going to bed, and I have to work tomorrow too." I meet her at the entrance to the closet and take the bag from her hands.

She sighs loudly in return and reaches for her bag. "You don't get to make every decision for me," she says stubbornly as we tug the bag back and forth between us.

"I know this," I tell her, tugging the bag a bit harder and out of her grasp.

"Drew!" she warns, reaching for the bag that I hide behind my back. "Give me my bag."

"Stay with me. We're going to the same place tomorrow," I remind her. "It just makes sense you stay here and we go to work together."

She snorts. Loudly. "Yeah, that's going to go over really well. You bought our company on Friday, I bedded you over the weekend, and we show up hand-in-hand on Tuesday? Can you even imagine what that would look like, let alone what people will say?"

"Quite honestly, Gracie, I don't give a fuck. I began bedding you before I bought the company, not knowing that you were an employee of said company. Our relationship started before my ownership."

"You don't understand." She closes her eyes, as if losing patience with me. "I need this job. I need the support of my co-workers to help me be successful. If they know we're..." She pauses. "...doing *this*, they're going to lose all respect for me."

"There is nothing wrong with *this*," I promise, trying not to sound irritated. "We'll keep it out of the office if that makes you more comfortable."

"It will make me more comfortable to go home tonight, sleep in my own bed, and show up at the office on my own tomorrow morning."

Now I'm the one sighing in defeat. "Fine." My tone is short and childish. I have to accept her feelings and honor them. While I don't like it because I want her here with me tonight, I have to remember this is a partnership; we both give and we both take. She wins tonight. Begrudgingly, I hand her the bag and she takes it, never pulling her eyes away from me.

"Thank you," she says sweetly and continues to put her clothes in the bag.

"But I'll be escorting you home," I insist.

She shakes her head in disapproval. "I can take the train, Drew. I do it all the time."

"Not anymore," I muster through gritted teeth. I surrendered when she wanted to go home. I'm not bending on this.

She zips her bag, dropping it to her feet as she steps over it and wraps her arms around my waist, pulling me into a hug. Burying her face in my neck, she squeezes me tightly. A hug I can't help but savor. I wrap my arms around her, holding her just as tightly in return.

She presses a soft kiss to my lips, then reaches up to rub my dimple. Her finger traces the small crease and she smiles.

"You come back here tomorrow night," I tell her. It's not a question, it's a demand. I pull her closer to me, already missing her.

"Wednesday night," she mumbles against my chest.

Gracie's stubbornness is going to be the damn death of me.

TWELVE

Gracie

As Tony pulls up to my building, I reach for the door handle, but Drew reaches across me, stopping me before pulling my hand into his.

"Stay with me tonight," he pleads.

This man is incorrigible and frustrating, and so goddamn sweet, my heart flutters in my chest, but I can't. I won't. I need tonight to clear my head. I need to be by myself for a few hours to settle into everything that's happened over the last five days.

"Drew," I let out a longsuffering sigh, "we're at my place. I'll see you in the office tomorrow." I lean in and press a soft kiss to the corner of his mouth.

He exhales and presses his forehead to mine. "You're right. One night apart won't kill us. But you're staying with me tomorrow night." He flashes that mischievous grin of his at me. He's right, one night won't kill us, and honestly, with how fast everything is happening, I need the space.

"We'll see," I tell him and wrangle my hand out of his grasp. As I open the door and slide out, I feel Drew right behind me. "Stay here; I'll be fine," I tell him, but he shakes his head.

Tony pops the trunk of the Town Car and Drew grabs my bag, slamming the trunk closed when he's done. "The only way I'm leaving you tonight is if I walk you to your door and I know you're safely inside." He carries my bag in his right hand and grabs my hand possessively with his left. "Lead the way," he urges me.

"Do I need to remind you I've lived here for two years, I go out all the time, and surprise," I wave my hands in the air in mock surprise, "I'm still alive!" He rolls his eyes at me and I fumble with my keys when I get to the main doors. No doorman here to greet us, only the scent of a musty one-hundred-and-ten-year-old building. We walk the narrow stairs, Drew following closely behind me because we wouldn't fit side-by-side up the staircase. When we get to my apartment door, I slide my key into the old door and shove it open.

With a loud squeak, the door opens into my small kitchen and I reach for the light switch on the wall. A dull yellow light fills the small dated space. "Thanks for walking me up," I say, turning to Drew.

His eyes scan the kitchen, the small living room, and trail over to my bedroom as if he's looking for something before he nods at me. "You're welcome," he answers, pulling me into his arms and into a hug. "I don't like you staying here, Gracie."

"I've lived here for almost two years," I remind him. "It's my home, and I'm safe here."

He sighs in frustration.

"Plus, the Four Seasons is so stuffy." I shudder in mock annoyance. He rolls his eyes at me and I let out a little laugh. "Now go!" I nudge him toward the door. "I want to take a shower and crawl into bed and read."

"You can do that with me at the stuffy Four Seasons." I continue shoving him toward the door and over the threshold right out into the hallway.

"I can't imagine you leaving me alone long enough to read," I tell him.

"Touché," he says with a wicked grin.

We stand, taking each other in. Our first night apart since we met. "See you tomorrow, Mr. McPherson," I whisper.

His wicked smile turns sweet. "Goodnight, Ms. Morgan."

I close the door and lock the deadbolt. It takes a minute before I hear his heavy footsteps descending the creaky old staircase. I pad across the small living room and push aside one of the thrift store curtains to see Drew jogging to the waiting Town Car. Before he gets inside, he turns and looks up at the building and spies me in the window. He smiles before ducking into the car. I watch the black car drive away, the red tail lights fading into the sea of other cars traveling down my street.

I do exactly as I tell Drew I was going to do. I take a hot shower and slip into a pair of yoga pants and a long-sleeved t-shirt before tying up my wet hair. Finally sliding into my bed, I shoot off a quick text to Jamie, who has texted me no less than eight hundred times this long holiday weekend, and I've casually ignored every single one.

Me: I'm alive and home. We'll catch up tomorrow. I love you.

I see the three little bubbles pop up indicating that she's responding and I wait, but nothing comes through before they disappear. I finally power down my phone and reach for my book. I used to roll my eyes at the cheesy instalove romances that I enjoy reading, never believing that love could happen so easily. Now I'm proof that love happens on its own timeline. A brief glance across a room, or a brushed shoulder in the grocery store, even a one-night stand after a night of drinking...love can happen instantaneously. I truly believe that now.

Even though the hot shower helped clear my head, I find it hard to read. I can't stay focused with thoughts of Drew at the forefront of my mind. I had no intention of falling for him, but every minute we spend together is making it harder for me to believe I'll be able to let him go. I barely read a chapter before I find myself falling asleep. Leaning over, I place the book on my nightstand and shut off my lamp before sleep takes over.

The next morning, I wake up feeling refreshed. I even make myself a piece of toast with bread I keep stashed in my freezer. A dollop of glorious peanut butter spread over the toast makes my stomach happy. I'm out of coffee grounds, so coffee will have to wait until I get to the office.

Sometime overnight, thunderstorms moved in and it's pouring rain outside. I love the rain, so it doesn't bother me in the slightest. I slide a pair of heels into my bag and throw on a pair of flats to commute in. I also toss an extra pair of black pants and a shirt into my bag just in case my half-broken umbrella fails me. Collecting my purse, I manage to leave my apartment on time at six forty-five in the morning, which never happens on the day after a long holiday weekend. I'm anxious to get to the office to see Drew and catch up with Jamie, however, I'm also glad I spent the night at my apartment. It's given me time to regroup and I feel refreshed this morning.

Fortunately, luck is on my side. The rain seems to have temporarily lightened and I wait for less than a minute before my bus arrives. Two transfers later and I arrive at the subway station to catch the train that will take me to Manhattan. I've done this commute so many times, I could do it in my sleep. I see familiar faces, although they're complete strangers. In Montana, we would have become friendly seeing each other daily. Here, everyone keeps their heads down, noses in their phones, and earbuds in, in an attempt to keep to themselves.

I score a seat on the train, another rarity, and mentally run through what I need to get done at the office today. I can feel my phone buzzing in my bag, but I ignore it.

By the time I get off at my stop and get up to street level, the rain has begun to come down in sheets. My rickety three-dollar thrift store umbrella barely gets me to the office, but I manage without getting too wet. Cloyd, greets me with a plastic umbrella bag and I offer him a kind smile as I shake water off my jacket and do my best to tame my hair that has now frizzed up due to the humidity.

Arriving on the floor, I glance over at Drew's office. The door is open and the lights are off. He's not here yet. The office is just starting to come alive when I slide into my cube. The weather—on top of it being the first day after a long holiday weekend—has everyone getting a late, lazy start. I fire up my laptop just as Jamie comes gliding across the floor, carrying two cups of coffee. I smile at her, and she smiles back. I wouldn't know what to do without her.

"You always have my back, don't you?" I say as she shoves the cup of steaming cardboard at me.

"Always." She side-eyes me sarcastically. "Except when you ignore my texts and calls for an entire weekend."

I glance away from her and hold the coffee between both of my hands, letting the contents of the cup warm my fingers. "Guilty," I manage between sips of the hot liquid. "And I'm sorry. It's just been so crazy, I don't even know what to tell you or where to start—"

She cuts me off in her endearing, commanding way. "How about we pick up where we left off on Friday." Her eyebrows raise knowingly, and I pinch my eyes closed, feeling awful for ignoring her.

I glance across the office and notice that Drew's office lights are still off, which means he hasn't arrived yet. I heave a sigh of relief, knowing that he's not here and I can catch up with Jamie before he arrives. I stand up and reach for Jamie's hand.

"Conference room," I tell her, nodding toward the dark room. I drag her down the hall and the room lights up when we enter thanks to the motion sensors. I close and lock the door, drawing the privacy screens next so people can't see us.

Throwing herself into a chair, Jamie grins at me. "Must be good if we have to talk about it in a conference room." She spins in her chair like an excited little girl.

"I can't have anyone in the office knowing about this," I tell Jamie seriously. "I can't have this jeopardize my career or have anyone thinking I'm doing anything inappropriate," I start.

Her eyes widen like she knows this is going to be juicy, but she says with all seriousness, "I know. I didn't mean it like that—"

"Jamie," I cut her off. "I need you to promise me you'll keep this under wraps. I need this job, I love this job. I've loved this job long before Mr. McPherson bought the company…"

"Is that what you call him? Mr. McPherson?" she interrupts with a giggle. "Deeper, Mr. McPherson," she jokingly says and I roll my eyes. "Okay, sorry. I'll be serious now." She straightens up in her chair and pulls her coffee to her. "Tell me everything."

I sit next to Jamie and start from Friday night. I tell her about the elevator, our night at the hotel, condo shopping, dinner, furniture shopping, and even about our picnic. I tell her I confessed about my money problems, problems even Jamie doesn't know the gritty details of. She knows I've got shit to take care of, but she doesn't know the extent of it. Jamie listens intently as I tell her everything. When I finally finish, she simply stares at me.

"Damn," she murmurs, dazed. "You guys jumped right into this, didn't you?"

I can't do anything but nod my damn head in response. "I know, and it fucking scares me."

There's a loud knock on the conference room door that startles both Jamie and me. She jumps up and opens the door, just as Eddie pops his head inside.

"Sorry to interrupt, ladies," he starts. "We have the conference room reserved for a client meeting in five minutes."

I glance at my watch and see that it's almost nine o'clock. Jamie and I have been in here for almost an hour.

"Shit," I mumble, grabbing my empty coffee cup. "I have to get to work."

"Me too," says Jamie, following me from the conference room back toward our desks.

I stop abruptly, causing Jamie to run into my backside when I see Drew standing in my cube, staring out my window over a cloudy, rainy Manhattan. His hands are shoved into his pockets and his dress shirt is rolled up to his forearms. Tan, muscular arms stick out from under that crisp dress shirt. Even casual, he looks like the powerhouse CEO that he is. My heart rate kicks up a notch at the sight of him.

As Jamie nudges me forward, I clear my throat as I do my best to look unaffected by his presence.

"Mr. McPherson," I acknowledge him, but don't look at him. I slide into my desk chair and enter the password to my computer, bringing the screen back to life.

"Good morning," he says from behind me and I still keep my eyes trained on my computer. "And good morning, Jamie," he says, acknowledging her.

I glance up at Jamie and see her smile at him knowingly. Dammit, Jamie.

"Morning, Mr. McPherson. Busy weekend getting to know

New York City?" she asks him with the kind of innocence only a skilled liar could pull off. I'm going to fucking kill her. I narrow my eyes at her and she winks at me.

I spin around in my chair to look at Drew, whose eyes jump back and forth between us, and I can see he's picked up that I've filled her in. I hang my head in shame and shake my head.

"It was a wonderful weekend," he tells her honestly.

"Do anything exciting?" she asks, her tone snarky and her questions intruding. "Or anyone?" she says under her breath and I choke.

"Are you okay?" Drew asks me.

"Fine," I cough out, tossing a glare at Jamie, who giggles and slides into her desk chair. I pick up a pen off my desk and throw it at her. It hits her back. She bursts into laughter and Drew shakes his head in amusement at us.

He leans over my shoulder and whispers into my ear, "I missed you last night." His warm breath causes me to shiver and catch my breath. "I didn't like waking up and you not being there," he continues, knowing the effect he has on me.

I shift in my chair and sit up straight, trying to drown out the throbbing that has started between my legs.

I spin slowly toward him and stop, his face mere inches from mine. "I slept remarkably well," I tell him.

He smiles. "Liar."

"I'm not lying," I whisper.

"You are." He brushes a knuckle over my top lip and my skin breaks out in goosebumps. "When you lie, your upper lip twitches." Jesus Christ, this man has me all figured out.

I hold his gaze and my heart stammers in my chest. Looking at him, I can't help but feel that I've missed him too.

"I'd like to meet with you later to go over a few things," he says, standing up. "How does eleven thirty in my office sound?"

"Sounds fine," I muster out.

"See you then, Gracie."

Drew saunters out of my cube and down the hallway. I can't help it as my eyes follow him as he walks through the rows of cubes until he reaches his office. I notice Jamie watching him too before she spins around in her chair and faces me.

"Holy fuck," she hisses. "That man has it bad for you." I look back at Drew's office and watch the door close before I look at Jamie again.

"I know." And sadly, I have it just as bad for him.

Just before eleven thirty, the art department sends over three different advertising design concepts for one of my potential clients, a large privately-owned hospital here in New York City. I examine each of the concepts thoroughly, finally landing on one that I propose they choose, and in turn hire me and AM Global Advertising to manage their advertising needs. However, I want all three concepts presented because, honestly, all of them are amazing. It's unusual to have three strong concepts where all of them stand out both artistically and content wise. This is an account manager's dream. Copy and concepts that will work with print, social, and radio advertising, and all of them are fucking fantastic.

I set up a meeting with my media buyer to discuss budget proposals and channel planning. I want magazine, newspaper, radio, social media, and television all on the table. I want a solid proposal with budget lined up to present when we meet with the client.

I'm feeling great about my progress for the day until I realize it's eleven thirty on the dot. I quickly lock the screen on my laptop and nervously run my sweaty palms over my dress pants. I grab a notebook from my desk and head toward Drew's office. I knock on the door and wait until I hear him say "Come in" before entering.

"Hey," I say casually, intentionally leaving the door open as I wait just inside his office.

He gestures toward the small, round office table that sits in the corner of his office. "Have a seat." His tone is professional, not a hint of casualness in his voice. Maybe this is a work meeting.

I like that he can be professional at work, not everything between us having to be sexual. He walks over to the office door that I left open and closes it, twisting the lock on the handle before joining me at the table. He doesn't sit across from me, but instead pulls out a chair right next to me and sits down, edging himself in closer to me. My heartrate spikes as his arm brushes mine and I feel like a fifteen-year-old school girl with her first crush.

He sets a manila folder on the table and turns to me. "I missed you last night." He looks amazing in his perfectly pressed black dress pants and blue dress shirt, sleeves rolled up to expose his forearms. I swallow hard, not knowing how to respond. I missed him too, but at the same time, the distance was needed. Everything is moving at warp speed and I needed a night to just be by myself.

"You already told me that," I tease, "and it looks like you survived." A smile tugs at my lips.

He shakes his head and leans back in his chair, propping his right leg over his left knee.

"I know I can survive without you, Gracie, but maybe I don't want to." His forefinger traces the outline of the manila folder and I remember that finger tracing every curve of my body.

I pinch my eyes closed, pushing back the memory. "I missed you too," I begrudgingly admit and inhale a sharp breath.

He grins at my admission. "Tonight, you're staying with me." It's a statement, not a request.

I don't even bother arguing with him. I simply nod. Good thing I packed an extra outfit in my bag for the rain.

"Good, now that we've agreed to that," he starts and can't stop smiling. He slides the folder in front of me. His face drops into something more serious.

"What is this?" I question, resting my palm flat on top of the envelope.

"Options."

"What kind of options?" The folder is about a half-inch thick and I trail my fingers across the cover to the edge to open it.

"Options that will hopefully help you."

Oh, Jesus, what has he done? I flip the folder open and see page after page of loan companies listing terms, payment amounts, and interest rates. My stomach drops when I see the amount of information he's collected and presented to me. Work I've been too intimidated, too afraid to do.

"Drew—" I start, but my voice breaks as my eyes scan the pages of information.

"Listen," he begins, his voice quiet and steady. "It's just for you to look at. You don't need to make any decisions today." He clears his throat and reaches out his hand, resting it on my forearm. "These are legitimate companies that won't take advantage of you. All I did was compile the information. That's where my help will end unless—"

"No!" I snap at him nervously. "This is perfect." I shuffle the papers back into the folder and slap the folder closed. "Thank you." My voice is clipped, abrupt.

"—unless you need me," he finishes his sentence hesitantly. He knows I don't want to talk about this with him. "I can co-sign, I can help—"

"You've done enough already. Thank you." I just want to end this conversation. All of this makes me so uncomfortable and it's embarrassing. "I should really get back to work," I tell him as I stand up, hoping to make a fast exit.

He nods, but not before reaching out and clasping his hand around my wrist. "Tonight," he says softly, a gentle reminder this conversation isn't changing my agreement to stay with him tonight. I nod quickly and get the hell out of his office as fast as I can.

I spend the rest of my afternoon doing my best to get through emails, the media proposal, and three conference calls, but I'd be lying if I said I haven't been distracted by the folder from Drew sitting dead center on my desk. I thumb through the pages over and over, wondering how he was able to collect so much information so quickly. I rub my forehead as I think about it, but then I remember who he is. He has access to the best of everything—accountants, financial advisors, and bankers. I'm sure he made a call and, *bam*, this is what I got.

While I'm thankful, I'm also humiliated. I hate that someone else knows about my situation, even though it was my choice to tell him. The loan information on the documents lists the exact amount of debt I have, having grown by the tens of thousands since I last checked. Fucking interest.

I rest my head in my hands and fight back tears. Angry tears. Angry at everyone and everything. Rationally, I know that's fucked up, because this is my own doing.

"You okay?" His voice is concerned and quiet. I glance at him quickly as he looks around to see if anyone is nearby, and fortunately, no one is around.

I want to tell him no. I feel nauseous. I want to cry and scream and make it all disappear, but this is what my life is.

I raise my head and look at him. "I will be," I muster out. "It's just overwhelming."

Drew chooses not to say anything, and for once, I'm grateful for his silence. Nothing he could say would make me feel better in this moment. He's done so much in just getting me the information I need to get me on a better financial path and that means more to me than I can even express.

Drew steps in closer to me, but not so close that it's inappropriate in a work environment. "It's five thirty. I've wrapped up everything important on my to-do list. Shut down and meet me downstairs in fifteen minutes. Tony is waiting on the corner of Forty-Seventh Street. I'll be in the car waiting for you."

I don't have the energy to argue, so I nod my head as my eyes fill with tears.

"Hey," he whispers. "I promise you everything is going to be just fine."

I want so badly to believe him. Taking a deep breath, I let his words sink in. Drew squeezes my shoulder in a gesture of comfort before heading back to his office. I see his office lights shut off before he makes his way to the elevator. After firing off one last client email, I gather my belongings, shoving the folder in my large shoulder bag next to my purse.

Jamie is still in a client meeting that should have ended almost an hour ago, so I scribble a quick message to her on a sticky note and leave it on her desk. I stop by the restroom to freshen up before heading downstairs. From the lobby, I can see the rain still falling heavily. I pull my shitty broken umbrella from my bag and wave to Cloyd on my way out.

Just as Drew said, Tony and his Town Car wait on the corner of Forty-seventh Street. As I jog over to it, the back door opens and Drew steps out, allowing me to slide in.

"That was quick," he remarks.

"I'm so over today," I tell him, fighting to close my broken umbrella. He pulls it from my hands, and in one swift movement, gets the damn thing closed. Despite wanting to hug him, it makes me exasperated. There isn't anything this man can't do perfectly.

"Then let's get you home."

Home. I've known Drew for less than a week, but when he says that word, it resonates deep within me. He is my safe space right now. He is my comfort...he is my home. I swallow hard against my dry throat at this thought, but I allow it to comfort me instead of pushing it away.

Even though we're only going a few short blocks, it takes us over a half hour in rainy Manhattan rush hour traffic. Drew is sending emails from his phone, and I sink into the plush back seat of the Town Car, enjoying the silence. Something about the dark sky, the rain, and the quiet is soothing me.

We arrive at the Four Seasons and Drew ushers us straight up to the room. Once inside, he takes my jacket and my bag and orders me to the couch, where he tosses me the remote control and a blanket. It's like he's figured me out in a few short days.

"Dinner is on the way," he says, kicking off his shoes before joining me on the couch. "What's our poison tonight? HGTV? Chip and Johanna?"

"God, I love you." I chuckle, then my whole body stiffens as I realize what I've said. "Because you get me," I say quickly. "I love that you know I need HGTV and food to make me feel better."

His mouth pulls into a smile and he lets me stumble over my words. He doesn't try to correct me or coerce more out of me and I appreciate that, but it also doesn't scare him away. He pulls me closer and I settle into his side. His arm falls over my shoulders and I feel safe here pressed against him.

"Home," I whisper to myself as I rest my head on his shoulder.

THIRTEEN

Drew

Gracie steps into the bedroom to change her clothes just as dinner arrives. Instead of eating at the dining table, I set up all the boxes of Chinese food and bottles of water on the large square sofa table in the living room. Tonight is all about comfort and casual. I threw a lot at her today and I know it's weighing heavily on her. I can see the tired circles under her eyes and the way her shoulders hang heavily.

"What did you do?" she gasps as she comes out of the bedroom wrapped in her silk robe. Her eyes are huge as she takes in the twelve boxes of Chinese food at the center of the table.

"I wanted to make sure to get something you'd like." I start opening the boxes and set a plate and chopsticks next to me, where I motion for her to sit.

"You could've just asked me instead of ordering everything on the menu!" She laughs, tossing a throw pillow on the floor next to me where she sits on top of it. After reaching for a box of chow mein, she uses her chopsticks to pull some onto her plate.

"There's fried rice, egg rolls, some chicken entrees, beef entrees, and who knows what else," I tell her, looking at the boxes. "I told the concierge to order us a variety and clearly she did." I chuckle.

"I'm taking some of this for lunch tomorrow," she says, scooping some broccoli beef onto her plate. "This smells so delicious."

I can't remember the last time I packed a lunch, I think to myself as I help myself to some fried rice.

She takes a bite, and I can visibly see her mood change. The color comes back to her face and her eyes sparkle again. "Thank you," she says softly, twirling her chopsticks around the noodles.

"For what?"

"Feeding me," she pauses, "and helping me." She sets the wooden sticks down on the side of her plate, wipes her mouth on her napkin, and then looks at me. "I've never had anyone offer me help before."

She's talking about the financial paperwork and options I was able to compile for her. "Thank you for letting me help you," I return. "I promise I won't overstep, Gracie, but I want to help you. I want to ease this burden for you."

The corners of her mouth turn up slightly, but her eyes are touched. "You already have." She twists her long hair and pulls it over her shoulder. "You've provided me everything I was too scared to do. Now I just need to sit down and put it into action."

I nod once and reach for my bottle of water. "I'd do anything for you." It feels weird saying that, but I mean it. I would do anything for her.

We fall into an easy routine. We clean up our dinner, have sex, shower, then sleep. If I could do this every day with her, I'd die a happy man. I will never be bored of Gracie.

I wake up at four in the morning, per usual. I'm an early riser and I know Gracie isn't. She's wrapped around me like a spider monkey, a death grip so tight, I can barely move. But I'm happy. She's here with me and the sound of her breathing comforts me.

I shift slowly, unwrapping her arms from my chest and unhitching her leg from around my waist. I decide to hit the gym and let her sleep. Only a few more days and my condo will be ready to move into. I've emailed my assistant back in San Francisco, who is on standby to send anything I need; however, I think it might be worth a trip back to California to manage it myself. Last thing I need is Tiffany sorting through my underwear drawer, not that I don't trust her, but it's weird.

I hadn't planned on staying in New York until I saw Gracie sitting at that conference room table the morning I walked into Williams Global Advertising. Seeing her face changed everything. After our night together, something inside me changed. I didn't know I wanted anyone, or better yet, needed anyone until I met her in that bar. Her innocence, her kindness, her naivety drew me to her like a moth to a flame. Now she's an addiction I don't want to fight.

I quietly collect my things and head to the hotel gym. I would've preferred a run outside, but I can still hear the heavy rain pinging against the windows. The gym is empty this early in the morning, so I grab a treadmill and turn the attached TV to CNN to catch up on world events. I've been so involved in the company transition and Gracie, I feel out of touch with what's happening in the world.

I get in a quick five miles and some weights before heading back to the room an hour later. I find Gracie still peacefully sleeping, a sheet wrapped around her and the light sounds of rain still hitting the windows.

Grabbing my clothes, I head to the bathroom to quickly shower and then order us breakfast. She doesn't eat much in the morning, so I keep it simple: muffins, fruit, and coffee. I arrange for my driver to meet us at seven thirty and check my emails while I wait for Gracie to get up. I have ten emails from my designer, Shannon, providing me updates on the condo design. The furniture is almost done. I paid a pretty penny to expedite the custom furniture, but the space required it. There's no way I could've gone into a store and picked furnishings that would fit the space properly.

Shannon has measured the windows for coverings, which are scheduled to be installed before I move in, and she has also scheduled the delivery of all the remaining interior furniture she shopped for. She left no room untouched. She even designed and ordered all of the furniture and equipment for the outdoor space.

Every single design board she's sent me with links to what she's picked out I've approved. She's proved to me that she has the eye for detail I was looking for. Though how she's managed to pull this off in a matter of days is beyond me. It's clear she's an expert and has the right connections in New York City.

I also gave her a handsome budget, which I'm sure helped with the expediting. However, if she can actually pull off what she said she can do, she'll be rewarded with an excellent tip.

This condo is important to me. I have this primal need to make sure Gracie is comfortable and isn't living in that shit hole building in Red Hook. Just the idea of her going back there upsets me. I appreciate the work she's put into getting her place and calling it her own, however, my level of discomfort when she wants to stay there trumps my appreciation for her hard work.

She'll be at home with me. *Our* home in Chelsea.

I hear the shower turn on and realize Gracie is awake. Finishing up with emails and approvals for Shannon, I email the concierge to get dinner reservations for Gracie and me tonight.

I message Tiffany to book two first-class tickets from New York City to San Francisco for the following weekend and also ask her to arrange a car from the San Francisco airport to my apartment. If I'm taking Gracie to California, she's going to see more than San Francisco. I plan to show her Napa too. We'll have one week in our new condo before I sneak her away for the weekend so I can wrap up my loose ends in California.

"Morning." Gracie's voice is raspy, but she looks refreshed. Her eyes are bright and her face is pink from her shower.

"Morning," I say in return and stand up. She walks right over to me and wraps her hands around my waist. I can smell the coconut scent of her shampoo in her damp hair and I wrap my arms tightly around her in return.

"Sleep well?" I ask and she nods against my chest. "Good. Breakfast will be here soon. The car is coming at seven thirty."

That's when I feel her tense. "I'm just going to take a cab," she says. "I don't want anyone to see us—"

"No one will," I interrupt her. "We're dropping you off. I have a meeting with my lawyers first thing this morning and I need to sign paperwork for the house, so I won't be in until later." I feel her body tense and she inhales sharply. "But, Gracie," I continue before she says anything, "you're going to have to get used to riding in the car with me to and from the office. We'll maintain a strictly professional relationship in the office, but people will eventually find out about us. The only thing we can control is how we act. We'll be nothing but utterly professional in their presence and show them there is no favoritism, and they have nothing to worry about. Least of all, us riding in a car together. That is not unprofessional." I say this as I lightly sway us back and forth.

She doesn't respond, but she also doesn't argue. Baby steps. "I'm going to go finish getting ready," she says, pulling out of my embrace. Fifteen minutes later, she comes out in black dress pants and a white blouse with ruffled sleeves. Her long legs look even longer in the black pants and black high heels. Her hair is down and she's brushed through her waves so her hair is almost straight. Her make-up is simple, but damn if she isn't the most beautiful woman I've ever laid eyes on.

A knock on the door tells me our breakfast has arrived. I have them set up everything on the dining room table. Gracie checks her phone and packs up the large shoulder bag she carries with her every day before sliding into her chair at the table. When I say "her chair," I literally mean it. The woman is a creature of habit. I've learned a lot about her in the last week. She sits in the same spot at the table every day. She also sits in the same chair in the conference room at the office. She powers up her laptop first before she does anything else and checks that the ringer on her phone is off twice before she's confident it really is.

I love that about her. She has her quirks and I love all of them. "I got you a present," I say before shoving a piece of croissant in my mouth. Her hand pauses, sending her coffee swirling around the mug mid-air.

"Why?" she asks, her eyes narrowed in confusion.

"Because I saw something you needed." I shrug.

She argues with me. "I don't need anything, Drew."

"I beg to differ."

Now she's annoyed. She sets her mug down on the table with a thud and sits back in her chair. I know she can take care of herself—she's more than proven that—but I want to take care of her, and I hope she'll let me.

"Here." I reach under the table to pull the bag off the empty chair next to me. I hand her the small bag and she takes it.

I hear her sigh when she looks inside and pulls out the new umbrella.

"Drew..." she says, twisting it in her hands.

"I told you that you needed it," I say smugly. On the inside, I feel all fucking warm watching her turn the thing over in her hands.

Her eyes are full of gratitude as she sets it on the table. "Thank you," she says, taking a sip of her coffee. "I appreciate it."

"You're welcome," I tell her. I mean it. I like helping her, even if it's just the littlest of things. I want to be that person for her. Her person. If she'll let me.

Two hours later, I'm sitting in my lawyer's office, reviewing the final closing documents for my new condo. Thankfully, everything is perfect and there are no last-minute issues. Janet actually got this pulled off in four days instead of five. She's definitely getting her extra three percent. Who would've thought that two weeks ago I'd be relocating my life from the West Coast to the East Coast? Certainly not me. If any one of my friends had considered relocating their life for a woman they met in a bar, I'd call them crazy. I guess I'm crazy.

One quick stop by the bank to finalize the wire transfer and I'm all set. It was a long yet productive morning opening a new chapter here in New York and my heart thrums with excitement.

Tony drops me off in front of my office and I jog inside, the rain still coming down in sheets. Something about the dark skies and rain reminds me of San Francisco and my stomach turns in eagerness as I think about bringing Grace there. I can't wait to take her to the wharf and show her the Golden Gate Bridge. But Napa, wine country, will be exceptional.

The elevator drops me in the main lobby of AM Global, and I greet the receptionist with a smile. I mentally make note of a few lobby improvements I'd like done, starting first with the name on the office suite. That needs to be updated as soon as tomorrow.

The office is abuzz when I come through. I glance at my watch, which tells me it's only two thirty in the afternoon, far too early for happy hour or late afternoon office shenanigans. Then again, I'm not sure what the office is used to. Everyone has been working so hard since I purchased it, I realize I haven't gotten to know the team on a personal level. Well, except for Gracie.

A large group is gathered around Gracie's and Jamie's desks. I can't see what's happening, but everyone is laughing and the air is buzzing with energy. "Are we celebrating something exciting?" I ask, shouldering my way through the group. I like that everyone is happy and cheerful; it makes for a great work environment when people get along and have fun together.

The crowd grows silent before parting when they realize it's me who is asking, but it's what I see that causes the blood drain from my face. There is Gracie pressed against Aaron Maxwell.

Aaron. Fucking. Maxwell.

He whispers something in her ear and twirls her away from him in some sort of fancy dance move before pulling her back and wrapping his arm around her waist.

"And that's how it's done, ladies and gentlemen!" Aaron announces. Everyone laughs and claps while I stand back, seeing fucking red. Aaron smirks when he finally sees me and Gracie's smile falls when her eyes meet mine.

"To my office, NOW!" I bark at Aaron. I notice Gracie flinch at my tone, but I can't explain now. With that, the fun is turned off like a switch. Everyone scatters like mice.

Gracie narrows her eyes and tilts her head in confusion. "He was showing everyone a dance move one of his clients in L.A. just perfected on that show where they get judged—" Gracie starts.

I simply hold out my hand to silence her. It's a dick move, but I'll explain later. I need to deal with Aaron right now.

"To my office," I grumble under my breath to Aaron, who stands with his arms crossed, an evil grin on his face.

"I don't know where your office is," he says in a cocky tone, taking a step toward me. He's about an inch taller than me, with lighter brown hair. He looks every part the bastardly Southern California publicist that he is.

I simply point to the only office with an open door and he nods before shoving me hard with his shoulder when he passes me by. *Asshole.*

"Nice to see you too, *brother,*" he mumbles.

Gracie's eyes widen in surprise when she hears him and I can see her connecting all the dots.

She pulls her hands over her face to hide behind them, before whispering, "I didn't know."

I'm so angry with Aaron right now that I don't even bother trying to explain all of this to Gracie. I simply walk away and try to convince myself not to murder my brother in my new office.

FOURTEEN

Gracie

"What the hell just happened?" Jamie asks as the entire office falls into an eerie silence. You can barely hear the sounds of keyboards clicking as people get back to work. I slide into my desk chair and sink real low, resting my head on the high back as I let out a deep sigh.

"Aaron is Drew's brother," I say quietly, processing the last five minutes.

"Aaron Maxwell is Drew's brother?" Jamie blinks.

I nod my head and close my eyes, recalling our dinner where Drew shared very limited information about his brother with me. I didn't make the connection with the different last names and a sudden wave of nausea hits me.

"Huh," she says with a shrug. "They're nothing alike."

I couldn't agree more. I had no idea who this cheerful Southern California boy was when he waltzed into our office this afternoon. He gleefully walked through the office, stopping at every desk to introduce himself as Aaron Maxwell, the managing director of the Public Relations division of AM Global

Advertising in California, and he was here for a meeting with Drew, so nothing seemed out of the ordinary to me.

I know of Aaron Maxwell. Everyone does. But what I didn't know is that Aaron Maxwell is Drew's brother. Maxwell? I shake my head, trying to think. Where does that name come from? My mind is all over the place trying to piece all of this together.

Regardless, that boy has charm and a dimple that could drive a girl crazy. A dimple just like Drew's. I saw the way Jamie was looking at him, but for some reason, he honed in on me. He found me, introduced himself with a handshake he wouldn't release, and then took a seat right on my desk, showing me photos of his clients in today's online tabloids as if we were old friends.

He's friendly, engaging, and downright adorable. But it was when he started talking about the competition dancing show, the most popular show on television right now, that a crowd gathered around us in the office. He has two celebrity clients competing against each other and the stories he was telling had everyone intrigued.

But then he decided to show the group some of the dance moves one of his clients is performing. He yanked me from my chair to demonstrate, and that was when Drew appeared out of nowhere. Just as Aaron slid one hand around my waist and pulled me close, so close, before dipping me back and twirling me around. I couldn't help but laugh at the insanity.

But the look on Drew's face was absolute rage. So far, I've never seen Drew angry or snap at anyone in the manner he did with Aaron.

"Earth to Gracie!" Jamie snaps her fingers, getting my attention. "Are you going to go in there?"

"Where?" I ask, rubbing my temples harder.

"There." Jamie points to Drew's office across the hall.

The sounds are muffled but noticeable. Two grown men shouting at each other.

"You can hear them fighting," she whispers.

I groan. "Everyone can hear them fighting."

One glance around the office and I can see everyone sitting still and doing their best to listen to the argument behind the closed door.

"I don't think I should go in there," I tell Jamie. Just the thought sends my heart fluttering in panic.

"You have to," she tells me, one bossy eyebrow raised. "Drew can't do this in the office; it's unprofessional." She waits, then adds, "And he's your boyfriend, so go make it stop." She smirks at me.

"Dammit," I grumble, pushing out of my chair. My knees are knocking against each other, I'm so nervous.

I stand in front of my desk, both palms resting on the surface as I will myself to go to Drew's office and stop whatever madness is happening in there.

"Hurry up," Jamie urges me along, clearly not worried about my impending doom.

"Shut up," I hiss at her. "I'm going." I narrow my eyes at her as I pass her desk and she breaks into a fit of laughter. I promptly raise my middle finger and she throws her head back, laughing even harder now.

"Go get 'em, tiger!" she whisper-yells at me.

Ugh. I wish I was a tiger, fearless, intimidating, and ready for a fight. But I'm not. I'm scared and full of worry of what I'll find behind that door.

My feet feel heavy as I take my time getting across the office. I pause just outside of Drew's door, where I can hear every word of their argument clearly.

"Fucking touch her again and I'll murder you!" Drew shouts and I hear laughter in return. It's Aaron laughing at Drew. I raise my hand and rap lightly on the door, only their loud voices drown out the sound.

"It's like you can already hear her screaming my name while I fuck her, huh, Drew?"

Oh, shit. I shove the door open just as Drew's fist connects with Aaron's face. With a loud thud, Aaron slams into a wall and Drew lunges at Aaron to get in another punch.

"Stop it!" I yell, reaching for Drew's arm, and I catch his elbow to my face in the process. "Shit!" I sink to my knees, white stars filling my vision.

"Oh, shit, Gracie." Drew's voice breaks as I feel his arms pull me into him. "Oh, fuck," he says, both of his hands now cupping my face. My cheekbone feels like it's on fire. Automatic tears flood my eyes because of the sting.

Drew tries to pull my hand away to assess the damage.

"Stop!" I yell as I catch Jamie running into the office. I can barely make out her form through my blurry eyes, but I hear the office door close and she steps into action immediately.

"Gracie," she says with worry, bending down to get a better look at me.

"It was an accident," I tell her. "I was reaching for Drew and caught an elbow," I tell her, wiping the tears from my cheek.

"Mine was not an accident," Aaron grumbles from the floor behind us. He must have slid down the wall because he's now sitting with his back pressed against it and his knees propped up. He's wincing and covering his left eye with his hand.

Jamie stands up and walks over to Aaron, bending down to check him out. "It's like fucking toddler time on the playground in here," she admonishes, pulling Aaron's hand away from his eye. "Instead of using our words like adults, we're resorting to temper tantrums and beat downs." She turns her head and glares at Drew.

"Gracie," Drew says quietly, ignoring Jamie. His voice breaks and I hold up my hand to stop him.

"What is this all about?" I ask, looking between him and Aaron.

Aaron smirks but doesn't say anything.

"Gracie," Drew starts again.

"Answer me!" I tell him, glancing between Drew and Aaron. And something about the sight of them both sitting on the floor, something inside me stirs, something that can't be explained, but I start laughing. Uncontrollably laughing. Three adults sitting on the floor of Drew's office looking like we just had a bar fight. Drew, the owner of AM Global Advertising—the now owner of the best advertising agency in New York City—getting scrappy over what I presume is me.

"You're all certifiable." Jamie clucks her tongue, standing up. "I'm going to get ice for you two." She points at Aaron and me. "Don't open this office door. If anyone sees you all like this, they'll think you're nuts...and honestly, they wouldn't be wrong."

Jamie opens the door only a few inches and shimmies out, but not before peeking her head back in, directing what she's about to say to Drew and me. "And keep your voices down or everyone in this goddamn office is going to know you two are fucking and Aaron wants in on the action." She huffs indignantly then shuts the door, and I burst out in laughter again. It's a case of the giggles and I can't stop. Because all of this is simply ridiculous. My left hand holds my cheek as more tears come, but this time from laughter, not the bruise I feel forming on my cheekbone.

Drew and Aaron sullenly look between each other before their eyes land on me. I'm a mess. Crying *and* laughing with my blouse untucked and my hair wild. My cheek still burns, but honestly, I'm fine. It startled me more than it injured me. But here I sit, cackling like a lunatic, looking like I'm drunk.

"Why are you laughing?" Drew's brows pinch in confusion.

I try to catch my breath as I look around the office at us. He stands up and straightens his suit jacket, tugging at the arms to smooth the expensive material. He bends over and reaches his hand out to help me up. I take it as he gently pulls me up and into a hug. His arms hold me tight and he presses his chin to the top of my head. "I'm so sorry, Gracie."

I feel his body trembling. To ease him, I reach around and hug him back.

"It was an accident," I tell him.

Aaron snorts.

"Fuck off, Aaron," Drew says sharply. "I'd never lay a hand on her, ever." And I know he means this. He's been nothing but gentle and caring with me. Something inside me tells me he'd never intentionally hurt me, physically or otherwise.

"Is she why you bought Williams out?" Aaron asks, now pushing himself up. He stands with his back pressed against the wall while he straightens his disheveled clothes.

Drew releases me and I take a step back, tucking in my shirt and smoothing out my hair so that we all look professional again.

"No," Drew snaps. "You know I've always wanted to expand, especially to the East Coast, and I got an offer I couldn't refuse."

"Bullshit." Aaron's eyes narrow with suspicion. "You bought a company based on some pussy you got a taste of."

Drew yanks his fist back like he's going to go for Aaron again, but I stop him with my hand to his chest. But then, instead of talking to him, something inside me snaps and I march straight across the office to Aaron Maxwell and, without a second thought, slap him across the face. Hard. I've never hit anyone in my life, ever.

Aaron yelps, "Whoa! Easy there, slugger. I don't need a matching bruise on my right side!" And he smirks. The asshole smirks at me. Obviously, the slap wasn't as hard as I thought it was. With his golden hair, blue eyes, and perfectly straight white teeth, he fucking smirks and then he winks at me.

"She's feisty," he says, looking impressed. "Just how I like them."

I roll my eyes, knowing he's only saying this to get a reaction out of Drew. I turn around and give Drew a look that tells him I have this handled. Taking another half step closer to Aaron, I narrow my eyes and whisper, "You'll never know how feisty I can really be."

He smiles, licking his lips and lowering his eyes to my chest just as I raise my leg and knee him square in the nuts.

A loud gasp fills the office and Aaron doubles over in pain. Now it's Drew who is chuckling as he pulls me away. The office door opens and Jamie enters quickly with two bags of ice from the kitchen before closing the door again.

"Jesus Christ, what the hell happened now?" She looks at Aaron.

"Unfortunate accident," I respond, feeling triumphant, though my heart is beating so hard, it might leap right out of my chest.

Jamie stops in front of me and lifts my chin to get a better look at my cheekbone before handing me a Ziploc baggie full of ice. She exhales disapprovingly. "There might be a little bruise. Hold the ice on it, and by tomorrow, you won't even see it. Foundation will cover it up if it turns purple, but hopefully, it won't."

"Spoken like a true fighter," I tell her and she winks at me. Jamie is the one who's been in scuffles before, not me.

"And you," she says to Aaron as she strolls over to him. "Need to stand up so I can look at your eye."

"Can't. Right. Now," he mutters between groans as he holds on to the side of the small table in Drew's office to balance himself.

I press the bag of ice to my cheek and Drew rubs his head, obviously upset about this entire situation.

"Man up!" Jamie says to Aaron and tosses him the bag of ice. He groans as he straightens and Jamie grabs his face. "You're going to have a nice shiner tomorrow. Get the ice on it now." Spinning around, she glances at me and Drew. "You two get out of here. I'll stay here with Aaron and make sure to contain the office gossip."

The words "office gossip" make my heart drop. This is exactly what I didn't want. Drew glances at his watch and nods, but I shake my head in disagreement. I refuse to let Drew or Aaron, or any of this, come between me and my work. "I still have work to do."

"Bring your laptop and do it at home," Drew says unthinkingly.

"Home?" Aaron mumbles. "You two live together already?" How this asshole manages to talk through his pain and still piss me off is a true talent.

Drew throws his head back in frustration with Aaron, and in lieu of another argument, I submit, "Okay, but I'm working." I look pointedly at Drew. "No distractions." He studies me carefully, but before he speaks, I continue, "And you leave first, without me. Send the car back for me in an hour."

"I'm not leaving you here with him." He gestures angrily toward Aaron, who just rolls his eyes.

"Couldn't try anything if I wanted to. She broke my dick," Aaron grumbles.

Jamie's eyes widen and she huffs out a laugh.

I look back to Drew to signal that all is going to be fine. He studies me for a moment, looking for something. A lie? Anger? But then his eyes soften when he sees I'm being serious and this isn't open for negotiation. "Deal."

I offer a tight smile to Jamie in appreciation for her help and take another moment to make sure I'm composed before leaving

Drew's office. I take a deep breath, pull my shoulders back, plaster the most sincere smile on my face, and leave.

Once in the hall, heads rise and eyes meet mine as I saunter as casually as possible back to my desk. That's me putting on the air that not a damn thing unusual happened. And I must be believable, because heads simply fall back to their desks, phones, and laptops. I'm pretty sure it worked. If I could pat myself on the back, I would.

FIFTEEN

Drew

I slide into the back of the Town Car and bark out an order to Tony to drop me off and head back to get Gracie. I should be pissed, I should be furious, and I was, but now I'm just stunned. Why is Aaron here? I left him a voicemail the morning of the merger. I told him I'd be in touch when there was anything that impacted his end of the business, but until then, it was business as usual. But to walk into the office, see him, hear his voice, and observe the way he was looking at Gracie sent me back to a place of rage I never expected, and in the process, I hurt Gracie.

My stomach rolls when I think of her falling to the ground, injured because of me. I clench my fists and take some deep breaths as I try to force back my rage. Then the logical side of my brain kicks into gear. Tomorrow morning, first thing, I need to call an all-staff meeting. I need to introduce Aaron to the team.

I check my email and I'm suddenly grateful everything else has fallen into place without any complications. The condo will be ready and furnished sometime on Friday. We'll move in that day or night, depending on when it's ready. *We'll*, I think to myself. Everything is moving so fast with Gracie and I see her fear, I see her concerns, and I see her bravery for allowing me to take control of this...of us, but I still worry. I worry she'll run away from me, and I can't let that happen.

As we pull up to the Four Seasons, I let myself out, reminding the driver to go back for Gracie. Instead of heading up to the room like I should, I find myself at the bar, ordering a double shot of whiskey, neat. I follow that shot up with another, and then another. Six shots later, my stomach burns, but I'm numb. To Aaron and our history, but I'm not numb to the fact that I hurt Gracie.

I throw two one-hundred-dollar bills on the bar and grab my briefcase, heading up to the room to catch a quick shower before Gracie gets back. I let the hot water burn my skin as it hits my back in a massaging pattern, and my head gets fuzzy from a combination of the steam and whiskey. Pressing both of my hands to the cool tile, I hang my head low, allowing the hot water to consume me.

When I actually feel myself getting dizzy, I quickly shampoo my hair and wash my body. Stepping out of the shower into the bathroom that hangs with steam, I dry off and wrap a towel around my waist.

I find Gracie standing in the bedroom when I exit the bathroom. She stands still, looking at me, her hands at her side and the blouse she was wearing in one hand. She promised me she'd come and she did. I try to gauge her mood by her body language. I snapped today and I'm so fucking ashamed. I don't think I've ever been this ashamed of myself. She's never seen this side of me, but then, it's only been a week. There's a lot she doesn't know about me and a lot I don't know about her. Guilt rolls through me, and instead of saying anything, I need to show her how I feel.

"Come here," I tell her, but she doesn't move. She doesn't

recoil either, though, as I step toward her. That alone gives me some relief.

Stopping in front of her, I reach for the blouse in her hand and take it from her, tossing it to the floor. Her eyes flit to it as it lies in a heap at our feet before coming back to mine. Finally, they fall to my chest. She watches a drop of water roll down the middle of my chest, right between both pec muscles and down my stomach, where the towel catches it at my waist.

"I'm sorry," I tell her. I know I apologized earlier, but I need to say it again. I need her to know how truly sorry I am. Her eyes hold mine, but she doesn't react to my apology. She simply bites her lower lip and watches me.

Her chest rises and falls quickly as I reach for the strap of her white lace bra, sliding it over her shoulder and down her arm. Her breathing hitches as I do the same to the other side, pulling her bra completely off and adding it to the pile with the blouse on the floor. Her breasts hang heavily, her nipples pebbled into little peaks.

"Drew." She mumbles my name as I cup her breasts and watch her head tip back. I love the sound of my name falling from her lips. Reaching down, I unbutton her dress pants and they fall off the curve of her hips. She steps out of them without me even urging her. She's telling me she needs me as much as I need her. Her panties are last. I waste no time sliding the matching white lace bikini down her long legs, taking the opportunity to press my lips to the soft flesh of her inner thigh as I guide them off.

Standing up, I drop the towel from my waist, and it joins her pants on the floor. Naked and needy, we stand in front of each other, our eyes speaking what our mouths can't or won't. *I'm sorry*, I tell her with mine. *Touch me*, she says with hers. And I do. Without hesitation, I guide her to the bed and ease her onto the center of it. Her dark hair spills out from underneath her head and I hold her face with both of my hands as I lower myself between her legs. As much as I want to take her hard, I need to show her that I will always be gentle with her. That I'd never hurt her or harm her physically, on purpose.

In one deft move, I sink into her and she releases a long moan. I capture her lips with mine and feel her warm breath on my lips. Her fingers claw at my back as I move inside her with long, languid strokes. Slow, methodical, careful. I press into her and almost pull out of her completely each time. With each thrust, she moans and her eyes roll back before she closes them completely. Her body reacts to mine with every move, every touch, every kiss. She bites her bottom lip as I press my pelvic bone to her clit, grinding into her.

I can feel her nipples pebble against my chest and her hips begin to buck. I know she's getting close and I want to see her eyes when she comes on me. "Look at me," I ask of her, and she does. I make love to her with such need, my throat tightens. Her hazel eyes hold mine as I slide in and out of her. "I love you, Gracie."

I said it. Those three words I never thought I'd say or feel again. "I love you," I tell her again, my voice hoarse with emotion.

Her eyes mist over as I plunge into her, stroke after stroke, again and again. I want her to feel my love. She doesn't say it back, but I'm not worried. I feel it in her body. I see her heart, I hear the words she can't say.

Gracie arches her back and I feel her legs tighten around my waist, pulling me deeper into her. Her right hand cups my ass and she holds me still inside her as I feel her body pulsing around me. She's holding back her release.

"Roll over," she says suddenly, taking control. I roll my hips and we stay connected with her now on top, straddling me. Gracie rides me, up and down. Slow and fast, and it feels fucking amazing. Her breasts bounce with each plunge she takes. I roll her taut nipples between my fingers, twisting the hardened little peaks. With each plunge and each pinch of her nipples, her head falls back. With her face pointed to the ceiling, she moans in pleasure with each descent. She's fucking gorgeous. Her pussy finally clenches around me and she gasps loudly.

"Drew!" She calls my name as she descends one last time on top of me. I know she's going to come. She's wet and her body quakes around me. Reaching around her, I grab her hips and hold her still while thrusting myself into her over and over again. Her soft, wet pussy is tight around me. It takes only a few pulses and I'm spilling my release inside her.

She falls forward on top of me, panting heavily with her cheek pressed to my chest. I come down from my own release, but we stay connected. Fuck, I could live inside her.

We lie still, catching our breath, when I finally pull out of her. She carefully rolls to her back and lies next to me.

"You smell like whiskey," she says with a hint of humor in her voice.

"You smell like sex," I counter with a chuckle.

"I said I needed to get work done with no distractions, and you distracted me."

"You were a willing participant in the distraction," I remind her and she laughs, "and after this afternoon, I needed to stop by the bar." I feel her shift in the bed next to me.

"Drew, I'd never do what Melissa did to you." Her voice shakes as she says that.

"Sleep with my brother?" I ask, exhaling loudly and pinching my eyes closed.

"Your brother or anyone else." I appreciate her telling me that, but I never in a million years expected Melissa to fuck anyone else either, especially Aaron. I want to trust Gracie, but I'm guarded.

Silence fills the room for a few seconds. "Let's not talk about

Aaron right now, okay?" I just told her I love her. I don't want to ruin this moment.

I feel her nodding against my shoulder before she rolls to her side and traces her finger across my chest and down my abdomen. She spends minutes tracing and retracing every muscle.

We bask in the silence and just lie in each other's arms. There's something so content and peaceful about the quiet as we hold on to each other.

"Gracie." I swallow hard. She turns her head to look at me, her hair wild on the bed next to us. "You know I'd never hurt you purposely, don't you?"

She stares into my eyes. I used to see fear in them, but that has been replaced with trust. "I know you wouldn't," she says, her voice quiet but confident. "You're the first person I feel completely safe around."

Damn, my heart swells. I pull her into an embrace and hold her for what feels like hours. No words, just our hearts beating against our bare chests, and I know this is what love feels like.

We must have fallen asleep because I wake up at midnight and Gracie and I are still wrapped around each other. Her heavy breaths tell me she's sound asleep. She's going to be upset that she didn't get any work done tonight, but it's too late to wake her. And I know she needs the rest; we had a rough day.

I throw on a pair of boxer shorts and a t-shirt, grab my phone, and head to the living room, where I text Aaron that we need to talk in the morning. Instantly, three little dots appear then disappear. I never get a response to the message I sent him, but I know he saw it and that's all that matters.

Pulling out my laptop, I draft some meeting notes and finally head back to bed around two in the morning. Gracie fills the center of the king-sized bed in all her naked glory and I want nothing more than to make love to her again, but I ease into the tight space at the far side of the bed and let her sleep. She groans as I shift in the narrow space, trying to get comfortable. I pull her into my arms, pressing a soft kiss to her forehead.

"Love you, Gracie," I whisper to her.

"I love you too," she mumbles in her sleep, and goddamn if my heart doesn't nearly explode.

I may have slept the hardest I have in years, because when I wake up at seven in the morning, Gracie is gone and there's a note on the dining room table. *Meet you at the office,* with a little heart drawn underneath it.

My stomach drops, wondering when she left and where to. It's still early, and I don't like not knowing where she is. I send her a quick message, doing my best not to get worried.

Where are you?

She doesn't respond and my agitation grows.

Gracie?

Still no response, so I shower quickly and get dressed for the day, choosing a dark grey suit, white dress shirt, and red tie. I send a text message to Tony, who instantly responds he's stuck in traffic and will be at the hotel around seven forty-five to get me. Until he gets here, I work from the room.

My worry grows as Gracie still hasn't texted me back, but at five to eight, I get a message that the car is here, waiting for me downstairs. I grab my suit jacket, briefcase, and phone, and head down.

"Morning, sir." Tony nods at me and opens the back door of the Town Car.

"Morning," I say curtly in return, sliding into the backseat. It's still raining, and even though it's eight o'clock in the morning, the sky is dark. The fact that Gracie left only God knows when in the dark is still pissing me off.

"She's safely at home, sir," Tony informs me as we pull away from the curb.

"Excuse me?" I say, not sure I heard him correctly.

"Ms. Morgan. I got her safely home to Red Hook."

"She's in Red Hook?" I question. I don't know if I'm angry she's at home or happy that Tony got her there safely. Both, actually. "And how did she get in touch with you?"

"She didn't. I saw her leaving this morning around five. She was walking and fighting with an umbrella and I didn't think you'd want her out in this weather. I arrived early and was sitting in my car, enjoying some coffee, so I offered her a ride, which she accepted." He looks at me briefly in the rearview mirror. "There was an accident on the bridge on my way back into Manhattan, which is why I am late getting you."

Even though she left me—and for her shitty apartment, no less—my stomach calms as he tells me he got Gracie home.

"She said she needed clothes." He smiles at me through the rearview mirror and I shake my head. I'll make sure she has her entire damn closet at the condo. "Real sweet girl you have there," he says as we barely move in this Manhattan traffic.

"I'm very lucky," I respond. If it wasn't raining, I'd get out of this car and walk to the office, but the rain is coming down so hard again this morning.

"I offered to wait for her, but she insisted I leave."

"Figures," I mumble under my breath and Tony laughs. "I've never met a more stubborn, hard-headed woman in my life." I pause, reflecting on all these life-changing days. "But I love her."

He smiles again and nods as if he's not surprised. "The difficult ones are worth it. Trust me." He winks at me and I sigh. I know he's right. Gracie is worth all of this and more.

When I enter the office, I see Gracie at her desk, her face buried in her laptop. As much as I want to make a beeline straight to her, I don't. I head to my office and close the door as I wait for Aaron to get here. He still never responded to my text message from last night, but I know Aaron. He'll be here.

There's a light rap on the door and I answer, "Come in" without even looking up to see who it is. I know it's not Aaron because that asshole would have just opened the door and let himself in.

"Mr. McPherson," a soft voice says, pulling me away from my phone and the email I was reading. I look up to find a short woman with bright red hair, probably in her mid-forties.

"You must be Sue," I say.

She nods her head softly.

Kevin Williams asked me for one favor when I bought this company. To keep Sue as an employee. She's his niece and has been his personal administrative assistant for over twenty years. He swore she was top-notch and I wouldn't be sorry. She also happened to be on vacation last week when I acquired the company and her job.

"Please, come in and sit down." I gesture to the chair on the other side of my desk.

She's pale, and her large-framed black eyeglasses pop on her face in comparison to her ghostly white skin and bright red hair.

As she approaches the desk, I stand, reaching across to shake her hand, which she promptly returns with a soft smile. "I'm Andrew McPherson. I assume your uncle told you about me?" I question. Now that she's closer, I see a sprinkling of light brown freckles that pepper her nose and upper cheeks.

She nods and swallows hard before sitting down in the chair opposite me. I also sit and tuck my phone into the pocket of my suit jacket. Sue is nervous, wringing her fingers together in her lap and her neck has large red splotches all over. I smile in hopes of calming her before I begin.

"I'm sorry you found out about this acquisition while you were on vacation," I start. "I had a team meeting while you were gone and assured the team there is a spot for everyone in the new organization."

Sue's shoulders visibly fall in relief, but she remains stoic, showing no emotion on her face.

"I'd really, really appreciate it if you'd stay on as my executive assistant." I look away from her to the thick folder I have that lists every employee and their duties. "And in reviewing your position and workload, there may even be room to bring on another assistant if the work load increases any more. When that happens, that assistant would report to you. Is that something you'd be interested in managing?"

Her eyes widen and I see the first sign of emotion from Sue. "Yes, sir," she answers, looking flattered.

"Good." I give her a genuine smile. "Until everything settles down around here and we have a chance to reassess our needs, it'll be business as usual. First thing I need you to do right away this morning is to schedule an all-office meeting for eleven o'clock. And I know this is short notice, but is there any chance you'd be able to have lunch provided for that meeting? Maybe have it delivered for noon? This could take a couple of hours."

She nods her head quickly and her voice perks up. "I have a deli on speed dial that works with us on short notice. How does an assortment of sandwiches and salads sound?"

"That sounds perfect, Sue. I can't tell you how relieved I am to have you on my team."

She finally offers me a wide, delighted smile. "Anything else for this morning?"

"No. Just the meeting and lunch. Let's regroup this afternoon and discuss the rest of the week." With that, Sue steps out, closing my door behind her.

Ninety seconds later, an email arrives with an attached invite for the all-office meeting. She's good.

My mood shifts suddenly when my office door opens abruptly and closes, followed by my brother's arrogant voice.

"I was going to be pissed off about the black eye, but it got me a lot of attention last night." The asshole smirks and slides into the chair Sue just vacated.

"Please, have a seat," I say, matching his sarcasm. "Is that why you couldn't be bothered to text me back?"

Aaron reaches both arms above his head and stretches. "That and the fact that I was buried inside Ashley," he frowns, "or was it Amy?"

I shake my head and rub my eyes with the heels of my palms. Typical Aaron behavior.

"What?"

I huff. "You're always going to be an asshole, aren't you?"

Something about this, the words I said or my tone, strikes him. He shifts uncomfortably in his chair, his icy blue eyes glaring into mine.

Swallowing hard, he finally speaks. "Are you always going to hate me?"

Hate is such a strong word. At times in my life, I have hated Aaron. I've hated things he's done and things he's said. But he's my brother, and deep down, I could never hate him.

"I don't hate—"

"Bullshit," he cuts me off.

"I don't."

We stare at each other for several long seconds, not knowing what to say next.

"Gracie." He says her name quietly and the hair on the back of my neck rises. I hate that he called her Gracie, and I hate the way her name rolls off his tongue like he knows her. He'll never know her like I do. "I didn't know." He clears his throat and pauses. "I didn't know that you two—"

"It happened very fast," I start, but then stop, not wanting to share too many details with him. While he is my brother, I still don't trust him. I don't know that I'll ever fully trust him again. I'm not ready to talk about Gracie with Aaron. My relationship with her is new and private and something I'm holding close to my heart.

"You know I would never—" he starts before I cut him off.

"Don't, Aaron," I growl at him. "Don't make any fucking promises you can't keep."

He nods his head slowly and something like remorse flashes across his face. I'm not ready to get into the past and everything that happened with Melissa right now, so I change the subject.

"I called you here this morning because I want to introduce you to the team. While I don't have plans at this moment to expand public relations to the New York office, it can't hurt for you to give them some insight into your end of the agency and how we might partner for future clients."

He rolls his fingers on his knee and listens intently.

I continue. "Everyone seems to be fascinated with the celebrity clientele you keep, so I think it's important that you discuss confidentiality, as well as company social media expectations."

"Anything else, boss?" His voice weighted with sarcasm.

I can't help but chuckle. "Yeah. Tell a fucking fascinating story to the team on how you got that shiner. You're good at the art of spinning, so spin a good story for that one."

He huffs out a laugh and rolls his eyes.

It always amazes me how Aaron can be the ultimate professional when he needs to be. He moves around the conference room, wowing the team with his presentation and his energetic personality. He's presenting an overview of his team, his clients, and professional decorum on how we interact with our celebrity clients.

"As much as we want to believe these people are superstars, they're just normal people. They want to be treated with respect, confidentiality, and professionalism." He pauses, changing the slide on the PowerPoint. "At this time, we don't have any PR needs in the New York office," he starts, chancing a brief glance at me. "But I'm open to it. It makes sense that the advertising team is bi-coastal; the PR team should be as well."

My heartrate kicks up a notch, but now is not the time to argue this with him, especially in front of the staff. I'll let him have his five minutes and we'll hash this out later in private. I have taken notice that Aaron hasn't so much as blinked at Gracie for more than a brief second, which pleases me.

She sits in the same spot she always does, taking diligent notes in her notebook while Jamie sits next to her, arms folded across her chest. She can see right through Aaron's professional demeanor. She saw the real Aaron yesterday and she has a look on her face that says, "I'm not buying your bullshit."

I can't help but smile. If anyone can put Aaron in his place, it's Jamie.

"Any questions?" Aaron asks as he shuts off the projector.

Bethany, a quiet girl from accounting, raises her hand. "Who was the biggest nightmare client you've ever had?" The room erupts in laughter.

Aaron shakes his head. "Professional decorum," he says, pointing a finger at her. "Also, libel. I've got a handful of ex-clients who were nightmares, but I'm not discussing any of them." He smirks to woo the crowd.

Everyone laughs again. I forget how charming Aaron can be. The team has taken to his energetic personality. He's a professional storyteller, which is why he's fucking fantastic at his job.

As the conference room clears, Aaron takes a seat at the table and disconnects his laptop from the projector cords. "Whatcha think?" he asks, looking at me out of the corner of his eye.

"The team was fascinated, the presentation was professional, and I'm proud of you." I don't know why I say it, but I do. When our dad passed the company on to me, Aaron was anything but supportive. He didn't want the company, but he also didn't want me to have it. When I asked him to run the PR division, he all but promised to make my life a living hell...and he did, personally. He also decided to use his middle name as his last name *professionally* to create separation between the two of us. That's where Maxwell came from. Aaron Maxwell McPherson is known only as Aaron Maxwell in the industry.

I always gave Aaron full rein of the public relations department. I knew if things got bad, it was a department I'd cut from the company and sever ties with Aaron for good. I didn't count on him growing the department from five employees to over sixty, while he also manages hundreds of clients. He's proven he's more than capable of running the PR end of this business, and now I fear he'll leave me and open his own business, taking his clients with him.

"Thanks," he says, his voice contemplative. I think he's equally as stunned by my words. He slides his laptop into his messenger bag, stands up, and clears his throat. "Do you want to grab a drink after work?"

I had planned to take Gracie to dinner, but a drink with Aaron first should be fine. "Sure. There's a pub right around the corner. Five o'clock work?"

He smiles at me. A genuine smile I haven't seen from him in years. "Sounds great."

I forgot how quickly it turns dark in the fall, and I glance at the corner of my computer screen, where it tells me it's almost half past four. Gracie has been on her phone or in meetings all day. I shoot her an instant message on our company instant messaging system and it takes her nearly fifteen minutes to respond.

Me: Grabbing a drink with Aaron at five. Meet you back at the hotel for dinner by seven.

Gracie: I didn't agree to dinner.

This woman drives me mad. But she's right. I didn't ask her; I told her. It's the push and pull that works with us. I tell her, she pushes back. Something about this dynamic works and drives me insane at the same time.

Me: See you at seven. Dress casually.

There's about a minute in between my last instant message and the one that just pops up on my screen.

Gracie: Be nice to him.

Why would she say that? Maybe because I wanted to kill him yesterday.

Me: No promises.

She doesn't respond after that, but I see her on her phone when I leave the office with Aaron at five. She's one of the hardest workers here, proving time and again her dedication to her clients and AM Global. I make a mental note to get her salary history from HR, along with everyone else in the office, to assess the last time there were salary increases and what their last annual review reflected.

Kevin Williams only hired the best and I know he treated his staff like family, so I'm sure he took care of them, but they're my responsibility now and if I want AM Global to be successful, I need to treat these employees like they are the best, and that includes their salary.

"Stop being creepy," Aaron whispers as he nudges me.

"I'm not being creepy."

"You're staring at her."

"I am not." I aggressively hit the down button on the elevator six or seven times in annoyance.

"I've never seen you like this before," Aaron notes as the elevator doors slide open and we shoulder our way in.

"Like what?"

"So fucking pussy-whipped." He laughs like it's the funniest thing he's ever said.

"Whatever," I mutter under my breath.

Aaron and I used to jab at each other like this all the time. We were always joking around and trying to get under each other's skin. Everything between us changed after Melissa, and rightfully so. I could barely stomach looking at him, so it's uncomfortably strange to see us falling back into our old habits with so much still left unresolved between us.

We exit the elevator and Cloyd offers me a parting wave. "Goodnight, Mr. McPherson," he calls with his deep voice.

"Night, Cloyd," I offer back as we push our way through the glass doors and out onto the bustling Manhattan streets.

The rain has stopped, but it's humid and grey. Reminds me of the Bay area. The sidewalks have puddles that we dodge along with the other New Yorkers, who look like they're playing hopscotch through Midtown Manhattan.

"So where's this pub?" Aaron asks, stuffing his hands into his pockets.

"Just around the corner." I point to the street corner that we're approaching. "Little Irish pub with amazing Guinness," I tell him, damn well knowing he hates dark beer.

"Sounds great," he says without the sarcasm I expected.

I shake my head, wondering when Aaron changed so much.

As we step inside the pub, the hostess greets us and seats us in a small booth in the back corner. Our server arrives and Aaron orders us two pints of Guinness and a warm pretzel.

"I'm hungry." He rubs his stomach and smiles.

"I've only got an hour and a half," I tell him. "I have dinner plans with Gracie."

He nods his head knowingly. "She told me."

My eyes narrow angrily. "She told you?"

He shrugs like it's no big deal. "Yeah, we grabbed a coffee this afternoon."

Big. Fucking. Deal. My heart is thumping with rage. "What?"

"Relax," he gripes. "I asked her to go get a coffee so I could apologize for yesterday."

I'm going to kill him. My jaw tightens, my fists clenching. Angry heat crawls up my neck.

He rolls his eyes like he doesn't think I'll do it. Not here anyway. Maybe he's right. "Look. I felt bad for saying some of the things I said, and I know she heard them."

I'm trying to control my breathing as I think back to yesterday's fiasco in my office.

"She's a nice girl and I shouldn't have said those things." He shrugs.

"Then why did you?" I barely get out through gritted teeth.

"To get at you."

Not like I didn't know that. At least he has the decency to look sheepish.

"Do you feel better?" I reach for the pint of beer just as our server arrives with it. I manage to choke down a large swallow, allowing the thick liquid to burn against my dry throat.

"Actually, I don't," he says, also taking a drink of his beer. "For all intents and purposes, I came here to make things right with you, but when I saw your reaction to me dancing with Gracie, everything that happened between us came rushing back."

I stare at him and clench my jaw. Despite the sincerity in his eyes, I just don't know that I believe him.

"You always had everything," he starts. "You had the girl, the grades, all of Mom and Dad's attention, and then finally, you got Dad's company. I've always been second best to you, Andrew." He calls me by my full name. "When that shit went down with Melissa, it wasn't because I wanted her." He clears his throat, his neck turning red with shame. "I wanted to hurt you."

"Mission accomplished," I grind out.

He sighs and runs his finger around the rim of his pint glass. "And when I did, it was the worst fucking feeling in the world." His voice breaks on that admission. "You were the one person I always respected and I betrayed you in the worst possible way because I was angry. When I saw how hurt you were, I knew I had the upper hand. I spent years doing anything and everything to piss you off, and all it did was destroy us."

"Why are you telling me this now?" I spin my own pint glass around in my hand, my stomach turning in disgust as he speaks. I can't even bring myself to drink my beer.

He shrugs again. "It was time. That's really why I came to New York. To apologize to you. I'm sorry. Very sorry."

Everything he's saying and the way he's looking at me tells me he's sincere. But these last years can't just be erased. He betrayed me in the worst possible way. How can I ever fucking trust him again?

I simmer in my thoughts, making him squirm.

"Say something," he says, and all I can do is shake my head while the last five years play like a slide show through my mind.

"You're my brother," I manage to get out before pausing. "The one person I should've been able to trust more than anyone."

He nods, his eyes dropping to the wood table between us. "I know."

More silence. The laughter and conversations in the bar fill the void between us. "Will you ever forgive me?" he asks, looking at me.

"I forgave you a long time ago," I manage to say. "I let what you and Melissa did eat away at me for a long time, and I lived in the hate I had for you until one morning I couldn't do it anymore. I forgave you. I had to, for me." His eyes widen in surprise. "I just haven't liked you very much." I smirk and take a long swallow of beer, suddenly feeling better getting all of that off my chest.

"Rightfully so," he answers.

"I appreciate your apology," I finally tell him, and he nods. There's a look of relief in his eye.

Our server delivers Aaron's pretzel and a large bowl of melted nacho cheese. This was Aaron's favorite snack when we were growing up, one he only got a handful of times at ballgames or at the movies. He slides the plate closer to me and offers me some first.

I shake my head. "No thanks, not really hungry."

"Same." He frowns.

I think about it and sigh heavily. "I assume this is why Gracie told me to be nice to you." I let out a small laugh.

"She did?" His brows twist in confusion.

"Mmmhmm. How'd she take the apology?" I ask, feeling a fraction more at ease now.

"She's a spirited one." He chuckles.

"Yeah, she is." I shake my head.

"She accepted the apology. Told me if I ever hurt you again, she'll rip my balls off." He shudders.

I nearly choke on my beer. "She said that?"

"Yep. And said she wasn't apologizing for slapping me or kneeing me in the nuts. That it was deserved and you don't apologize for things that are deserved."

We both laugh at that, the mood lightening, and Aaron finally takes a piece of his pretzel, dunking it in the cheese.

"I like her," he says with a shrug. "She's good for you."

She is good for me. "I love her," I respond. This is the happiest I've felt in five years. Mending fences with my brother and falling in love with Gracie all in one week. But I have to add, "And if you touch her again, I'll be the one cutting your balls off."

SIXTEEN

Gracie

"So were you going to tell me you had coffee with my brother?" Drew asks, raising his eyebrows as he opens the door to the pizzeria where I assume we're having dinner.

I shrug. "Were you nice to him?"

"As nice as I could be," he says with a sly grin. "Table for two," he tells the hostess.

The pizzeria is around the corner from Drew's new condo. The atmosphere is moody and dark. Red candles sit in the center of the tables and just a few lighting fixtures cast a dim light throughout the small space.

After we're seated, Drew promptly orders a bottle of white wine and fried mozzarella cheese for an appetizer.

"So back to the question at hand," I say. "Were you nice?"

"We worked through some shit today," he says, leaning back in his chair, and I can tell he looks more relaxed than he ever has.

I smile. "Good. Aaron took me for coffee to apologize for yesterday."

He returns my smile, softly running his hand over where mine rests on the table. "I know."

The server brings an ice bucket with our bottle of wine and offers me a sip to taste. Pinot Grigio is my favorite. It's chilled, crisp, and perfect. After pouring two glasses, she leaves quickly.

"I accepted his apology," I tell Drew.

"As did I." He releases a contented breath. Something inside me flutters and makes my heart happy. "But don't get too excited that everything will magically be better. He's Aaron. He's unpredictable, stubborn, and moody."

"Sounds exactly like his brother," I tease, pulling the large wine glass to my lips to hide my smirk.

Drew shakes his head and laughs at me. Our appetizer arrives and Drew orders a pizza for us to share.

"I'll tell you more about Aaron later," he starts, "but I have something else I want to talk to you about first." His tone turns more serious and my stomach suddenly drops. Obviously, my face must also convey my concern because his hand tightens over mine. "It's good, I promise."

I let out a long breath and take another drink of wine to calm my fraying nerves. The cool liquid warms my belly and I offer Drew a stiff smile.

"Tomorrow the furniture is being moved into the condo. I'd like to hire some movers to bring your things to the condo at the same time."

I narrow my eyes at him and stare at him for a long moment. "I'm not moving in with you." What in the hell is he thinking?

He sighs loudly. "I thought you'd say that."

"I mean it. I have my apartment in Brooklyn. I like it. It suits me." It's the first place I've ever lived on my own, and while it's not in the nicest neighborhood in New York City, it's mine.

He drags in a long, patient breath. "And you agreed to stay with me five nights a week. Why can't you just move your stuff in, and if you ever decide to stay at your apartment, you'll bring a change of clothes. Just seems easier."

I purse my lips and blow an exaggerated puff of air out through them. "I said I'd stay with you, not move in with you." Is he crazy? Things have been fast—and wonderful—but he can't seriously think I'm moving in with him already.

"Same thing." He smiles softly at me, and I know he's playing the game. Push and push until I'm exhausted and can't refuse him. He's sneaky, but I see right through him.

"Totally different," I tell him, though watching the hope drain from his eyes makes me want to change my mind.

"Drew—" I start before he cuts me off.

"I know this is fast," he looks away and takes a deep breath, "and scary. It is for me too. But it's just right. Never have I fallen so fast and so hard for someone and just known this is how it's supposed to be." I see the vulnerability in his eyes as he says this and my heart swells. "Please, Gracie. Waking up this morning and not having you there drove me crazy."

"Then it sounds like you need a therapist." I'm being sarcastic, but his eyes widen and he looks at me like I've lost my mind.

"I don't need a therapist, Gracie. I need you. I need to know you're going to be at our house when I wake up in the morning, or when I come home from work late, or on the weekends. I want you to cook in that kitchen—"

I cut him off. "You do not want me to cook anything, trust me."

He laughs and squeezes my hand. "I want you there with me. I understand your need for space, and I'll give you space when you need it, but I about lose it whenever I know you're in Brooklyn and I'm in Manhattan."

"I can take care of myself," I interject.

"I know you can, but maybe I want to take care of you." He pauses and gives my hand another squeeze. "Please." The man is damn near begging and I swear to God he's breaking me down.

I let out a longsuffering sigh. "I don't even have anything to move. You saw my closet; it's literally twenty-four inches wide. I have like seven shirts, a dress, and some jeans."

One side of his mouth quirks up, like he was hoping I'd say exactly that. "Then let me help you stock the closet at our house."

"You keep saying *our* house, like it's *ours*. It's yours, Drew," I correct him.

"It's ours, Gracie. I saw the way your eyes lit up in that kitchen. I saw the way you ran your hand over the countertops, the way you twirled around in the rain on that terrace. That place is *ours*. I get it, I see your reservations. We've only known each other a week. It sounds fucking insane. I know, Gracie, but…I'm ready for this. Already. I can't see myself in that place without you."

I look at our intertwined hands and my heart flutters in my chest. How did this man capture my heart in one week? He acts like my flaws are cute quirks, treats my baggage like it's his own. His tenderness has broken my walls and cut through the deep spaces in my heart I didn't even know I had.

"And I know you want to keep your apartment, Gracie—"

My jaw tightens, my stubbornness and independence rearing their ugly heads. "Don't tell me to give it up. I won't."

He holds up his hands. "I've been thinking about this but was hesitant to share it with you. Just hear me out. If you lived with me and didn't have the apartment, your rent money could go toward the debt you're working to pay. You could double your payments and maybe get ahead for the first time. It's a win-win on all fronts."

It's a good argument, and I chew on it for a moment, but I just can't. "No. That place is the only thing that I've accomplished on my own and I'm so proud of that—"

"As you should be," he interrupts. "But are you going to put your pride before your finances?" He raises an eyebrow at me. As much as I want to continue arguing with him, it's a lost cause, because he's right. He's always right.

I hate it.

I love it.

And...I love him. I do. I can tell myself over and over again that I don't, but I do.

"My lease is up in two months. Let me consider it at that time." I tip my glass toward my lips and finish my glass of wine, then hold out the glass to Drew and he refills it.

"What do I need to do to convince you?" he asks, setting the bottle of wine back in the ice bucket.

I mull it over for a minute. "I'll agree on one condition," I say, and take another drink of wine.

His lips twist into a small yet victorious smile. "What's that?"

"We put a library in the office."

"Deal. This is just the beginning of great things, Gracie." He slides out of his chair and pulls me from mine before pulling me into a caring embrace.

"I hope so," I say, pressing a kiss to his lips. "But I'm not getting rid of my apartment yet," I remind him.

"Yet." He winks at me.

Everything is happening so fast. I walk into the office at seven thirty in the morning and Aaron is setting up a makeshift office in one of the empty offices next door to Drew, and by eight o'clock, a man shows up asking for my apartment keys.

Of course, Drew is nowhere to be found. He dropped me at the curb, left with his cell phone pressed to his ear, and barely a kiss to my cheek. I'm hesitant to give a stranger my key and, therefore, access to the few possessions I actually own, but the man stands, impatiently tapping his work boot on the carpet and showing me a work order that states he's to pick up my key and move my stuff today.

You've got be fucking kidding me, I growl internally.

"Just give him the damn key, G," Jamie says with an eye roll. "If anything goes missing, you know your boyfriend will gut him." The man suddenly stops tapping his toe and looks at Jamie.

"He mob or something?" His thick New York accent is on full display.

"Something like that," Jamie says, flicking her long hair over her shoulder.

I roll my eyes and pull the small keyring from my purse and toss it into the man's calloused hand, mumbling a prayer under my breath that he doesn't steal anything from me. Not that anything is worth a dime, but it's mine.

He winks at me. "Don't worry, doll. No one is going to take shit. Work order says to box all clothes, toiletries, and two bookshelves."

"Bookshelves?" I reach for the paper in the man's hand and rudely take it from him. "No. Those stay."

"Says it right here." He points to the bulleted list of items Drew told him to move.

"Ignore what it says," I bark at him. "Bookshelves stay."

He eyes me hesitantly. "Yes, ma'am." He twirls my keyring around his finger and takes a step back. "Anything else you can think of that needs to be moved?"

"Just the clothes. That'll be all."

He nods. "We'll be out of your place by three o'clock. The key will be delivered to the address in Chelsea." With that, he spins, his heavy booted feet making all kinds of noise as he leaves.

"This is too fast," I grumble under my breath and rub my temples.

"Roll with it," Jamie responds, spinning around in her chair. "It's just clothes, and you're with him all the time anyway."

"It just seems so. . ."

"Serious?" She answers my thought.

"Yeah. We went from zero to sixty in a week. A *week*, Jamie."

"Oh, please." She waves her hand dismissively. "You're dating and moved some clothes to his place. Zero to sixty would be a one-night stand to pregnant." She winks at me and laughs, although that doesn't make me feel any better. "Look," she says with more sincerity. "Enjoy this. I haven't seen you this happy in a long time."

"I'm not happy."

"Pfft," she snorts. "You have a permanent smile on your face, so either you're happy or he fucks like a God."

I blush at her remark and bury my face in my hands.

"Oh, I see. It's both." Now we're both giggling. "Just have fun, G. Don't overthink this."

I let out a long sigh. "It's hard not to."

She offers me a tight, sympathetic smile. "I know. You're always the responsible one. The one who takes care of everything, fixes everything. The one who figures shit out, the one who makes one hundred lists on paper and in your head every day. Just roll with this, okay? Let things happens without overanalyzing everything. You deserve to be happy, you deserve to have fun, and you deserve to have someone take care of you once in a while."

She's right. Jamie is always right, just like Drew is always right. It's just that I need to be in control, and with Drew, I have zero control. He calls the shots, he fixes things, and he takes care of me. This is out of my comfort zone, but I need to heed Jamie's advice.

"I'll try," I say.

A wide smile spreads across Jamie's face. "Atta girl! Now finish up work so you can go home to your new condo."

"It's still his condo," I mutter defiantly.

Now she's the one who sighs. "You just said you'll try. You're already failing," she points out.

Now it's me who's laughing. "Okay, I'll try harder."

I slide back into my desk chair and send off some ad concepts a client has been waiting for and schedule a meeting with the art director for another client. Thank goodness I have a busy day of meetings ahead of me to distract me.

At six o'clock sharp, Tony is waiting for me at the curb, just like he waits for Drew every day. The man is never late and always in the exact same spot. How he does that in Midtown Manhattan on a daily basis is an act of God.

"Ms. Morgan," he greets me with the door open.

"Hey, Tony." I slide into the backseat and sink into the soft leather seat. This is definitely a luxury. Normally, I'm shouldering my way onto packed trains and buses, and here I am getting a ride a few short blocks to Chelsea.

"Ready to see your new place?" he asks as he buckles his seatbelt and eases into the bumper-to-bumper traffic. I won't correct his error because, like I promised Jamie, I'm trying harder.

"I am," I answer, looking out the window. I wonder how long it'd take me to walk from the office to the condo. Sometimes I appreciate the fresh air and a walk after work, and this seems like it'd be the perfect distance. Another plus to living with Drew.

"Should have you there in twenty to twenty-five minutes, depending on traffic."

I close my eyes and take in how crazy all of this is. Two weeks ago, I would have never imagined this might be my life, but here I am in the back of a Town Car heading to what is very likely my new home.

A short twenty minutes later, Tony turns onto the tree-lined street and pulls up to the nine-story building. I can't help but pause and look out the window at the top floor condo, taking it all in. My stomach flutters as the reality of all this hits me. I inhale sharply just as Tony opens the door.

"Ready?" he asks, reaching for my hand.

"As I'll ever be." I smile and he helps me out from the seat. I adjust my purse on my shoulder and wave goodbye to Tony. Excitement continues to flutter in my belly as I approach the entrance.

The doorman opens the door and greets me, "Evening, ma'am."

"Hello." I smile at him warmly. Just inside the doors, I find Drew standing in the lobby, leaning all casually against the concierge desk. He greets me with a giant smile and tight hug.

"Why are you down here?" I ask him when he finally releases me.

"I've been waiting for you. I want us to go in together." He wraps an arm around my shoulders and we walk together to the elevator.

"Wait, you haven't been here all day?"

He shakes his head. "I've been with lawyers all day, finalizing the acquisition." I assumed he was here micromanaging the hell out of the movers.

"Is everything okay with that?" I thought everything had been finalized.

We step into the elevator and the doors close slowly behind us. He swings a keyring with a single key around his finger and rocks back on his heels. "Everything's great, just some final documents that needed to be signed."

I nod, letting my curiosity go. Everything about this building is exquisite and luxurious, even the travertine tiled floors of the elevator. The elevator doors suddenly open and I hadn't even realized we moved.

"Ready?" he asks with a giant smile as we approach the door. A nervous energy rolls through me and I nod my head quickly. "Let's do it," he says. He inserts the key he was just swinging and his hand twists the lever handle while he pushes the door open.

I gasp when I step inside the foyer. The last time I saw the condo, it was stunning. Now there are no words to describe it. Shannon did an exceptional job.

"Oh my god." My shaky hand covers my mouth as I take it all in. The furniture, the window coverings, and even the kitchen. I drop my purse on the console table in the foyer and kick off my heels.

"Where do we even start?" I ask, my eyes jumping from one thing to the other. Drew laughs and holds out his arm in a gesture telling me to take my pick. I move to the kitchen and start opening drawers. Nothing was left untouched. Shannon has drawers filled with silverware, towels, pot holders, and utensils. The cupboards are stocked with plates and cups and everything you could imagine needing in a home. Even the pantry has been stocked. The small butler's pantry has a state-of-the-art coffee machine and a mixer.

"It's too much," I say softly, overwhelmed and feeling a bit emotional all of a sudden. I've never seen anything this luxurious and beautiful.

"It's not," Drew says, pulling me into an embrace. "It's perfect and I can't wait to share it with you."

SEVENTEEN

Drew

Seeing Gracie get emotional stirs something inside me. "Why are you crying?" I pull her into a hug and she buries her face in my chest.

"It's just too much," she says, sniffling.

"It's not. You deserve this."

She shakes her head and pulls out of my embrace. Wiping her tearstained cheeks, she walks into the living room. "I've never seen anything so beautiful," she says reverently, running her hand along the soft fabric of the oversized sectional. "Everything is stunning and perfectly matched," she snorts. She's comparing this condo to her Red Hook apartment that she pieced together on her own.

"Come here." I reach for her hand and lace my fingers through hers. We walk through the living room and down the hallway. When we get to the office, I open the double doors and flip on the light. She gasps again when she sees the office.

"That desk!" she says, running her hand over the generously sized wood desk. A large slab of reclaimed wood sits atop metal legs, giving this desk an edgy, modern feel with a touch of old world charm.

Her fingernails trace the rough edges and she turns to look at me. "Did Shannon pick this out?"

I nod. "She picked out everything except the colors of the fabric. You and I did that. But that's not what I wanted to show you." I place my hands on her shoulders and turn her around. Along the back wall, nestled around an oversized chair, sits the two bookshelves from Gracie's apartment.

Tears roll down her cheeks and her chin quivers.

I stand behind her and squeeze her shoulders tenderly. "I know you told the mover to leave them, but I wanted a piece of you here."

She wraps her arms around her waist. Shannon filled the shelves with books from Gracie's apartment and then finished off the shelves with other accessories and plants.

"They're perfect in here," I remark, and she nods her head but doesn't say anything. I swallow hard, hoping I haven't overstepped. "Are you upset?"

She turns to me and wipes her eyes. "I'm not. I'm just surprised."

"Why?" I asked, perplexed.

"Because those were bargain finds; they don't really work in a place like this."

My jaw tightens. This hurts me. Gracie feels like her belongings aren't good enough.

"They're exactly what this office needed," I tell her, "just like you're what I needed. Those bookshelves fit into this place, like you fit with me."

"Drew." She whispers my name and reaches for me.

Before anything can happen, I say, "There's one more thing I want to show you." I shut the lights off in the office. "Tomorrow, you can spend all day going through all the nooks and crannies of this place."

We take a right down the hallway all the way to the end. The lights in the master bedroom are already on and she steps inside. This time, she doesn't gasp, she doesn't cry, she doesn't move. At all.

Her eyes shift from the bed to the dresser, to the patio doors that lead outside. Shannon decorated the bedroom in a light grey. The walls have a grey textured wallpaper and she used white, cream, and natural woods sparingly in here, with a light-colored burnt orange for accent pillows and throw. I would have never picked this color, but it's stunning. It amazes me how she mixed colors and textures and how everything just seems to flow perfectly.

"Do you like it?" I ask.

Gracie turns to me, a stunned expression on her face. "It's so..." She pauses. "Simple and elegant."

Just like my Gracie. I grin, tucking her hair behind her ear.

"I would have never imagined all of this together like this." Then she tips her head back and looks up at the coffered ceilings. "And then to have a chandelier like that in here." She points to the crystals hanging in the center of the room. "It's remarkable."

That's the perfect word for this. Remarkable. "The closet is through the bathroom." I gesture toward the open door off the other side of the room. "Your clothes are in there and all your toiletries are in the bathroom."

She nods in understanding and pads over to the French doors that lead out to the terrace. Twisting the lock, she opens the door, the sound of honking horns and New York City traffic suddenly filling the room. She steps outside and turns around, a large smile spread across her face. Fucking perfect. She's fucking perfect. There is nothing better than seeing Gracie happy, and there is nothing I won't do to make her happy.

"Drew!" she says, her hand over her heart. "Look at this!" I follow her out the doors and I'm taken aback at the beauty that is the terrace. Plush outdoor furniture fills the space, along with rope lights and large planters full of plants and small trees. Shannon more than outdid herself.

"I could live out here." She sighs, walking over and throwing herself down on the outdoor chaise. I take a seat next to her, and suddenly, life feels perfect...content. Like this is what I've always been missing. Not the luxury condo, but Gracie.

She loops her arm through mine and rests her head on my shoulder. We sit on the terrace, listening to the cars nine stories below, but there isn't another place in this world I'd rather be right now than on this terrace with Gracie.

We must have sat outside for hours because there's suddenly a chill in the air. "Pretty soon we can use the gas fire pit," she says, and clasps her hands together in excitement.

"We can make s'mores—"

"And wrap ourselves in blankets and lie out here for hours," she finishes, a soft curve touching her lips.

I imagine us lying out here under blankets and staring at the sky. "Maybe even on really clear nights, we can see the stars."

She tilts her head. "The sky in New York City isn't as clear as Montana, but maybe." She tucks her feet under my leg to keep her toes warm and I chuckle.

"I'd love for you to take me to Montana someday," I tell her.

She looks at me out of the corner of her eye. I see hesitation there, but she doesn't outright shut me down.

"Maybe someday," she comments vaguely.

"I'd love to meet your mom." With this, she tenses. Maybe

I'm pushing for too much too soon. She doesn't respond to that admission, and I don't push it further.

"Let's go inside," she says, rubbing her hands over her arms. "It's getting cold."

I slide off the chaise and help her up.

Once we're inside, she slips into the bathroom and I hear the bath running. I feel myself relax when I realize Gracie feels comfortable here. She's making herself at home and there is no better feeling.

I fix a tea kettle of water on the stove and pull mugs down from the cabinet that Shannon has fully stocked. I'm still in awe of her. There wasn't a detail or item she missed. I shoot her a quick email, thanking her for her work while the water boils in the kettle. I also send her a tip I believe she'll be most grateful for.

Walking into this place and knowing I didn't have to lift a finger or purchase anything so I could focus on making Gracie comfortable meant the world to me. The tea kettle starts hissing and I fill the mugs with the steaming water. Shannon purchased an assortment of teas and I choose a peppermint lavender tea for us.

Carrying the mugs down the hallway to the bathroom, excitement flutters in my stomach. I can't believe this is my home and Gracie is here with me. I set the mugs on the nightstand and knock on the bathroom door before opening it.

Peeking my head around the door, I find Gracie neck deep in the tub, soaking in bubbles. "I can barely see you in there," I say with a chuckle.

She raises her head up to see over the mountain of bubbles on her chest. "This tub is the greatest thing I've ever experienced," she says.

I can't help but laugh. "I made us tea." I walk back into the room and grab her mug, carrying it over to her. "Caffeine-free peppermint lavender," I tell her as she reaches for the mug.

She takes a sip and hands the mug back to me. "Set it on the bathroom counter. I'm almost done." The bathroom is almost all white, with Carrara gold marble counters, floors, and shower tile with grey counters. It's sleek and modern, yet warm with gold accents. Shannon finished off this space with plush throw rugs and gold accessories. There is not a space in this house that isn't perfect. Even the damn laundry room is welcoming as well as functional.

Gracie has set a large bath towel on the edge of the counter and I set her tea next to it. "Take your time and relax," I tell her as she slinks back down into the bubbles and I laugh. "I'm going to go explore some more."

Before I leave the bathroom, I check the master closet and find that the movers grabbed what looks like all of Gracie's clothes, however, there are still empty shelves we'll need to fill for her. The other side of the massive closet has only the clothes I brought with me to New York, so our closet looks a little weak at the moment. We'll fix that soon.

Back out in the kitchen, I rummage through the refrigerator to see what Shannon and her staff purchased. She mentioned she was having food staples delivered and I saw in the pantry an assortment of crackers, canisters of flour, sugar, pastas, bread, and all the things a kitchen should have. There is a slender cupboard full of spices and seasonings and the fridge has every condiment known to man. Ketchup, mustard, and mayonnaise, along with milk, cheeses, lunch meats, eggs, and even fruits and vegetables. It's been so long since I've cooked, I don't even know what to make, but it's going on nine o'clock, and I know Gracie must be starving.

Just as I'm about to Google food delivery, I hear a knock at the door. It has to be someone from Shannon's team or the movers because this is a secure building and those are the only people I've given access to.

I weave through the living room and out to the foyer to get the door just as I hear Gracie holler from the bedroom, "Who's here?"

"Not sure," I respond, then the bedroom door closes.

Opening the front door, I find Aaron, his face buried in his phone and a large brown bag sitting at his feet.

"'Bout time you answer the fucking door," he says, bending down to grab the huge paper bag by the handles. He shoves it at me and shoulders his way past me and right into the condo.

"Come on in," I say sarcastically. However, the smell of garlic quickly takes over and my stomach rumbles. "What is this?" I kick the door closed behind me.

"Dinner. Figured you'd be hungry, so consider this my housewarming gift." He smirks at me. "Lasagna, salad, and garlic bread, so don't get too excited."

Excited isn't exactly what I'd say I am feeling, but hungry is. The gesture is also nice and that doesn't go unnoticed. "Sit." I gesture to a seat at the kitchen island, and he finally pulls his face from his phone and sets it next to him.

"You didn't have to do this," I tell him as I set the bag on the island so I can fish out some plates and utensils.

"I wanted to." He shrugs like it's no big deal. "Figured eating was the last thing you were thinking about."

"You couldn't have shown up at a better time," I explain. "I was just digging through the fridge, wondering what to make."

"Hey." Gracie's voice calls from behind us. She joins us in the kitchen, wearing a pair of yoga pants and a tank top, her long, wet hair falling over her shoulders. She walks over to Aaron and offers him a courteous but short hug. Two days ago, that would have bothered me, but not today.

"Brought you guys some dinner." He gestures suavely to the bag like he's trying to impress. I roll my eyes but let it go. It's like he can't help himself sometimes.

"It smells amazing." She peeks inside the bag. "What's all in here?"

Aaron drags the bag over to him and starts pulling containers from it. "Lasagna, salads, bread, and I think there's dessert too." As he's pulling the containers out, Gracie starts opening them.

"You'll join us, right?" I ask Aaron, surprised at how non-begrudging I sound.

He hesitates before shrugging. "If you don't mind company."

"Stay." Gracie grins. "We'd love to have you."

Taking the three plates from me that I've pulled down from the cabinet, she sets them on the small round table that sits off the kitchen, our informal dining space. There's a large formal dining room off the other end of the kitchen, but I don't foresee us using it often, maybe for entertaining or for holidays if we have guests.

While they're transferring the takeout to the table, I gather some utensils and napkins, then join them. We all sit down and pass around the food, filling our plates. Gracie and Aaron fall into easy conversation and something inside me stirs. Not rage, like before. Not jealousy. Not possessiveness or protectiveness. No, it's something else.

Peace.

Never did I envision this. My brother, my girlfriend, and me all sitting down together in my house.

"What's wrong with you?" Gracie asks when she finds me staring at my plate of food—a weird expression—something between a cheesy grin and confusion spread across my face.

"Nothing." I pause. "Just happy." I look between Gracie and my brother and I finally relax in my seat. "Just happy," I repeat.

Gracie reaches for my hand. "So am I," she says quietly, her eyes twinkling.

Just as I take a bite of the lasagna that smells like heaven, I hear Aaron chime in, "Me too."

EIGHTEEN

Gracie

When I wake up, Drew is still sound asleep. I can hear the light sound of his snoring coming from his side of the bed, and in this moment, I'm thankful Shannon had blackout curtains made for the bedroom. With almost an entire wall of windows in here and French doors that lead out to the terrace, this bedroom would be bright as hell without them.

I put myself to bed last night after dinner when Aaron and Drew moved to the living room and started talking about one of Aaron's more difficult clients. Aaron was asking Drew for advice and it was nice to see them interacting and not beating the shit out of each other. Aaron still has a slight purple hue under his eye from the escapade the other day, but it's hardly noticeable if you didn't know it was there.

I know Drew wanted to "christen" our bed the first night here, but within seconds of my head hitting the pillow, I had fallen asleep. I barely remember brushing my teeth.

Usually, he's the early bird, but it's nice waking up to him still in the bed. I decide to let him catch up on some much-needed rest, so I tiptoe quietly across the room through the bathroom, and into the closet, then slide on a silk robe before sneaking out of the bedroom and closing the door silently behind me.

I'm so thankful it's Saturday and we can relax. It's my turn to explore the condo and see what I can drum up for breakfast for Drew. Little does he know I can't cook to save my life, but I can bake the hell out of some pastries. Cookies, cakes, muffins, rolls; you name it, I can make it.

On the way to the kitchen, I stop by the office and just take it all in again. I know I originally didn't want my bookshelves here, but now, seeing them anchoring both sides of the chair, I can't help but feel happy. I was hesitant to have Drew move the bookshelves from the apartment, but when he told me it was because he wanted a piece of me here, my heart melted. It was such a touching gesture and I'm glad he didn't let the mover listen to me.

Next, I peek inside both guest rooms. They are each complete with a bed, dresser, and a small chair in each corner. Each room is set up exactly the same, just a different style of bed and color scheme. Each room is tasteful and beautiful in its design.

The laundry room has a state-of-the-art washing machine and dryer that I'll definitely need an instructional manual to use, and the storage this place has is insane. Built-in cabinets fill the entire perimeter of the laundry room. There's a small utility sink in the corner and even a built-in ironing board. I've never seen a place have everything one would need. My time spent in shitty laundromats has definitely made me appreciate having a laundry room in the condo.

Finally making it to the kitchen, I pull up Pinterest on my phone and find a recipe for homemade blueberry muffins with a crumble topping. Fortunately, all the ingredients I need are already here. I get to work pulling the mixer from the pantry and washing the fresh blueberries, allowing them to dry on a kitchen towel. I mix the dry ingredients in one bowl, including the flour, sugar, and baking powder, and the liquid ingredients in another.

I find a muffin pan in the cabinet next to the stove and I preheat the oven, greasing the muffin tins before I mix everything together. I love spending time in the kitchen and hope to learn to cook more meals. Warming up cans of soup and Easy Mac is getting old, but I can't complain, it's kept me alive since moving to New York City. Funny how you learn to appreciate what other people snub their noses at.

Finally mixing all the ingredients together, I then fold in the blueberries. I spoon the batter into the muffin tins and mix up the crumble topping, sprinkling the brown sugar and butter mixture on top of the batter before I slide the tins into the oven and set a timer.

Coffee sounds amazing, but I stare in bewilderment at the large machine that looks like it belongs in a coffee shop and not in a private residence. There's no way in hell I can figure out how to make coffee with that contraption. I make a mental note to save some money to buy one of those easy drip coffee makers.

"Smells good." A groggy voice startles me and I yelp in fear.

"Jesus Christ!" I turn around, my hands flying to my chest to cover my pounding heart.

A low, rumbling laugh fills the space and I find Aaron's light brown messy hair and blue eyes peeking over the back of the sectional couch.

"Sorry to scare you," he mumbles, rubbing his eyes. He pushes himself up to a sitting position.

"I didn't know you were here," I respond, feeling oddly self-conscious. Especially after realizing I'm in a short, silk robe with nothing on underneath it. I tighten the belt and hold the top closed with my hand. And I obviously didn't look around the condo hard enough to notice the sleeping man on our couch.

"Obviously," he responds with a chuckle. "You know you talk

to yourself, right?" he asks, joining me in the kitchen. "I thought I was dreaming because I kept hearing a girl talking and then I realized it was you talking to yourself."

I roll my eyes. "You and your brother have both pointed that out to me."

"It's kinda cute," he says, tapping the tip of my nose with his forefinger as he walks past me. He's shirtless and built exactly like Drew. Broad shoulders and a muscular chest that narrows down to a taut waist. I try not to look, but dear God, you can't *not* look at him. His jeans are slung low around his hips and his perfect V is on display.

"Coffee?" he asks, running his hand through his mussed-up hair.

"Machine is right there." I point to the industrial-sized beast. "But I have no idea how to use it."

"I'll figure it out," he mumbles and starts twisting knobs and pushing buttons.

"I'll be right back," I tell him and scurry down the hall to the bedroom to throw some clothes on. If I had known Aaron stayed here, I would have been dressed more appropriately.

I put back on the same clothes I was wearing last night and pull my messy, wavy hair into a bun. Drew is still sound asleep, and I rejoin Aaron back in the kitchen. Of course, he figured out how to work the coffee machine. To my utter relief, there are two cups of piping hot coffee on the island, right next to where he's sitting on the counter. Like literally *on* the counter. His denim-clad legs hang off the edge of the island with his bare feet dangling.

I do my best to ignore his Adonis form and reach for my cup of coffee.

"Drew and I stayed up late talking," Aaron says, picking up his own cup of coffee. "He told me to crash in the guest room, but

I didn't quite make it there," he says, blowing the steam off his coffee.

"It's your brother's place. I'm sure you're welcome here anytime," I tell him with a shrug, "and thank you for the coffee." I raise the glass in a show of thanks before taking a long, soothing drink. Nothing beats the feeling of caffeine in the morning.

He nods just as the timer goes off for the muffins. "Muffins are done," I tell him, setting down my coffee before I pull the hot potholders from the drawer. I open the oven and pull the warm muffins from the rack and slide them on top of the stove to cool for a minute.

"I want one while they're warm," he says, sliding off the island. He pulls some small plates out of the cupboard and offers me one. "Is there butter in the fridge?" he asks, yanking the huge stainless-steel door open.

"Middle shelf," I answer, dumping the muffins carefully from the pan onto another kitchen towel. I arrange them carefully so they can cool.

Aaron grabs two of them and splits them open, slathering each side with a ton of butter. He pushes himself back up onto the kitchen island and takes a giant bite. "There's nothing better than fresh muffins," he says around a mouthful. He looks like a little kid, all messy and talking around a mouth full of food. I can't help but laugh.

"Dude!" Drew's booming voice pulls my attention away from Aaron. I turn to see him sauntering down the hallway in a pair of joggers and tight grey t-shirt. "Put a damn shirt on."

Aaron smiles and winks at me. "Nah, I'm good, man."

When Drew is close enough, he smacks Aaron upside the head. "And get off my kitchen island."

I'm laughing again. These two. Watching their dynamic shift so quickly the last few days has been a rollercoaster, but it makes me happy.

Aaron doesn't budge from his perch on the island. He smirks at Drew and shoves another piece of muffin in his mouth.

Drew slides right up to me and presses a kiss to my lips. "Sorry, I didn't want to wake you to tell you he was staying," he whispers against my lips before kissing me again.

I wink at him and smile, letting him know I'm not upset. In fact, I'm elated these two seem to be mending bridges. He pulls away from me and grabs a coffee mug from the cupboard.

"How do you work this thing?" Drew asks, jiggling knobs on the coffee machine.

"I got you," Aaron says, sliding off the island. He brushes his hands on his jeans and shows Drew how to make the perfect cup of coffee.

I settle onto the couch, a muffin in one hand and my coffee in the other. I was so resistant to moving in here, but waking up next to Drew, in his bed, is a routine I could easily get used to. I can see us making breakfasts and enjoying mornings on the terrace.

To my utter relief, Aaron picks his shirt up off the floor and puts it on before joining me on the couch. He cradles his coffee cup in both hands and sinks into the oversized cushions. Drew is still in the kitchen opening drawers and cupboards, obviously looking for something. I'd offer to help, but I'm useless at this point. I also have no idea what we have or where it'd be.

Aaron reaches for the remote control that sits on the large ottoman and turns on the TV. Drew joins us on the couch and promptly puts himself between Aaron and me, even though there is another entire side of the couch. Now we're all three squished into one small section and I can't help but chuckle. Possessive Drew can be awfully adorable. Well, when he's not trying to convince me to leave my apartment behind.

Aaron smirks but doesn't say anything.

"What are our plans for the day?" Drew rests his hand on my thigh, giving it a little squeeze.

I have to think about it for a second. He's always the one who makes plans for us, so my side-eye glance and deafening silence must explain my confusion.

"I mean, do you have any plans today?" he asks me.

I shake my head slowly. "I never have plans. Not really."

I don't know why, but Aaron huffs out a laugh. I'm not really embarrassed. It's been my life for so long, I don't really care. Until Drew, my weekends usually consisted of the New York Public Library and the laundromat. Not wanting to actually embarrass myself, I don't tell him the details.

Drew grins. "What do you say we show my brother around New York City?"

Aaron snaps his head in our direction and looks between the two of us, like how could we possibly want to spend a day with him.

I shrug. "I suppose we can if we have nothing better to do."

Drew tips his head back in laughter just as a throw pillow hits me in the face.

"Hey!" I yell and toss it back at Aaron, who is obviously faster than me and catches it with his giant man hand.

"You know you're dying to spend time with me," he counters with a sarcastic tone.

I roll my eyes.

Drew sits between us laughing and pulls the throw pillow from Aaron's hand. "Go back to your hotel and shower and change. Meet us back here in two hours and we'll give you the ten-cent tour."

Aaron has barely closed the door to our condo before Drew is suddenly ripping my clothes off of me. In less than ten seconds, he has me completely naked and spread out on the couch, drooling over me like I'm a feast before him. I'm all for it.

His lips twist into a sly grin as he settles between my legs and his tongue finds that spot on my neck just below my ear that he loves to torture. "You have no idea how much I wanted to do this last night," he mumbles between kisses, nipping at the sensitive skin on my neck. How he manages to undress himself and drive me wild with his mouth and hands at the same time takes true talent.

Before I can collect my thoughts, he's disrobed and plunging deep inside me. My body accepts him fully before he starts making love to me. The room is cool, and goosebumps prick my skin.

"You're so warm," Drew murmurs, capturing my lips in his. His thrusts are slow and deep, every nerve of mine on high alert. "Every. Room," he says between kisses. "We're doing this in every room."

I smile, biting my bottom lip as he works my body into a frenzy. Every stroke, every brush of his lips, every graze of his fingertips has me on sensory overload.

"And I'm going to bend you over that kitchen island and fuck you so hard from behind." His rhythm picks up, and good god, that does it. Every part of my body shudders around him. My fingers grip his ass as he slides in and out of me.

"Promise?" I respond and he slams into me harder, causing me to see stars as he hits that bundle of nerves he knows how to expertly work. I've never been able to come as fast and as hard as I have with him. Drew knows how to work my body and he takes advantage of that.

He presses a kiss to my forehead. "Promise, baby." I love when he calls me this, and hearing anyone else called baby would normally make me gag, but from Drew, I love it.

"Why are you walking funny, Grace?" Aaron asks, laughing as we weave through the crowded sidewalk. I swear this man is like a fourteen-year-old boy.

"I'm not." I smack his arm hard as we walk down Twenty-third Street.

He flinches in mock pain but glances at me out of the corner of his eye with a coy grin.

"Leave her alone," Drew admonishes him tiredly, like an old dad.

Aaron laughs, knowing damn well why Drew wanted two hours with me before we left.

"You could have just said you needed some *alone time*," he points out, raising his fingers into air quotes.

Drew narrows his eyes at his brother. "Do you want to see New York City, or would you like a beat down right here on the corner?" But it's hard for Aaron to take him seriously when Drew's tone is light and joking and both men start laughing, elbowing and nudging each other like brothers do.

"While a beat down sounds fun, I prefer when that happens in the bedroom, in the form of sex, and from a woman, not my brother," Aaron lambasts and Drew shakes his head. "Plus, I'm still recovering from the last one." He points to his eye. The purple has faded, and you'd never even know he had a black eye unless he pointed it out.

"We should've taken the car." Drew sighs, holding my hand as we cross the street.

"Nonsense! Real New Yorkers walk." I loop my arm through his and lean into him. The weather is turning cooler. Fall is definitely upon us. We still have some warm days, but the cooler, rainy weather tells me those won't be around for much longer.

"Where are we going?" Aaron scans all the buildings as we pass them.

"Ever heard of Serendipity?" Drew asks.

Both Aaron and I look at him.

"Like the movie?" I ask.

Drew nods.

"Never heard of it," Aaron says. "But if Gracie has, you know it's some chick flick."

I elbow him in the ribs, and he busts out laughing again. I love that we're all in a good mood and enjoying each other's company. "We're really going there?" I ask, almost hopping with excitement. I've always wanted to go there, but I never found it reasonable to splurge on something like this for myself.

"Really," Drew answers. I pull my arm from his and clap my hands like an excited little girl, and Drew frowns at me. "I'm surprised you haven't been there yet."

I bite my lip, once again feeling the divide between us. Me the poor girl and Drew the wealthy CEO. "I haven't been to many places in Manhattan. I spend most of my time in Brooklyn," I remind him.

"Well then, this will be an experience for all of us." He pulls my arm back into his and we continue our stroll. It takes us an hour to get to the Upper East Side since we walked, but we got to show Aaron all the New York City sights along the way. We walk past Rockefeller Center, the Empire State Building, and so many other points of interest I'd been hoping to see. I've been to Times Square a million times. Aaron was fascinated by it in the daytime, but it's truly spectacular at night. He also pointed out every Broadway show he wanted to see, which surprised me. He doesn't seem like the Broadway kind of guy...not that I would know. I can't afford a Broadway show, even the cheap tickets you can buy hours before the show starts.

At Serendipity, we get a table and I peruse the menu full of delicious treats. The only thing I want is a frozen hot chocolate. The guys can't decide between sundaes and banana splits. Watching their decision-making process is amusing.

"Bananas are healthy," Aaron tries to rationalize, "but then I want the frozen hot chocolate too."

"So get them both," Drew says, his face still buried in the menu, like it's no big deal and people just eat two desserts all the time. "I'm doing a caramel hot fudge sundae," he announces and tosses the menu in the center of the table.

"Fuck it. I'm doing both," Aaron finally says, tossing his menu on top of Drew's.

We all sit quietly for a moment while we rest and wait for our dessert before Drew breaks the silence.

He clears his throat and folds his hands on his lap before looking at Aaron. "When are you headed back to L.A.?"

Aaron flips his phone around in his hand and shrugs. "Was thinking about staying here for a while. Something about the New York vibe I kind of like." He sets his phone down on the table and rubs the stubble on his chin, not making direct eye contact with Drew. I can tell he's trying to feel Drew out on this topic and there's an uncomfortable silence between them.

Drew looks at me and then back to Aaron. "But the L.A. office needs you."

I cringe. They've been getting along and this sounds like he's trying to get rid of him.

"They really don't, though," Aaron replies, a hint of disappointment in his voice. "And maybe it's time to expand into New York." He leans back in his chair and looks pointedly at Drew. "Ashley has been basically running the L.A. office for the last year. It'd be a great promotion for her and an opportunity for me to focus on getting New York up and running."

Drew holds Aaron's gaze, showing no emotion one way or the other. I swallow hard, shifting uncomfortably in my chair. Just as

I'm about to interject to ease the tension, our server appears and delivers all of our desserts. I flash her an uneasy smile because she knows she just interrupted something. There's a weird vibe in the air and I wish we could just go back to the chummy mood of five minutes ago.

Drew picks up his spoon and stabs his caramel hot fudge sundae before scooping out a large bite and shoving it in his mouth. I nervously swirl the straw around my frozen hot chocolate, my stomach twisting in knots as I wait for him to say something, anything.

Drew stabs the ice cream again before releasing the spoon. Leaving it in the large mound of dairy deliciousness, he leans back in his chair.

"Realistically..." He pauses and I about vomit with anticipation. Things have been going so good between them that I don't want a confrontation now. "It's not a bad idea." Drew picks up a napkin and wipes his mouth. "But we have to sit down and build out a business expansion plan."

My stomach jumps in excitement, and the corners of Aaron's lips pull into a small smile. I feel like maybe the cloud has lifted, but Drew puts up a hand.

"Before you move across the country, let's figure out what our business needs are and see if it makes sense."

"That's fair," Aaron responds, picking up his own spoon and digging into his banana split.

My stomach settles and I reach for my frozen hot chocolate, finally taking a drink. Drew catches my eye, winks at me, and my heart swells with happiness. This weekend feels a whole lot like new beginnings for all of us at this table and I couldn't be happier.

NINETEEN

Drew

It's unreal how easily Gracie and I have fallen into a routine. We spent the rest of the weekend getting acquainted with the condo, exploring our new neighborhood, and even spending time with Aaron. He now refers to himself as "the third wheel" because he's been out with us twice, once while we ran errands. He made a joke about us being a "threesome," and I almost lost my fucking mind. Almost. I was able to laugh it off and that's when I knew I was making progress, beginning to let go of some of the rage and betrayal I feel toward him. Baby steps.

The beginning of this week has been hectic. The last three days, Gracie has been in and out of the office with client meetings and is now pitching to two new prospective clients. She's stressed, but I've seen what she's doing with her pitches, and with the support of her team, they are phenomenal. She's truly one of the most talented account managers I've ever worked with. She's wise beyond her years.

I haven't told her my plans to take her to California for the weekend, although I've asked Sue to clear her calendar for Friday

—which she's graciously done—and Gracie either hasn't noticed or hasn't said anything yet.

At three o'clock, after a full day of conference calls and meetings, I send an email to Grace asking her to please come to my office. She doesn't respond, per usual, but about five minutes later, there's a light knock on my office door.

"Come in," I say.

Grace enters the office and cocks an eyebrow at me. "Mr. McPherson," she says, glancing over her shoulder to see Sue typing away at her desk. "You requested a meeting with me?" A playful smile tugs at her lips.

I grin. I love when she tries to be all professional in the office. "I did. Come in." I gesture to the chair across my desk. She narrows her eyes at me in question, but she obeys and closes the office door before taking a seat.

"Does this have anything to do with the vacation request for Friday that Eddie approved, and I didn't submit?" She purses her lips and taps the arm of the chair with her hand in mock annoyance.

"Maybe."

"Don't you think you should talk to me before using my vacation days? Maybe I was saving them for something—"

"Like what? It was one day," I point out, genuinely curious what she'd use her days for. In the human resources system, it shows she still has twenty days to schedule out and she's allowed twenty-five days per year. It's mid-September and she's only used five days this year.

She shrugs. "Maybe I was going to go home for Christmas."

"For the entire month?" I frown. "We're closed the week between Christmas and New Year's and you have twenty days of vacation left, Grace. I requested one day for you. Please humor me and use it."

She sighs loudly. "It's going to look weird if we're out of the office at the same time," she whispers, as if anyone can hear her from inside my office with the door closed.

"It's a Friday. Do you know how many people take Fridays off? Half the damn office is gone on Fridays, Gracie."

She rolls her eyes at me but concedes. "Fine. What are we doing?"

I get excited thinking about taking her to California. "It's a surprise. Tonight, when we get home, though, you need to start packing a bag. We leave Friday morning. Pack casual. Jeans, long sleeve shirts, and a jacket."

"I don't like surprises," she reminds me.

"Well, I do." I wink at her. "Just trust me. You're going to love this." I hope.

Thursday passes by in a blur. The office was crazy, and I barely saw Gracie except for at home. Home. I love the sound of that. We're falling into our routine there too. We try to cook but usually end up calling for delivery after one of us royally screws up our sad attempt at making a meal. Then we spend our nights watching TV, making love, sleeping, and then start our days all over again. It's a routine I'm absolutely in love with. Just like I love her.

Thankfully, it's Friday, and I get to whisk Gracie away for a short weekend.

"The airport!" she hollers and smacks my arm when Tony pulls up to the curb at JFK airport. "I've never been on a plane," she admits, her fingers gripping my wrist. "I'm afraid of planes."

This admission stuns me. "How did you get to New York City from Montana?"

"Bus."

I blink at her. "You rode a bus from Montana to New York City?" I ask, thinking she can't be serious.

She nods quickly. "Yep, took three days."

I'm amazed she had the willpower to ride a bus for three days. Then again, when resources are limited, I imagine you do what you have to do. This makes me love her even more and I want to spoil her with experiences that she'll always remember, like her first plane ride.

The back door opens, and Tony stands there waiting for us to get out. When he sees Gracie's contemplative face, he begins unloading luggage from the trunk while I try to calm her.

Squeezing her hand, I tell her, "It's going to be fine. I'll be in the seat next to you and nothing is going to happen, I promise."

"Drew." Her voice is shaky as she drags a breath in through her nose and exhales.

"Trust me." I press a kiss to the corner of her mouth. "I'll never let anything happen to you." My meaning is much deeper than this flight.

Her misty eyes lock onto mine and she nods, but I also hear her mumble under her breath, "You can't control airplanes, asshole," and I laugh. She hasn't lost her spirit at least.

With first class tickets, we breeze through security and get to our gate where Gracie shuffles from foot-to-foot. She's so nervous, she can't sit down. She stands at the window and watches the ground crew load luggage onto the plane while she chews on her thumbnail. She's fascinated, watching as they also fuel the plane. She hasn't noticed the electronic board that tells her we're flying to San Francisco, or if she has, she hasn't said anything.

When the gate agent finally makes an announcement that first class can board, Gracie grabs my hand and shakes her head. "I can't do this." I can see the fear in her eyes.

"You can," I urge her.

"Drew..." She sounds like she's about to throw up.

"Gracie." I squeeze her hand. "Trust me."

"Okay," she whispers and laces her fingers through mine.

I have our boarding passes on my phone and get us through the gate with no issues. However, I have to all but drag her down the jetway to the plane. I'm thankful we're in first class, so we don't have to go as far. I guide her to the window seat, trapping her there. Thankfully, she's too busy fidgeting with everything—her seatbelt, the window shade, and her tray table—to let her nerves get the better of her. Before takeoff, I order two glasses of wine, hoping it will help take the edge off her nerves.

Fortunately, it does the trick. She's as cool as a cucumber when the plane is lifting into the air, although she does have a death grip on my hand.

"We're good," I tell her quietly. She nods, her attention focused out the window and the New York City skyline.

"It's gorgeous," she muses.

"It is." Except I'm not looking at the skyline, I'm looking at her.

"San Francisco! Eek!" Gracie exclaims excitedly.

I chuckle, wrapping my arm around her shoulder. My heart swells with her growing excitement.

"Will you show me the Golden Gate Bridge?" she asks as we wait for our luggage at baggage claim.

"It's on the agenda," I tell her, yanking her suitcase off the luggage carousel. I've arranged for a car to pick us up and take us to my apartment in downtown San Francisco for tonight. Tomorrow, we'll head to Napa before heading back to New York City on Sunday.

Once we've collected our luggage and found our driver, we're on our way into the city. As much as I love New York City, I've missed San Francisco. In a sense, I grew up here, learned everything about advertising here. I also experienced the most pain here, and it's bittersweet to be back.

Gracie smiles out the window as she takes in the sights of San Francisco. Thankfully, traffic is light, and it takes us less than a half hour to get to my building. The driver helps me unload our luggage and I manage to get it all over to the elevator. Gracie keeps trying to help, but I've got it under control. I want her to enjoy this weekend and not lift a finger. It's about her relaxing. I can imagine she hasn't had a vacation in years, if ever. I never broached the subject with her because I didn't want to make her feel uncomfortable.

Once we're in my place, I breathe a sigh of relief. Tiffany did everything I asked of her. She had the cleaners come so the apartment is pristine, and the fridge is stocked with a few things to get us through tonight and tomorrow morning.

"This apartment is gorgeous," Gracie breathes, throwing herself down onto the leather couch. It's the opposite of my New York City condo. Everything here is dark and masculine. Dark leather, dark cherry kitchen cabinets, clean lines, and edgy décor. "But I like your New York City place better." She smiles at me.

"Our place," I correct her, but she doesn't acknowledge it, and I agree with her. Our place in New York is more her. It's light and bright and homey. This apartment was the old me. Dark and cold. It amazes me how quickly I've been able to let go of San Francisco and embrace New York City and I know it's because of Gracie.

I pour us a couple glasses of wine and join her on the couch. I tell her all the San Francisco history I can drum up, and she asks a million questions until her eyes become so heavy, she falls asleep. I knew she was exhausted when we landed. I should put her to bed, but I can't bring myself to just yet.

Instead, I watch her, running my fingers lightly through her hair. She's stunning, even when she's sleeping. Her hands are curled under her cheek and she rests her head on the arm of the couch.

As I slide my arms under her to carry her to the bedroom, she wakes, her eyes heavy with sleep. "I didn't mean to wake you up," I whisper, pressing a soft kiss to her temple.

"I didn't mean to fall asleep. I'm just really tired." She yawns, stretches, then pushes herself up from the couch, following me to the bedroom. She strips down naked, dropping her clothes in a pile on the floor before sliding into the center of my king-sized bed and wrapping her entire body around a pillow. I do the same, sliding in behind her and wrapping myself around her.

I wake to an empty bed and the sound of a toilet flushing. It's still dark and I crack an eye open to see the clock. Three thirty-seven in the morning. I hear more sounds and the toilet flush again before I finally get up to see if Gracie is okay.

"G," I say, knocking on the bathroom door.

"Go away," she mumbles back, then the sounds of the toilet flushing again.

"Are you okay?"

"No. I'm dying."

I hear her spitting into the toilet, and my heart sinks for her. I think back to yesterday and wonder if she ate something bad. She had fish on the airplane.

"I think I have food poisoning," she says, flushing the toilet again.

I'm hesitant to go in, knowing that she wants some privacy, but I also want to make sure she's okay.

"Can I get you anything?"

"A new stomach," she answers. I'd chuckle if I didn't feel so bad. Even when she's sick, she keeps her snark at the helm, prepared to use it at any time. That's when I remember I have

Pepto Bismol in the kitchen. Hopefully that and a glass of tea will help settle her stomach.

When I return to the bedroom, tea and medicine in hand, I find her back in bed and already falling asleep. I set the medicine and tea on the nightstand closest to her side of the bed and slide in behind her. I press a gentle hand to her forehead to see if she has a fever, but she feels fine. Hopefully, whatever she ate has passed and we can still have our weekend away.

Gracie moans when she finally wakes around seven thirty. I've been up and sorting through clothes I'm going to have shipped to New York.

"Morning." I walk over to the bed and sit down next to her. She reaches for my hand and I gently massage her palm while she wakes up.

"Morning," she musters out and rolls to her side.

"Feeling any better?"

She groans again, but then makes a cooing sound as I hit that pressure point between her thumb and forefinger. "Not really. I shouldn't have eaten that fish on the plane. I thought it smelled funny." She grumbles and rolls onto her back.

"Let me draw you a bath." I lay her hand on top of her stomach. "Soaking in some warm water might help, oh, and there's some Pepto Bismol." I point to the bottle of pink medicine on the nightstand.

While I get her bath ready, Grace must have rewarmed her tea. She's carrying the mug and the bottle of Pepto into the bathroom in all her naked gloriousness. Sighing, I reach for both items while she slides into the tub and moans in pleasure as the hot water covers her.

"Relax," I tell her. "I'm just going to get a few more things together to have shipped to New York. Hopefully, this makes you feel better, because I have one more surprise for you this weekend."

She offers me a tired smile and nods her head. I know she's not feeling well when she doesn't argue with me about another surprise. "Thank you for taking care of me," she says, her voice weak.

"Always." And I mean that. I'll always take care of her if she'll let me.

Gracie perked up after her bath. I can tell she's still not one hundred percent, but Tylenol, some Pepto Bismol, and ginger tea seemed to bring some life back into her. She said she's still nauseous and her body aches, but she's powering through, and for that I'm grateful.

Early this morning, I sent a text message to my mom to tell her I was coming for the night and bringing someone. This prompted nearly one thousand additional text messages wanting all the details. Being the horrible son that I am, I didn't respond to a single one. She can wait and form her own opinion of Grace in person, just like everyone else.

Tiffany also had my car cleaned and filled with gas, so it's all ready and waiting for us in the parking garage.

With a tea for the road, and everything we'll need for the night, Gracie and I begin our hour trek north to Napa.

"Where are you taking me?" she asks.

"Another surprise." I wink at her and she groans. "But we're going over the Golden Gate Bridge first."

This changes her mood. She smiles and stares out the window into the foggy San Francisco morning. The fog will break in the next fifteen minutes or so, but I'm glad she gets to experience what we get nearly every morning in the city.

She's in awe of the bridge and closes her eyes for most of the remainder of the trip. I'm hoping the short nap will help her feel better so she can enjoy Napa. The drive is painless, which isn't always the case. Traffic out of San Francisco is almost always as bad as traffic in New York City.

I pull into the long drive that leads up to the house I grew up in. The house sits on five acres and is surrounded by vineyards. Vineyards we don't own, but the five acres our house sits on is nothing short of amazing. There's a creek that runs through the property behind the house and oak trees line the perimeter. It's like a mini forest behind the house and it was everything Aaron and I loved growing up as kids.

We hid in those trees, played in the creek, and helped my mom work in her huge garden. The house, while familiar, has changed dramatically. After my dad died, my mom renovated the house from top to bottom, both inside and out. Now it looks more like a massive modern farmhouse than the two-story Craftsman style home we grew up in, but as I've learned, change is good. My mom loves the house, and as long as she's happy, I'm happy.

"We're here," I gently wake Gracie and she startles.

"Oh, my gosh, I was so tired!" She stretches and notices the house we're parked in front of. "Where are we?" She looks at me and back to the house.

I smile nostalgically. "This is where I grew up."

Her eyes widen as she takes in the massive house in front of us. "Holy crap." Reaching for the door handle, she steps out of the car. I meet her on her side just as I hear footsteps.

"Oh, my god!" I hear my mother's voice before I see her lunging down the stairs and right toward me. "Andrew!" she says, wrapping me into a tight hug.

"Hi, Mom." I kiss her cheek. "I want to introduce you to

Grace. Grace Morgan." My mom unwraps herself from me and bounces over to Gracie, pulling her into an equally obnoxiously tight hug. She looks at me over Gracie's shoulder and gives me a surprised look. I haven't brought anyone home since Melissa.

Gracie smiles and hugs her back. "So nice to meet you, Mrs. McPherson."

"Stop that." My mom swats at her playfully. "Rose. You call me Rose, honey."

And that is my mother. Rose McPherson. Over the top, but the most loving person I've ever met. She is exactly what Aaron and I needed in the absence of our father. Someone to smother us with hugs and kisses. Someone who was always in our business and front and center at every game, at every school play, and the only person who was a constant in our lives.

"You're acting like you haven't seen me in years," I chide her.

She smiles. "When you're as old as I am, weeks feel like years," she says, brushing me off.

"You're only fifty-nine, Mom."

Gracie laughs at this. My mom acts like she's eighty, but she plays tennis four days a week, still manages her garden on her own, volunteers at the hospital, and still hosts a girls' dinner twice a month. She's hardly immobile or ready to die.

Mom laces Gracie's arm through hers while I unload the luggage and she steers them up the front steps of the house, pointing out things along the way. I knew my mom would love Gracie the moment she met her, just like I did, and I'm also sure I've lost my girlfriend to my mom for the next hour.

I was right. My mom has given Gracie the grand tour and even put her in the ATV and took her out to the edge of the property to show her the creek. Gracie comes back with a huge grin on her face, her cheeks pink, and her hair windblown. Even sick and windblown, she's the most beautiful woman I've ever seen.

"I can't believe you grew up here," she says with a hint of envy as she steps down off the ATV. I've been sitting on the back terrace with a glass of wine, waiting for the ladies to come back after putting our luggage in my old room, which is now a guest room. My mom sits in the chair to my left and Gracie picks the chair to my right.

"It was definitely a fun place to grow up," I tell her, remembering all of the fun Aaron I had hiding in the woods and playing in the creek.

"I'm so glad there wasn't all those electronics when you were kids," my mom says, glancing at my phone.

I shake my head at her. "We had video games, Mom. Aaron and I just spent more time outside."

She nods but doesn't say anything at the mention of Aaron's name, so I decide it's time to fill her in.

I pour her and Gracie a glass of wine as I start. "Speaking of Aaron..." I slide each of them a glass of crisp, white Pinot Grigio, Gracie's favorite. Thankfully, one of the things my mom added to the house when she renovated was a wine cellar. She has every wine known to man in there and close to a hundred bottles of Pinot Grigio. "Aaron and I have been talking."

My mom chokes on a sip of wine and coughs loudly. "What did you say?" she asks, as if she misheard me.

I inhale and sigh out the exhale. "Aaron and I are finally speaking. We're working through our shit."

"Don't curse," she admonishes me, as if the word shit is more important than the fact her two sons who've barely looked at each other in the last five years are finally speaking. I laugh and she takes another drink of wine. "How? Tell me everything."

Gracie sips her wine and smiles as I tell my mom about our recent conversations. She knew about me purchasing Williams Global, but she had no idea Aaron showed up in New York City unannounced. I give her the high-level overview of everything that's happened these last few weeks and she sits stunned, speechless, and a little teary-eyed.

"I don't even know what to say," she says quietly. "I wasn't sure I'd ever see you two come back together." Her chin quivers and I reach for her hand.

"If there's one thing I've learned, it's that life is too short to hold on to anger." I squeeze my mom's hand and she squeezes mine back. Gracie looks relaxed in her chair as she watches us, a small smile pulling at her lips. My life has really come full circle in just a few short weeks. Meeting Gracie and reconciling with Aaron were two things I didn't expect, but I couldn't be more content than I am right now.

Late afternoon, I find Gracie and my mom all wrapped in blankets on the large sectional in our family room. The weather has turned colder and rainy and my mom started a fire in the fireplace. I'd planned to take Gracie to a local vineyard for a wine-tasting and dinner, but I can see she's still not feeling great.

"How are you feeling?" I sit down next to her on the couch and she rests her head on my shoulder.

"Getting better, but my body is still achy."

"Maybe you have the flu," my mom chimes in. "I've heard it's already hitting people this year. Make sure when you get back to New York, both of you get your flu shots," she orders. She wouldn't be my mom if she wasn't still telling me what to do.

Gracie chuckles and pulls the blanket over my legs. "I've never had a flu shot," she admits.

My mom audibly gasps. "Don't tell me that!"

Now Gracie and I are both laughing. You'd have thought Gracie just admitted to killing puppies as a hobby.

"She's a germaphobe," I tell Gracie.

My mom narrows her eyes at me. "I'm not a germaphobe, Andrew. I just believe if there are preventative measures in place to protect you, you best take them. I'm a big fan of vaccinations, condoms—"

"Mom!" I yell at her and Gracie tips her head back, laughing even harder.

"Please tell me you two use protection." She eyes us probingly.

And now I want to die. I feel like I'm fifteen again.

Gracie blushes, covering her face with her hands, and I pull the blanket over us to hide our faces.

"Your line of questioning is too much," I yell from under the blanket and Gracie giggles.

"I'm your mother, Andrew," she says chidingly. "It's my job to make you uncomfortable." She laughs darkly, and I pull the blanket down and glare at her.

"We're never coming to visit you again," I tell her jokingly and we all laugh together. It's nice to see Gracie laugh and I love that she gets along with my mom, even when those laughs come at my expense.

I mentioned to my mom about my plans to take Gracie out tonight, but I don't think she understands how sick Gracie is feeling. Gracie still finds it within her to laugh with us, but her eyes are red and glossy, and I can tell from her demeanor she's not going to manage a night out.

"I think we're going to stay in tonight," I tell my mom. "Gracie isn't feeling well, and I hate to take her out in this weather."

"Let me make dinner!" Mom jumps up from the couch and shuffles into the kitchen.

Gracie rests her head in my lap, and I massage her temples in hopes of helping her relax. It takes less than five minutes before she's sound asleep.

Gracie wakes just before my mom calls to get us for dinner. Whatever she's cooking smells amazing and Gracie looks like she's turned a corner.

"That smells so good," she says, stretching her arms above her head. I'm glad that she's asking about food. She hasn't eaten since the plane ride from New York.

"Do you have an appetite?"

She shrugs and pushes herself up from the couch. "Only one way to find out." She reaches her hand out and she helps pull me up. "How long did I sleep?"

"Maybe an hour." I toss the blanket onto the couch before we head into the kitchen.

My mom has the table all set up with a white tablecloth and centerpiece made of candles and pinecones. No doubt, her fall décor came from our very own backyard. But it's when I notice only two place settings, my heart tugs in my chest. She did this for Gracie and me.

"It's almost ready," she says, wiping her hands on her apron. "I hope you like tri-tip and asparagus," she says, pulling a pan from the oven. "My baked asparagus is to die for."

I smile at my mom as she transfers the asparagus to a small platter that also holds the tri-tip that has already been sliced.

"You didn't have to do this," I say.

Gracie nods her head in agreement. "And I hope you're planning to join us."

"Can't. I have plans." She winks at Gracie.

"Plans?" I wonder where my mom would be going after eight in the evening. Then I remember, she's a fifty-nine-year-old widow, not an eighty-five-year-old wife, and I need to treat her like that.

"Yes, plans," she says cryptically. She pushes her reading

glasses up onto her head and pulls her apron off. "Now you two enjoy dinner while I go get cleaned up." She pulls Gracie into a hug. "I hope you feel good enough to eat, sweetheart." When she lets go of Gracie, she moves to me. "And you better take good care of her." She leans in and presses a kiss to my cheek.

"I plan to," I whisper, and she smiles at me.

TWENTY

Gracie

Whatever illness I have, it's kicking my ass. I'm able to get a few bites of dinner down, and while it's delicious, my stomach turns and I have to stop. However, just sitting at this table with Drew, knowing how much love Rose put into this dinner, makes my heart swell with happiness. I love his family, even Aaron. Everyone has welcomed me with open arms and open hearts and I can't help but fall even more in love with Drew because of it.

"Go rest." Drew shoos me away from the table. "I'll clean up and meet you in the bedroom when I'm done." As much as I want to help him clean up, my body is weak and tired. And honestly, I'd be more of a hindrance than a help.

I carry my plate to the sink, and Drew pulls me into an embrace before I leave. He holds me tight and I wrap my arms around his neck, allowing him to comfort me. Something about being in his arms makes me feel safe, content...loved.

He kisses my cheek before sending me on my way. "Go."

A half hour later when Drew finally joins me in bed, he pulls me into him.

"Can we come back here again when I'm feeling better?" I ask him.

He pauses. "You want to come back?"

I nod and slide my fingers in between his. "I do. I like it here and I love your mom. I'd love to spend more time with her and actually get out and see Napa."

I can feel him smile as he presses a kiss to the top of my head. "She loves you too," he says quietly. "I'm so glad you got the chance to meet her. I just wish you felt better. And yes, we'll come back again."

"Good." I close my eyes and sink into his warmth. There's no place I'd rather be than right here with him wrapped in his arms.

"Babe," he whispers in my ear and presses a gentle kiss to my temple. "You need to get up or we'll miss our flight."

I grumble and roll over, feeling disoriented. "What time is it?"

"Six in the morning. We have to leave in an hour."

I groan. No. I don't want to get up. My head is pounding with a headache. "I'm going to shower and then I'm going to need a cup of coffee."

Drew massages my neck and I moan in pleasure. "Don't make those sounds, baby," he breathes into my ear. "You know what that does to me."

I turn my head and smile over my shoulder. "Maybe you should join me in the shower," I tease him.

He groans, and I can't help but laugh. I love the effect I have on him. Even though I feel miserable, I've missed his touch and our connection. I know he's giving me the space I need to get better, but I also need him.

"I wish," he says. "You know I do. But you need to recoup.

When we get back to New York, I'm all yours." He presses a kiss to my temple and slides out of bed. "I'll get you coffee. Go get in the shower."

I do as I'm told, sighing with such contentment as I step into the hot shower. After I'm all clean, I wrap a large towel around me, brush my teeth, and towel dry my hair. I try not to sigh at myself in the mirror. My reflection isn't inspiring confidence today. My face looks ashen and my eyes are still red, but I do feel better than yesterday. Hopefully by tomorrow, I'll be back to normal.

Drew greets me in the bedroom with a cup of coffee and our bags are almost packed. "My mom wants to see you before we leave," he says, handing me my coffee.

A twinge of sadness strikes me when I think about leaving Rose. I've barely met her, but I adore her, and I feel sad that both of her boys are moving across the country and away from her.

He nods toward the door. "Go see her. I'll finish packing up."

I dress quickly and carry my coffee to the kitchen where I find Rose, her nose stuck in her Kindle. "Good morning," I greet her.

"Good morning!" She perks right up. "How are you feeling?"

"Each day gets a little better," I tell her and take a sip of my coffee.

"Good." She smiles at me and sets her kindle on the table. "Come with me." She opens the back door and guides me outside to the covered terrace.

We sit down at the outdoor table, and I breathe in the cool Northern California air. My lungs expand with each deep breath and my head seems to clear with each cleansing inhale.

"Thank you," she says quietly.

My brows pinch in confusion as I glance at her. "For what?"

"For loving Andrew." Her smile is genuine, but there's a hint of sadness on her face. "I assume he told you about Melissa?"

I nod and swallow hard. After getting to know Aaron, it's almost difficult for me to imagine him betraying Drew in such a terrible way.

"He was so broken," her voice breaks and she pauses, "I wasn't sure he'd open his heart to love ever again, but Grace, the way he looks at you...he's never been happier."

I smile at her. "I love him too," I admit. I'm not sure I've even told him that, but I tell Rose because it's the truth. I love him.

She reaches over and grabs my hand. I see a tear slip from her eye and she squeezes my hand as she takes a deep breath. "Be patient with him."

I'm not sure what that means, but I nod. "I will."

"Good. He's lucky to have you, sweet girl."

I think it's the other way around. "I'm lucky to have him." And that's the truth. Rose and I enjoy a few minutes of quiet with our coffee and we take in the beautiful Napa Valley fall morning before Drew announces that we have to leave.

Even though we barely know each other, Rose and I say a tearful goodbye. Drew looks at us like we're crazy. Aside from being sick, this was a much-needed break and I'm so thankful Drew wanted me to meet his mom.

As much as I loved seeing San Francisco and Napa, there's just something about New York City that calls to me. It's where I belong; it's home.

Tony is waiting for us in the car when we arrive at JFK, and being the efficient driver he is, he has us home before dinner. Drew lights a fire in the outdoor fire pit on the terrace and orders us Thai for dinner. After dinner, we curl up under blankets on the outdoor chaise and relax in each other's arms. Something shifted in me while we were in San Francisco. I no longer look at this condo as Drew's; it's ours. It's where I belong, with Drew.

"Thank you for going home with me, even though I know how much you hate surprises." Drew leans in and places a gentle kiss to the tip of my nose.

"Thank you for taking me with you. I loved meeting your mom and seeing where you grew up."

He's quiet, contemplative, and I'm curious. "Are you going to miss California?" I know that's a loaded question, but I also don't want him to give up living somewhere that he loves.

He turns his head and gazes at me before shaking his head. "No. I'm not. I've got everything I've ever wanted right here in New York." His eyes hold a softness and sincerity in them and my heart swells.

"So do I," I say quietly. He pulls me closer and presses a sweet, gentle kiss to my lips. "Sick," I mumble and pull away from him, reminding him of my flu or stomach illness, whatever it is.

"Worth the risk." He smirks at me.

The weather is cooling off in New York City and it's the perfect evening to spend on the terrace all bundled up under the blankets. Drew shares his plans for expanding the public relations department into New York City and how that will impact the Los Angeles office. He seems excited to have his brother working alongside him, and nothing makes me happier than seeing him genuinely happy and at peace with Aaron.

This week flies by. Aaron has been back in Los Angeles, tying up loose ends, and Drew has been slammed with new contracts and other acquisition-related meetings.

I have had three different potential client meetings, and I pitched new ad campaigns to two existing clients. This is what I

live for. The craziness of the advertising business. The thrill of
the pitch and relief of the catch.

All three potential clients have agreed to come on board with
AM Global and I could not be more excited and proud of this
achievement. Jamie was a godsend in helping me get my pitch
prepared, even though she has her own client needs. She stayed
late with me every night and listened to my proposed pitch for all
three different client campaign strategies multiple times. Her
feedback gave me the confidence I needed to land these clients.
Of course, I also couldn't have done it without the support of my
favorite graphic designer and the design team, as well as the
media department. Together we make a strong team. Everything
was top notch, professional, and on target. We were all on our A-
game and it showed in our presentation.

Of course, Drew was always nearby, but he kept his distance,
allowing me the space to do my job independently. I knew he was
listening, yet he gave me the courtesy and respect to do my thing.
I knew if I needed him, he'd be there to help me, but this was
something I wanted—no, needed—to do on my own. I needed to
prove to myself I could do this alone, and I did.

Now that the week has come to an end, Drew made me
promise that tonight I'd leave the office no later than six o'clock.
Of course, I'm exhausted and want nothing more than to spend
the evening sleeping, but I promised Drew we'd celebrate over
dinner tonight, and that's what we'll do.

At five forty-five, Drew saunters over to my desk and, without
a word, reaches across me and hits the power button on my
laptop. I watch my monitor flicker and then go dark before I turn
and look up into Drew's piercing blue eyes. His lips are twisted
into a smug grin and he's leaning back, resting his ass against the
side of my desk with his arms crossed over his chest.

"What did you do that for?"

"To get your attention."

"You got it." I cross my arms across my chest to mimic his stance.

"Tony will be here in ten minutes and we have dinner reservations for eight-thirty."

"Okaaaaay?" I question, glancing at the clock on the wall. It's not even six yet.

He leans over and whispers in my ear, "I want to do all kinds of dirty things to you before dinner, so we need to leave on time."

A chill runs down my neck and through my spine, stopping at my core, which suddenly throbs in anticipation. Even though I'm still not feeling one hundred percent better, my body craves Drew and his touch.

I tilt my head, my eyes holding his. "We're not going to have time." A mischievous smile tugs at my lips and I take a deep breath as an idea pops into my head. "With traffic, we'll be lucky to make it home, clean up, and get out the door on time to make it to our reservation." His eyes fall from mine to my chest and I see him lick his bottom lip.

"Then we'll eat fast so we can have dessert at home." He rubs his hands together as if he's solved world hunger.

Only I have a better idea. "Or maybe we'll have dessert *before* dinner." I quirk my eyebrows and push my chair back, putting some distance between us. He leans back, resuming his previous position, his eyes watching me intently, not understanding where I'm going with this. On my desk sits three large cardboard campaign displays I used for my client pitches this week. I pick them up and stand, walking over to Drew. Now I lean into him and whisper in his ear, "Meet me in your office, Mr. McPherson. I have a proposal you need to see."

His eyes widen in surprise and he swallows hard, his Adam's apple rising in his neck. Thank God most of the office staff is gone and Jamie isn't at her desk. She'd never let me live this down, and she'd totally dog on Drew for not picking up the hint I just laid down. I walk away from my desk and down the hallway, glancing back over my shoulder to see Drew following me, leaving a casual distance between us.

His eyes scan the office, taking note of who's still here, but I feel him shortening the distance behind me. Thankfully, Sue isn't at her desk right outside of Drew's office. I walk right into his office and drop the display boards on his desk before turning around and leaning against it. He enters a few seconds behind me, closing his door.

"Is there something you want to show me, Ms. Morgan?" He grins, damn well knowing where I'm going with this now.

I walk back over to the office door and twist the lock on the handle before sauntering back over to him, reaching for the belt loops on his dress pants. I pull myself into his firm chest where he stands next to his desk, one hip propped against the side as he watches me intently. I slowly work the leather strap out of his belt buckle with my fingers, unbuttoning his pants.

"Graaace." He hisses my name when I unzip his zipper slowly and reach inside his pants, pulling his long, thick cock free from his boxer briefs. He's hard and warm, and without hesitation, I drop to my knees in front of him. Drew's hand twists in my hair and he holds my head steady as I pull him into my mouth. Just the tip. I swirl my tongue around the soft head and suck gently. He groans as my tongue glides around him again and again before I finally slow, pressing my tongue along the underside of his head. He pulls my hair harder when I do this.

"Jesus, Grace!" he grumbles and thrusts his hips when I finally take his full-length in. I take him as deep as I can, feeling the soft head of his cock press deep into the back of my throat. I tighten my lips around his shaft, feeling the tight, rigid skin with every glide back and forth, his hips thrusting to match my glides. "You're going to make me come," he groans softly as his fingers tighten in my hair and he tries to pull out of my mouth.

I grip his hips and work him faster with my tongue before squeezing his balls softly with my hand. I roll the tender skin gently in my fingers, offering a gentle squeeze as I suck him off. I feel him hardening even more. I want Drew to come in my mouth, I need to taste him and take this from him. I love him more than I thought I could ever love anyone. With one last groan, he denies what I wanted. He yanks his hand free from my hair and grabs both of my arms firmly. In one swift movement, he pulls me up from my knees just as I release him from my mouth.

I gasp, trying to catch my breath as his pulls me up and lifts my skirt all at the same time. He's aggressive with need and I stumble and fall forward onto his desk, my arms catching me as he bends me over. Before I register what's happening, Drew pushes my panties aside and slams his length into me as I yelp in a mixture of pleasure and pain.

My mind races as he grabs my hair at the nape of my neck and pulls my head back, twisting it to the side. Leaning in, he presses a kiss to my mouth as he thrusts fast and hard, in and out of me. Our breathing is loud and our bodies slick with each other's juices.

He pulls my hair and I gaze at him over my shoulder. "God, you're so wet, Gracie."

I groan in pleasure at his words, but also at how he works my body as I feel my climax building. "I want you in my mouth," I manage to get out between gasps and he slows his pace, his eyes holding mine, those blue eyes so possessive and piercing. He releases my hair and my head falls forward while my hands grip each side of his desk to hold myself in place.

He continues to thrust in and out, hard, almost completely pulling out of me with each glide. Drew hits that spot inside me that drives me wild and my body shudders around him. He knows exactly where to find it and uses that to his advantage.

"Drew," I mumble his name as he slows to long, languid

strokes. My entire body hums in delight as he hits that spot over and over again and my knees shake beneath me. I muster up the strength to stand up as he does his best to hold me in place, only I win this time. Freeing myself from him, I turn and drop to my knees in front of him, his length bobbing in front of me as he groans. When I reach for him, he humors me and grabs my head before sliding himself into my mouth again. I look up at him and he looks down at me as I work his cock in slow circles before moving to long glides.

He tips his head back and moans and I can taste the saltiness of myself on him. Normally, it would be a distraction, but my focus is solely on his pleasure at this moment. He moves his hips slowly, matching my long strokes as I take all of him in. His hands find my head again and he holds me in place as he thrusts slowly in my mouth, pressing himself to the back of my throat.

"I'm going to come, Gracie," he warns, giving me a chance to release him. Only, I want this. I want him. All of him. My hands grip his hips tightly and he suddenly stops thrusting as his cock tightens in my mouth. I smile around him when I feel the warm spurts of semen hit the back of my tongue and throat. As I swallow around him, he groans in pleasure before pulling himself completely from my mouth. He grips my arms and helps me up before placing a long, soft kiss directly to my lips.

"I fucking love you, Grace Morgan," he says when he's done kissing me. "More than you'll ever comprehend."

And I love him too.

TWENTY-ONE

Drew

I wake to the sounds of Gracie laughing and then a sudden bang, which sounds like a pan dropping in the kitchen. I step into a pair of pajama pants to go find out what's going on, but it's clear the second my feet hit the floor that Aaron is back from Los Angeles. I hear his exuberant voice echoing through the condo, and I can't help but wonder what he's doing here at eight o'clock on a Saturday morning.

"Morning, sleepy head," Gracie says with a giant grin, opening her arms for me as I approach. I slide right into her waiting arms and press a firm kiss to her lips. Her hair is down and she's wearing torn jeans and a Grateful Dead t-shirt. She always looks more beautiful in casual clothes than when she's all dressed up.

"Morning," I respond after peppering her lips with kisses. She bites her bottom lip and I glance at Aaron, who stands with an eyebrow cocked, watching us. "What the hell are you doing here so early?" I grumble, wrapping my arms around Gracie's waist. I rest my hands on her stomach and she leans back into me.

"Well, nice to see you too." Aaron smirks before taking a sip of his coffee. "Just took the red eye in from L.A. and wanted some of your lady's muffins, only she's holding out on me." He winks at her. I swear, if I suggested it, Aaron would move into one of the spare bedrooms just to annoy the hell out of me and beg for Gracie's blueberry muffins. "And I also wanted to talk to you. I was afraid if I went to the hotel and fell asleep, I wouldn't wake up until late this afternoon."

Talk to me about what? My face twists in confusion, but I nod at him and release Gracie before reaching into the cabinet for a coffee mug. I'm going to need caffeine before there's any chatting with my brother.

"Here, let me get that." Gracie takes the mug from my hands and tinkers with the coffee machine. Aaron must have finally showed her how to work it because she turns knobs and pushes buttons just before some piping hot coffee begins to fill the mug.

Aaron walks into the pantry and comes back out holding a container of oats. "Is this what you wanted?" he asks Gracie.

She nods. "Yes. Set it right there next to the pan." There's a small Dutch oven on the stove that has water that's just begun to boil.

"What else do you need?" he asks, propping his hip against the kitchen island. I find it interesting he's not asking what I need, because I know I'd be a smartass about it and tell him I *need* him to get the fuck out of my apartment and let me snuggle my girl in peace.

Completely unaware of my grumpiness, Grace answers him. "Salt, brown sugar, and there's some fruit in the fridge. Can you rinse the berries?" She pulls a measuring cup from the cupboard and pours the rolled oats into it.

"What are you making?" I ask, feeling left out. Aaron is fetching the items she requested and I'm simply an observer, sipping my coffee.

"Just some oatmeal. I used to eat this all the time as a kid."

She turns and smiles at me. "Except now it's not just plain oatmeal. We can spruce it up with fruit, and syrup, and things to make it taste delicious."

"And it's fiber!" Aaron pipes in, and Grace laughs.

"Spoken like an old man, bro." I smirk at him.

He throws a raspberry at me and I duck, the berry narrowly missing my head. This is the shit we'd do as kids and it would drive our mom crazy.

Gracie stirs the oats into the water and covers the pot. Aaron rinses a strainer full of strawberries, raspberries, blackberries, and blueberries as Gracie takes the strainer from him and dumps the berries on a kitchen towel. She gently wraps them and rolls them around to pull the excess water off of them.

"You two go talk," Gracie insists, nodding us toward the living room. "I'm going to go lie back down for a little bit." She holds her hand over her mouth and gives her head a little shake before she starts again. "In fifteen minutes, shut the burner off. The oatmeal will be ready. You two eat without me."

Aaron looks at Gracie with concern before looking to me.

"I thought you were feeling better," I ask, reaching out to touch her forehead.

"I was." She smiles like there's nothing to worry about. "Just a little nauseous all of a sudden. I've been so tired lately, I think I just need a day to sleep and let my body rest."

I press a kiss to her cheek before she dumps the berries back in the strainer and leaves Aaron and me alone. Aaron grabs his coffee and nods toward the kitchen table. I follow him there and we take a seat across from each other.

"What's up?" I ask, curious what this could be about.

"Need to ask a favor."

"What kind of favor?" I sip the hot coffee, diverting my gaze from him and down the hall to see Gracie close the bedroom door behind her. I'm glad she's going to rest. If she's not feeling better by Monday, she's going to the doctor.

"I need the name of your realtor."

My head snaps back. "Why?"

"To get a place, dumbass." Now he lifts his mug of coffee and takes a long sip. "On the plane, I started thinking about whether I should get an apartment or buy a place. It's a buyer's market right now, and I was hoping to put down some roots here...now that—"

"Janet. I'll get you her number," I tell him.

He looks at me, curious about my reaction. I'm not sure what to call it. I'm not excited, but I'm also not upset. He's weaseled his way back into my life, and Gracie seems to like him enough.

"Thanks." He sets the mug down and looks at me. "I figure if I decide New York isn't for me, I can rent it out. Dad always said real estate was a good investment."

I nod my head in agreement and lean back in my chair. So many things have come between us—my dad, the business, Melissa. It almost seems surreal that we're sitting at my kitchen table, having a normal conversation like brothers do. There's something to be said for time healing old wounds and maturity. Not that it's perfect, but it's definitely a step in the right direction.

"Dude, are you going to wake her up?" Aaron asks from the other side of the sectional where he's all stretched out. "It's almost three o'clock." Gracie has been asleep since she left the kitchen this morning. Aaron and I ate the oatmeal she made and have been on the couch, watching college football all afternoon. He's doing his best to power through and stay awake so he can sleep tonight—old trick of the trade to avoid the jetlag—and I'm just enjoying a few hours not glued to my phone.

"No, I'm going to let her sleep. Sleep is the best thing for your body when you're sick." We've been going non-stop since we moved into this place and her body hasn't had time to just rest. I'm thankful for a quiet Saturday where she can sleep and I can spend time with my brother.

"I hear Mom is smitten." One side of his mouth tips up. "She called me after you two left. Said Gracie is the best thing that's ever happened to you."

I glance over at him before averting my eyes back to the football game. "You know how Mom is," I start. "She was convinced I'd sworn off women—" I stop, realizing I'm headed back into Melissa territory.

Aaron picks up on where I was going and turns the conversation back to Gracie. "She said to me," and he brings his voice up a few octaves, doing his best Mom impression, "this is the one he's going to marry, Aaron. I can see it. They're meant for each other." Aaron laughs. "I mean, you two did get pretty serious, pretty fast." He looks at me pointedly, and I don't fight him on it. He's right.

"When you know, you just know," I say, keeping my attention focused on the game. I'm still not comfortable talking about my relationship with anyone, especially Aaron. It's still new, still sacred, still mine. I could care less about anyone's thoughts, judgments, or opinions.

"I like her," he says with sincerity.

I glance at him out of the corner of my eye.

He even looks serious. "She's good for you. She's humble, and beautiful, and fucking hilarious. And she doesn't put up with your shit."

Right again. I can feel the sides of my mouth turning up.

"I hope I find my own Gracie someday," he says quietly. It's the most honest I've ever heard Aaron.

"Thought you loved the bachelor lifestyle."

"Gets old." He props his arms under his head, trying to hide the loneliness I was all too familiar with. Before Gracie.

Now I feel complete, content. Like I have a future worth looking forward to. I'm fucking done with all the lonely nights. Losing myself in strange women, women I never wanted to see again.

"You'll find her," I tell him. And I mean it.

I see him nod, but he doesn't respond.

It's after six when Gracie saunters out into the living room in a pair of pajama pants and tank top. Aaron and I finally caved and ordered pizza. The side tables each have empty beer bottles scattered across them and Aaron screams at the TV when the wide receiver for Notre Dame drops the ball.

"Noooooo!" He throws one of the throw pillows from the couch onto the ground.

Gracie starts collecting the empty bottles and I reach out to stop her. "Leave them. I'll get them in a minute."

She smiles and leans in, pressing a kiss to my lips. "Let me just get these." She holds up three bottles in each hand. I hear her put the glass bottles in the recycling bin before she joins us on the couch.

"How are you feeling?" I pull her closer into me and wrap a protective arm around her shoulders.

She sighs. "Like a new woman. I can't believe I slept all day." She yawns and kicks her feet up onto the ottoman before resting her head on my shoulder. "Oh, Jamie is stopping by. She sent me a text while I was sleeping. She wants to check out the place, so I told her to come over."

Aaron twists his head and looks at Gracie at the mention of

Jamie's name, but he doesn't say anything. "You remember Jamie, right, Aaron?" Gracie asks.

He smiles at her before looking at me. "I remember everyone in the office, but yeah, Jamie is pretty unforgettable."

I eye him, sensing something from him when she mentioned Jamie's name and how he reacted. I quirk an eyebrow at him.

"What?" He throws his hands up. "You want to tell me not to dip the pen in company ink? Too late for that since you've already done that, huh?" he chides.

I roll my eyes. "I'm not going to tell you what to do," I begin, "but you better not do anything that is going to put our reputation on the line."

"Yes, sir." He salutes.

"Such a fucking smartass sometimes," I say. "No wonder I'm Mom's favorite."

I finish my beer. These conversations are never easy, especially when it's with Aaron. However, I feel like we've got a newfound respect for each other. He knows my professional boundaries are to protect the company, even when I look like a hypocrite because of my relationship with Grace.

A few minutes later, we get a call from the lobby, announcing that Jamie is on her way up. Gracie jumps up from the couch to meet her at the door, and I hear the two women talking in hushed tones before they enter the living room.

"Mr. McPherson," Jamie calls me with a smirk on her face.

I roll my eyes. "Drew, Jamie. Call me Drew."

She snickers and Aaron laughs.

"And you know Aaron," Gracie says, not introducing Aaron.

"What's up?" Aaron asks with a chin lift.

"Oh, nothing much, just coming to see my friend that your brother has kidnapped out of my life," Jamie jokes. Gracie elbows her before they both start laughing. "Show me around this place," she tells Gracie and they take off down the hallway.

If those two weren't polar opposite in appearance, I'd swear they were related. Same sense of humor, same wit. I now understand why they get along so well.

"She's fucking hot," Aaron says, adjusting his crotch like a Neanderthal.

"Aaron," I warn.

"I'm just sayin'."

We turn our attention back to the football game, but I don't like when there's tension between us. "You staying here tonight?"

He shrugs. "If you're cool with it, it'd be nice."

I chew on it for a moment. "You're always welcome here." I'm surprised that I actually mean it.

TWENTY-TWO

Gracie

"This place is fucking insane," Jamie shrieks when I take her out to the terrace. "I can't believe you live here."

I can't believe it either, and while it's technically not my home, I really do feel at home here with Drew. I feel like it's our home. We've fallen into domestic routines like an old married couple, and on one hand, it's comforting, and on the other, it's scary.

"It is," I remark, and we sit down on the chaise together, the same one I share with Drew when we're out here.

Jamie loops her arm through mine and rests her head on my shoulder. "If anyone deserves this, it's you."

"Stop it," I tell her.

"No. Gracie, you deserve the best this world has to offer. I've never had a best friend, hell, I've never even had a friend as loyal as you. You have my back, you support my crazy-ass ideas, and I trust you like a sister."

This makes me tear up. I never had a sibling, and Jamie is a sister to me as well.

"Jamie," I whisper, my voice breaking.

"Don't go getting all emotional on me." She turns to look at me just as I swipe a stray tear from the corner of my eye and take a deep breath. She frowns, her eyes concerned. "What's going on?"

I sniffle. "Everything is happening really fast. Him moving me in here, all the new clients at work, *us*. It's been the craziest month of my life."

Jaime sighs. "Life doesn't always happen at a snail's pace. Sometimes things happen fast and furiously. Don't let a timeline dictate how it should happen." She squeezes my arm supportively. "Gracie, that man loves you like you deserve to be loved. I can see it. It's hard to believe it, someone like him and you've only known each other for this short amount of time, but he's the real deal." Her voice turns soft. "Let him care for you. Let him love you."

I smile, because dammit, Jamie is always right. "It's scary," I admit.

"The best things always are." She winks at me.

I sigh and let it go for now, then I fill her in on the California trip. Even though we've been back for a week, I dove headfirst into those client pitches and we never really got the chance to catch up. I've loved every minute I've spent with Drew, but tonight, spending time with Jamie has been good for my soul. I need her, and I need to be better about making sure I get time alone with her. There is nothing more important than genuine female friendships.

We occasionally hear the guys inside yelling at the TV and we both giggle at their latest outburst.

"What is it about dudes and football?" Jamie asks before breaking out into another fit of laughter and before her tone turns more serious. "Can I ask you something?"

"Of course, anything."

"I know you mentioned you were sick in California..."

"Mmmhmm."

She hesitates before looking at me. "Have you seen a doctor yet?"

I scoff, "I don't even have a doctor."

"Grace—"

"I know. I have an OB/GYN, but I don't have a primary care doctor. I've always hit the Minute Clinic if I needed anything."

She swallows hard. "I'm worried about you...you know, with your mom's history and all."

That hits me hard for a second. My mom was diagnosed with colon cancer at such a young age, and I shared my concerns with Jamie that maybe I was susceptible to cancer at an early age.

But it can't be.

"I don't have cancer." I smile at her. "I'm positive it's the flu or some lingering virus—"

"Gracie," she warns, ignoring my nonchalance.

"I mean it," I promise. "I slept all day and I feel so much better already. I think I just wore myself down. Everything has been on high speed since the day I met Drew. We dove headlong into it, then work has been insane, and the long hours..." I pause. "I think I just haven't been taking care of myself. But it's a priority now. I promise. Sleep, eating better, and maybe even exercise."

Jamie laughs. She knows my aversion to exercise.

"What?" I shrug. "I mean, there's a gym right here in the building and I don't even have to pay for it." Now we both laugh. Because there could be a gym in this damn apartment and I'd probably just look at it and never actually use it.

She nudges me with her elbow. "Come to yoga with me. It's exercise, but I promise it won't kill you. It'll be our date night." She grins.

I make a face. "How much is it?"

"Gracie..." She sounds exasperated.

I smirk. "I have to ask."

"It's cheap. I promise."

She's lying, but I need my time with her, so I will make this work. "It's a date."

Aaron and Drew join us on the terrace when they've finally had enough football. "What are you two doing out here?" Drew asks, taking a seat on the plush outdoor couch next to the chaise.

"Girl talk," Jamie answers with sass. "And you don't have a vagina, so you're not invited."

"Whoa!" Aaron exclaims as he approaches. "I heard the word vagina and I'm a big fan of those. Whose are we talking about?"

"Jesus," Drew growls.

I laugh while Jamie rolls her eyes exaggeratedly at Aaron, who sits down next to Drew on the couch.

"Done watching those cavemen beat each other up?" Jamie asks, and Aaron rolls his eyes back at her.

These two act like toddlers around each other. Maybe they should date. That would be interesting. The thought makes me chuckle.

"I'd be hesitant to call them cavemen," Aaron starts and rolls his eyes.

"Oh, sorry, they've evolved since they wear helmets now, right?" She fires back. Jamie is playing with fire going toe-to-toe with Aaron. He's the king of the comeback. It's part of his job, always be quick to fire off a response, except this time, he doesn't. "You know football is rigged, right?" Jamie continues egging him on.

I see Drew chuckle as he looks at Aaron.

"Rigged?" Aaron raises a doubting eyebrow. "It's not rigged."

"Bullshit," Jamie fires back at him. "Those refs are all bought."

"Since when did you become an expert in football?" Aaron spits out, eyeing her up and down. "Looks like you spend more time at Nordstrom than on a football field—"

"All right, guys," Drew intervenes, cutting Aaron off. "Let's not argue over football."

"I'm not arguing." Jamie shrugs. "I'm sharing facts."

I grin. I've always loved how she doesn't give a shit what anyone thinks.

"Facts, huh?" Aaron scoffs.

Drew looks at me and his lips contort into a sly grin as Jamie and Aaron now banter back and forth at each other through huffs, eye rolls, and snarky comments under their breath.

"What time is it?" Jamie finally asks.

"Time for you to get the hell out of here," Aaron chimes in. We all know he's kidding, but I pick up one of the pillows and toss it at his head. The pillow bounces off him and lands at his feet.

We all laugh and the conversation turns lighter. Nothing makes me happier than spending time with three of my favorite people. There's something about the comfort and ease I feel with them that makes me content...happy, and Jamie and Aaron are absolutely hysterical together.

We all talk for at least another hour, thankfully without Jamie and Aaron killing each other. Earlier, Drew brought out blankets for all of us and started the fire to keep us warm. Jamie and I listened to Drew and Aaron tell stories from their childhood and Drew and I listened to Jamie and Aaron take comical digs at each other all night.

"I need to go," Jamie finally says, standing up and stretching. "Where's my phone?" she asks me.

"Your purse?" I suggest, not even remembering her having her phone with her out here on the terrace.

"I'm going to call an Uber."

"You can't get into a car with a stranger," Aaron remarks, like it's the stupidest thing he's ever heard.

"I do it all the time," she snaps back at him.

He scoffs, "And to think I thought you had brains under that—"

Jamie props both of her hands on her hips. "If you say blonde hair, I'm going to rip your balls off, bring them home, and feed them to my cats."

Drew busts out laughing, and Aaron covers his crotch protectively with his hands. "Should have known you were a cat lady," he grumbles and I double over in laughter.

"Traitor," Jamie bumps me with her shoulder. She knows I've never liked cats.

"Where do you live?" Drew asks Jamie.

"East Village."

Aaron pushes himself up off the couch and reaches his hands above his head in an over-exaggerated stretch. The hem of his t-shirt rises, and his muscular abs are on full display. "Being the gentleman that I am, I suppose I'll escort you home."

"Not happening," Jamie snaps back at him.

Aaron rolls his neck and cracks his knuckles like he's about to tackle something difficult. "Shut up, woman. Get your purse so I can deliver you safely to your East Side high-rise in the sky and get you to bed."

Jamie scoffs but doesn't argue and Drew looks at me with a surprised look. I shake my head, a non-verbal sign to keep his mouth shut. What those two do is their business and I'm staying out of it, at least for now.

"Love you," I tell Jamie as she pulls me into a hug. "Thank you for coming over."

"I love your place," she says before releasing me and pulling Drew into an awkward hug. This whole mixing business with pleasure has all of us in unchartered territory, but Drew rolls with it and hugs her back.

"Thanks for coming by. You're always welcome here," Drew tells her.

"Damn right I am." She smirks at him. "You're not the only one who gets time with my girl."

Drew smiles.

"Let's go!" Aaron says impatiently, shooing her off the terrace.

Jamie waves at us over her shoulder and Drew and I both shake our heads at them.

"The sexual tension between them is off the charts," I remark.

"Please don't talk about it," he groans as he shuts off the outdoor fire pit. "Those two are an HR nightmare waiting to happen. Oil and water."

"And we aren't?" I raise my eyebrows.

"No. We're not." He winks at me and pulls me into a long hug before pressing a gentle kiss to my lips. "Now let's go to bed. I need some alone time with you, and I thought they'd never leave." He palms my ass before dragging me off to the bedroom.

I wake up feeling worse than ever. My entire body aches and my head is pounding. I'm so weak, I feel like I can barely gather the strength to get out of bed. It's time to see a doctor, and not at the Minute Clinic.

Drew sleeps peacefully next to me as I reach for my phone and search for a clinic or urgent care that's open on Sundays. I'm lucky enough to find one a few blocks over that opens in an hour.

I muster up the strength to get out of bed and into some comfortable clothes. I brush my teeth and braid my hair in an attempt to look halfway presentable in public. By the time I make myself a glass of tea, it's time to leave. I jot a quick note on a piece of paper telling Drew I'll be back in a bit. No need to wake him or worry him, but I know he'll be happy I'm finally going to the doctor.

I'm the first one in the urgent care when they unlock the door at nine o'clock sharp. I sign in and take a seat to fill out the ten pages of paperwork they've given me. My headache makes it difficult, though, and I feel like I could vomit again at any minute.

When the medical assistant calls me back, she takes my vitals, weighs me, and sticks me in a room while she reviews my paperwork.

"Last period?" she asks. I intentionally left that blank on the paperwork because I can't remember. I've always had irregular periods, which is why I'm on the pill. However, for the last six months, even those aren't regulating me.

I explain this to her, along with agreeing to follow up with my gynecologist.

The doctor sees me right away, reviewing my paperwork, my vitals, and following up with more questions. She looks at my throat, feels the glands in my neck, looks in my eyes and ears, and does an overall general physical. She orders bloodwork, a flu and strep test, and even a urine test. She's definitely covering all the bases and asks me to rest until the medical assistant returns.

I've always considered cancelling my health insurance to give me more take home pay on my paycheck. Today, I'm thankful I didn't do that. I can only imagine what this visit would have cost me out of pocket. If I've learned anything, it's don't take your health or good medical insurance for granted.

After I've been poked, swabbed up the nose and in the back of my throat, and peed in a cup, I'm asked to wait back in the room. Drew texts me while I'm waiting, asking where I'm at, and I shoot him a quick response, telling him I'll be home shortly. If I told him where I was, he'd surely insist on meeting me here. I don't have the energy to argue with him right now, so I shut off my phone after responding.

I close my eyes and lie on the exam table until I feel a gentle squeeze on my arm. Dr. Friedrich coaxes me awake and I apologize for dozing off.

She sits down in a chair and props her laptop on her lap. "Grace." She says my name as her eyes scan the screen. "The good news is, overall, you're perfectly healthy. The bad news is you're fighting a little bug amongst some other things." She taps at the keyboard before setting the laptop on the small counter. "Your flu test was negative, as was your strep test. You weren't displaying symptoms of strep throat, but I wanted to check to make sure. It's that time of year where we've seen many cases of strep and some patients don't display the usual symptoms."

I nod my head as she rattles off her findings. "However, your white blood cell count is a little low, which tells me you're definitely fighting off an infection. Most viral infections contribute to an upset stomach, body aches, and general fatigue. Couple that with your pregnancy and I can see why you're miserable. I recommend a minimum of three days rest, continuous fluids, and an appointment with your OB/GYN in the next couple of weeks. Congratulations." She smiles at me and folds her hands in her lap, waiting for me to respond.

But I can't. I'm stunned.

I'm...what?

"Excuse me?" I finally say breathily.

The look on her face tells me she sees my hesitancy. "Grace, the pregnancy is early. The urine test didn't show the pregnancy yet, but your HCG levels are elevated in your bloodwork. You're definitely pregnant. I'd say you're probably five, maybe six weeks at the most."

I blink several times, trying to swallow this. My heart is pounding harder than my head now. "I have barely been having sex for that long," I explain, trying to convince her, or maybe myself, that she has this all wrong. This is a huge error.

She shakes her head and goes into the long medical explanation about how a pregnancy is determined from the time of the last menstrual cycle, not from the time of actual conception. Except, due to my irregular periods, I don't know when my last menstrual cycle was.

This is too much. My head begins to spin, and I feel like I might vomit right here in front of her. Drew and I have never even spoken of kids. We've discussed birth control and that's it.

My stomach continues to twist and turn, and anything else she's saying, I don't even hear. I simply nod my head as her lips move until she stands up and leaves the room. I do my best to use the breathing techniques I've learned to ward off an anxiety attack. In through the mouth, hold it, release slowly. I do this at least twenty times before the medical assistant returns with my release paperwork. I do my best to smile politely, but all I want to do is get the hell out of this clinic before I lose my shit.

I take a cab to Central Park, where I sit in the grass under a tree in almost in the same spot where Drew brought me on our picnic. There's something about the crisp, fresh air, the green grass, and the turning leaves that helps me settle my mind, even temporarily.

A million scenarios run through my head, like how I'm going to tell Drew and what his reaction might be. From good, to bad, to everything in between. I'm too numb to cry, too worried to predict, and too scared to tell him right now.

It's almost noon when I arrive back at the condo to Drew and Aaron standing around the kitchen island.

"There you are!" Drew says when I enter the kitchen. I take a deep breath and do my best to plaster a smile on my face, hoping to hide my worry. "You've been gone for hours."

"Sorry," I tell him as he pulls me into a hug. "I finally caved and went to the urgent care." I hold up the papers I've been carrying around as if he was questioning my whereabouts. "Looks like it's just a virus."

Aaron's eyes grow wide. "You have a virus? Are you contagious?"

"It's not the plague," I tell him sarcastically, "and I sure hope not. I've been at work the last week and would have exposed everyone in the office to it."

Thankfully, Drew doesn't seem suspicious. He pats my shoulder. "Go get some rest. Aaron was just filling me in on his evening with Jamie." He gives me a look that tells me it's more than I probably ever could have imagined it'd be.

"I don't know that I even want to know..." I hold my hand up, stopping Drew from telling me more. "You two enjoy."

Drew leans in and presses a kiss to my forehead. "I'll come check on you in a little bit."

I nod, tuck my paperwork under my arm, and disappear down the long hall to the bedroom, where I crawl into bed and cry myself to sleep. It's the first time I'm allowing myself to really feel the impact of how quickly my life is about to change.

TWENTY-THREE

Drew

Aaron and I spend the day together, again. It's been great reconnecting with my brother. When he unexpectedly showed up in New York, I wanted to fucking murder him, but in the last couple of weeks, I've actually gotten used to his pain-in-the-ass presence. Between Gracie agreeing to live here, reconnecting with Aaron and him deciding to move here, and AM Global taking on a record number of new clients, everything in my life is falling into place. This is what dreams are made of. These are the days I cherish and I'm so thankful for it, and for the first time ever, I truly feel blessed.

Around five o'clock, Aaron went back to his hotel for the night so that I could take care of Gracie. She's been asleep all day and I'm beginning to get worried. I find her sound asleep in our bed, burrowed under the comforter and all curled around a pillow. She's peaceful and beautiful, and I decide to just let her sleep. Rest is what she needs to heal.

My alarm goes off at five thirty in the morning. I set it early so I can get a work-out in before hitting the office. I've been so busy lately, I haven't set aside my normal time to work out and I can feel it manifesting physically and mentally. I need the release and if I have to get up early to get it, that's exactly what I'll do. I reach over to pull Gracie to me, wanting to feel her warm skin against mine before I leave, but I find an empty bed.

I find Gracie relaxing in the bathtub, her favorite place. "Morning," I say, peeking my head in the bathroom.

"Morning," she responds, rolling her head to the side to look at me. Her long hair is all tied up on top of her head.

"Feeling any better?"

She nods slowly. "Yeah, a little. Hopefully, once I'm up and moving, the body aches will go away."

I frown, still worried about her. "Maybe you should take today off."

She shakes her head quickly. "No. Too much work to do—"

I cut her off. "Gracie. All of it can wait. Plus, you have an amazing team that can pick up anything urgent."

Her face looks flush and I don't know if it's from her not feeling well or because she's soaking in a hot bath.

"I'm fine. I slept really good, I just need to soak my achy muscles." She knows I'm not buying her lies. "Really."

I'm not going to argue with her, because if the shoe was on the other foot, I know I'd be doing the same damn thing. "Okay. I'm going to go work out. Tony will be here at seven thirty to take us to the office. Anything you need from me before I go?"

She nods. "Will you make the bed? I'm just too tired. I'm going to soak for a bit longer in here."

"Sure."

She offers me a tight, unreassuring smile. "Have a good workout."

Even sick, she's the most beautiful woman in the world. I toss on a pair of joggers and a t-shirt before I pull the plush comforter up on the bed. I grab all the decorative throw pillows and begin arranging them on top of the comforter, but I'm doing a poor job at making them look nice. I knock a stack of papers off Gracie's nightstand, and as they fall to the floor, I realize it's her release papers from the urgent care.

I grab them, placing them neatly back into a pile when I see the words "pregnancy confirmation" with follow up orders to see an OB/GYN. I pick the papers back up and also see a note for pre-natal vitamins.

My heart stops dead when I see Gracie's name on the paperwork—Grace Morgan—next to her date of birth. The name, address, and telephone number of the urgent care is listed at the top of the paperwork, along with yesterday's date.

Pregnant.

I need a second, sitting down on the edge of the bed.

Fuck.

Nausea, vomiting, body aches, fatigue. All symptoms of pregnancy. Why in the fuck didn't I see this?

She lied to me. She's known since yesterday and said it was a virus. My hands tremble, the papers shaking wildly. This was not supposed to happen. "Fuck." I punch at the air, sending the papers flying across the bedroom.

"Drew?" Gracie's voice is weak, and then I realize she's out of the bath, standing in the bathroom doorway.

I bury my face in my hands. I cannot bring myself to look at her. I can hear her bare feet pad across the floor, and I can feel her next to me. My entire body shakes with anger as I breathe, trying to control myself.

I open my eyes to see Gracie wrapped in a towel, bending down to pick up the papers. She's shaking as badly as I am when she approaches, stopping in front of me. She sets the papers on the nightstand and wraps her arms around her waist in a protective stance.

"I was going to tell you—"

"You fucking lied to me!" I shout at her, cutting her off. "You said you had a virus."

She takes two steps backwards, her entire body trembling in fear. I've never raised my voice to her. I've never had her scatter away in fear and I feel like a fucking asshole, but right now, I'm too pissed to care.

"I didn't lie." Her voice is tiny, barely above a whisper. "I have a virus...and I'm also pregnant."

I don't know if it's anger or rage or hurt...but I pick the papers off the nightstand and crumble them in my hands, my hands balling into tight fists. "You told me you were on the pill."

Her chin quivers, but she raises it higher in an act of courage. She's always been a stronger, better person than me. "I am...was..."

"Then how—"

"I don't know!" she screams back at me before bursting into tears. "I don't know how it happened. I missed pills, Drew. You were aware of that. You didn't let me go home some nights. I have irregular periods...all of it. All of it happened and now I'm pregnant." She drops to her knees and buries her hands in her face, loud sobs filling the room. Her bare shoulders shake and her arms tremble with her cries.

"I didn't do this on purpose," she chokes out between gasping sobs. She sits on the floor in front of me, a crumbling mess, and as much as I want to comfort her right now, I can't. Because I'm a selfish prick and the only person I can think of is myself.

"I don't want a baby," I say. My voice is flat, devoid of emotion. "I can't do this."

Something happens almost instantly, and she stills. Her sobs come to a sudden stop and her entire body becomes motionless.

"I can't do this," I say again, barely above a whisper. My voice is hoarse. I wanted everything with Gracie, a house, a life, but we never discussed kids. The last thing I ever wanted was to be an absent father like my dad was, therefore, I decided years ago, kids weren't in my future.

She raises her head to look at me, her eyes holding mine, searching for answers, searching for support, searching for the love I promised her. Only I'm the fucking liar now. I promised to never hurt her and here I am, destroying her. My chest heaves with heavy breaths when her eyes finally fall to my clenched fists.

Tears fall from her eyes and roll down her face. Giant, wet tears soak her cheeks. Her lips tremble and her chin quivers as the weight of my words settle in. Without a word, she simply nods at me in understanding before standing up and walking away.

I hear the bathroom door close behind her before I hear her quiet sobs echo against the tile room, and that's when I know I broke her. The one thing I promised I would never do I did, and my heart breaks into a million pieces. I destroyed the one thing I love the most in this world.

It's been an hour since Gracie locked herself in the bathroom. I listened to her cry through the bathroom door, but not once did I try to get to her, not once did I apologize or try to be a rational human being. Not once did I call out to her, comfort her, or tell her we'd figure this out. I'm a fucking asshole. I finally left for the office, leaving her behind. I walked out on her, leaving her with the burden of this news.

I don't greet Sue when I arrive at the office. I simply slam my office door behind me and send her an instant message telling her to clear my calendar. There's no way I can function or think critically today. I rub my temples, trying to push away the growing headache that seems to be worsening by the minute.

At nine o'clock, there's a light knock on my door and I bark out at Sue, "Not right now."

Only Sue doesn't give a shit. She opens the door and steps inside. "Mr. McPherson, I think you're going to want this." She hands me a piece of paper that I snatch out of her hand. With it, she hands me Gracie's employee badge.

"Letter of resignation" is typed in the memo line, under Gracie's name and Red Hook address. Fury rages through me and I crumble the paper, much like I did the medical release papers this morning, and toss it in the garbage can. Sue simply glares at me, pursing her lips.

"I don't know what's going on, but Grace Morgan is the best thing to happen to this company—" she starts before I cut her off.

"Not now, Sue!" I bark at her like the asshole that I am. I don't even know who I am anymore.

"Fix it," she says, slamming my office door on her way out.

Not two minutes later, my office door flies open again and Jamie comes barreling through.

"Where'd Gracie go?" Jamie demands, furious. She cornered me once before and told me that if I ever hurt Gracie, she'd gut me, and for some reason, I actually believe she would. Grace is lucky to have a friend like Jamie.

"Don't know," I snap at her.

"What did you do to her?" She takes another step further into my office and narrows her eyes at me.

I throw my hands in the air and growl but don't answer her question. One, because I don't know if I can even vocalize what I'm feeling right now, and two, it's none of her damn business.

I see Aaron slide into my office and stand next to Jamie before he pipes in, "Uh, everything okay?"

I push myself up from my chair and stand with my hands

planted firmly on the desk to steady me. Sensing the seriousness of the situation, Aaron closes my office door, giving us privacy from all of the eyes that seem to be pacing the hall outside my office. Everyone seems to be acutely aware that shit is going down. But it's the two pairs of eyes standing in front of me that I have to answer to. My heart beats wildly in my chest and my stomach twists in knots as I replay what I said to Gracie. I'm disgusted with myself for the way I handled the news and how I pushed her away when she needed me.

I prop my hands on my hips and take a deep breath. "I don't know where she went," I tell them.

"What did you do?" Jamie seethes.

"Everything..."

"Dude!" Aaron starts, but I cut him off.

"She's pregnant." My voice is weak, and I find it hard to speak. I try to swallow against my dry throat, but struggle to. "I found out she's pregnant."

I hear Jamie gasp and I turn away from them, unable to look at either of them.

"Is it yours?" Aaron asks like a dumbass.

Anger courses through my veins at the insinuation it wouldn't be. "Of course it fucking is." Sighing loudly and rubbing my eyes with the heel of my hands, I suddenly find myself fighting back the rapid onslaught of emotions.

"You're not happy," Aaron says quietly, a statement, not a question, and I simply look at him. He's my brother. He knows me better than anyone. I don't even need to answer this because he knows; he lived the life I lived. We lived it together. I always swore I'd never bring a child into the world knowing that I couldn't or wouldn't commit the time to be the best father. My goal has always been on AM Global, and I'm just building that dream.

"It's not what I planned—" I begin before Jamie cuts me off.

"Whoa there, buddy," she says, clearly disgusted with me. Join the fucking club. "I don't know what's going through your head right now, but for one goddamn second, you best not be angry at or blame Gracie for this. Last I checked, it takes two to make a baby, and I can goddamn guarantee you she didn't plan this either."

"I know how a fucking baby is made," I bark at her.

She points a finger at me, her long fingernail right in my face. "What did you say to her? She left here crying, Drew," she asks through gritted teeth.

I take a sharp breath and lace my fingers together behind my head. "I don't even remember. I was so upset—"

"Bullshit. You know what you said." Jamie takes another step closer, almost nose to nose with me now. She's intimidating with her long blonde hair and New York accent. She also most likely knows how to have me killed and disposed of with her New York connections and she looks like she's ready to call in a favor and do just that. "What did you fucking say to her?" she asks me again.

I take a long pull of air into my lungs and pinch my eyes closed. "That I didn't want a baby—"

I don't know if I feel the smack or hear the slap first, but Jamie's palm meets my cheek and I lurch backward.

"What the fuck!" I yell as Aaron wraps his arms around Jamie's waist, pulling her back and away from me.

"You son of a bitch!" she screams at me, throwing her arms wildly like she wants a piece of me. "She deserves better than that...better than YOU!" she shouts at me, trying to break free from Aaron's grip. There is no doubt if she gets free, I'm a dead man. But my heart sinks at what she's said to me because she's right. Gracie does deserve better than me. She is the best thing to ever happen to me and I treated her like trash. I treated her and our baby like they were disposable—all because this didn't happen according to my plan or my timeline.

Because I wasn't in control.

"You're a selfish bastard, you know that, right?" She chokes those words out and I look at her. Tears fall from her eyes as Aaron keeps his arms wrapped around her waist. I turn away from both of them, my hand rubbing my cheek where the skin still stings.

On a sob, Jamie continues laying into me. "You don't deserve her, Drew. I knew you were going to hurt her. I fucking knew it."

With my back to Jamie, I respond with the most honest words I've ever spoken, only I should have said them to Gracie, not Jamie and Aaron. "I didn't want to hurt her either. I love her."

"Love her? You don't know what love is, you selfish prick." She snorts and I turn around to look at her. "If you love her, you wouldn't have let her walk out of here. For once in her life, she needed someone to have her back, to support her. Just once..." Her voice breaks. "She carries the burden of everyone else's problems, Drew. She never catches a break. I thought you were different. I thought you were a break for her. Someone easy for her to love, someone who'd take care of *her* for once. You are just like everyone else in her life...worthless. Guess I was wrong about you." Her face twists in disgust. "Gracie is the strongest person I know, and she'll raise this baby with or without you. But if you're not on board, you best get the fuck out of New York and never come back here. San Francisco is calling you back, you asshole."

With those words, she twists out of Aaron's grasp and flees my office. My throat closes as I think of Gracie being here with our baby, without me, and I feel like I'm suffocating. God, I fucked up. I run my hands through my hair as my stomach continues to twist violently.

"Why would you tell her you didn't want it?" Aaron asks, seeming genuinely concerned and disappointed in me for once.

I look at my brother and a million memories of our childhood flash through my mind. All the baseball games that I'd look out into the bleachers only to find my mom, and I can't even remember all of the birthday parties he missed, all because he was "at the office," building his company.

"Because I'm afraid," I choke out, my voice breaking. I clear my throat, swallowing back the lump in my throat. "Because I don't want to be like him."

He nods in understanding.

"Because I'm so fucking afraid I will be like him, and Grace deserves better than that, our baby deserves better than that. You remember what it was like…" I actually feel tears sting the backs of my eyes. I can't remember the last time I cried, but the thought of Gracie doing this alone, or worse, allowing someone else to raise my baby, is enough to make me want to vomit.

"I have to find her," I tell Aaron.

He nods. "Any idea where she might be?"

I shake my head. If someone wants to hide, New York City is the perfect place. "She could be anywhere."

"Red Hook?" Aaron asks, and I shake my head, doubtful that she'd go back to her apartment. Too easy. "I'll text Jamie," he says, pulling his phone from his back pocket. "We need to divide and conquer."

Aaron shoots a message to Jamie and I mentally run through all the places she might go. Central Park. The library. Jamie's apartment.

"Jamie is headed home," Aaron says, reading the text message she must have sent him. "She thinks she might be headed there."

"I'm going to check Central Park," I tell him. "It's her favorite place in the city." I grab my jacket off the coat rack and slide into it as I take off out the door. I hear Aaron behind me, but I don't wait for him. I have to find Gracie and make this right; that's the only thing I care about.

TWENTY-FOUR

Gracie

Hot tears sting my cheeks as I walk across the Brooklyn Bridge. It's been a long time since I've walked across this bridge, but walking has given me time to think about all the decisions I have to make for me and my baby. I spent the afternoon in Battery Park before walking the waterfront to the Brooklyn Bridge. The sun is setting and the sky darkening when I finally make it across and into Dumbo. I weave through the busy streets and make my way to the nearest bus stop. It's been a while since I've taken the bus, but ease temporarily settles inside me as I fall back into the routine that I was all too familiar with...before Drew.

This is my life—buses, not private cars and drivers. Red Hook, not Chelsea. I was only fooling myself thinking Drew could love someone like me, and he proved that today. I take a seat on the bench at the bus stop, my aching feet breathing a sigh of relief.

Twenty minutes later, I'm exiting the bus in Red Hook, a short three blocks from my apartment. Familiarity hits me here and something inside me stirs. A sense of comfort and ease suddenly envelop me. The smell of the Mr. Pirelli's pizza place

on the corner makes my stomach growl and the sight of the
bodega I used to frequent once a week calls to me.

I stop at the bodega and grab a can of soup and a bottle of
water, knowing I have nothing in my apartment—not that I ever
did. As I get about a block from my apartment, I hear a car slow
down next to me, but I ignore it and continue walking. From my
peripheral vision, I can tell it's a Town Car. Fucking Drew and
his Town Cars.

"Grace," the voice calls to me, and I realize it's Aaron, not
Drew. Figures he'd send his brother to do his dirty work.

"Leave me alone," I call back to him, fumbling with my purse
to get my keys out as tears sting the back of my eyes.

"Give me five minutes, Grace." The car continues to follow
me until I hear the brakes squeak and it finally stops in front of
me. A car door closes and I see Aaron jogging up next to me.

"I don't want to talk right now," I tell him, picking up my
pace. My apartment is just coming into view down the street.

A strong hand grabs my arm, stopping me. "Please, Grace.
I'm not here to apologize for my brother being a dick...because he
needs to do that."

He's more than a dick, but my throat is tight and I don't have
it in me to argue right now. I'm tired, both emotionally and
physically. I shake my head and feel new tears forming in my
eyes. I used to be so strong. I was able to bury my emotions. I
never cried, but something inside me broke today and I no longer
care about being strong. That's what I get for opening up my
heart.

"I don't want his apology," I choke out.

"Fair enough," he says. He reaches for the bag in my hand
and takes it from me. "Just let me make sure you get home safely."
He starts walking beside me. I can see him taking in the
surrounding sights of my street in Red Hook. Much like Drew
did that first day he came to my apartment, in silent judgment.

"I've walked these streets for two years and I've always been fine. Tonight won't be any different," I tell him, swatting away the now falling tears from my cheeks.

Aaron keeps pace with me but remains silent, simply carrying my bag. When we reach my building, I stop and turn to him, reaching for the bag with my soup and water.

"Please just give me five minutes, Grace," he pleads with me, holding the bag away from me. "I promise. There's just some things I need to share with you."

I sigh, and he reaches for my keys. Reluctantly, I release them into his waiting hand and he opens the door to my building. We walk the stairs to the third floor, the old wood creaking under our feet, and the musty smell hitting us as we ascend and finally reach my place.

As I take the keys back from Aaron and open my apartment door, dark, stale air greets us, a realization that I haven't been here in weeks. As I flip on the overhead kitchen light, Aaron drops the bag on the kitchen counter and walks over to the old thermostat on the wall to turn on the heat.

"Good luck getting that to work," I mumble. The temperature doesn't rise above sixty degrees in the fall and winter.

"It's freezing in here," he says, rubbing his hands together while taking in the sight of my dingy old apartment. An apartment I was once so proud of, but I'm sure Aaron is judging me for it. He doesn't say anything, but I notice the way his eyes take in the stark space, all the furniture I've collected from thrift shops and painted or tried to restore on my own.

"You have five minutes starting now," I tell him, wanting him and his judgment out of my apartment.

He joins me in the small kitchen that really isn't much of a kitchen; it's a miniature stove, a tiny fridge, and sink. There are two small cupboards and a tiny free-standing cart that doubles as a kitchen island. Another thrift shop find that I sanded and re-stained.

He pulls a sauce pan from the shelf under the cart and sets it on the stove, then reaches for the bag with the soup. "Can opener?" he asks as he pulls the aluminum can from the bag. I reach into a drawer and pull a handheld can opener out and hand it to him. While he works on opening the can of soup, he begins talking.

"I'm assuming Drew hasn't told you much about our life growing up," Aaron starts, glancing at me. I shake my head and hand Aaron a wooden spoon. "Everyone assumes that Drew and I had the perfect life growing up." He pauses as he dumps the chicken noodle soup in the small pan and slowly stirs it. "But it wasn't all that great," he continues. "I mean, our mom was the best." His lips pull into a smile as he speaks of his mom. "She kept the wheels on our family cart, so to speak." Drew rarely spoke of his family, but when he did, it was always of his mom. I always wondered about his father, but I didn't want to appear nosy. I was so thankful I got to meet Rose when we went to Napa, even though our trip was cut short.

He sets the spoon on the spoon rest I have on the counter next to the small stove. "But what no one knew was the anger Drew and I developed growing up in that house." He turns to me and rests his hip against the kitchen cabinet. "See, my dad was busy building an advertising empire—the one Drew owns and I work for—and we should be thankful for it, but it came at a cost. We lived a pretty cushy life in Napa, while our dad spent most of his time at his other home in San Francisco. He never attended one of our football or baseball games. He never once attended parent-teacher conferences or took us driving when we finally got our driver's permits." His eyes hold a sadness I've never seen before and he swallows hard before continuing once again.

"He was never around. Ever. He even missed our birthdays,

Grace." He sighs loudly. "When Drew and I were in college, we came home for Christmas one year and our dad never came to Napa to celebrate with us. We spent two weeks in Napa and didn't see him once."

Aaron pauses and grabs the spoon to stir the soup again. "Early on, I learned he wasn't going to be a prominent fixture in my life or Drew's. I guess I was unaffected by the lack of a relationship I had with my dad, but Drew, he always took it hard. He's the one who would act out in his absence. He always wanted the attention of our father, and our father was too busy to give a shit. He's the one that took it personally that our dad neglected us. Drew needed him and I didn't. We were just built differently." He shrugs, but I see how the pain has chipped away at his casual exterior. It affects him; he's just learned to control it.

And I guess I can see what he's saying, how he and Drew are different. Aaron seems disconnected from personal relationships, where Drew strives to grow them. Drew wants to know every intimate detail; Aaron wants the surface details. It's crazy how two men, the same blood, can be so vastly different.

"What I'm getting at is that Drew vowed from a very young age to never be like our father. Only, he's become the one most like him. When our dad was dying, it was Drew who said he wanted to own and run McPherson Advertising. I didn't give a shit about owning it. Drew wanted to manage the finite details, I just wanted a job. It was Drew's ambition that got McPherson Advertising to where it was when he bought Williams Global, and in doing so, he started seeing more and more of our father in himself. He mentioned it to me last week, and...it eats at him."

Aaron turns the knob to shut off the burner for the soup that's now boiling in the sauce pan. "After everything that happened with Melissa, he told my mom he never saw himself getting married or having kids because he thought he was becoming exactly what he said he'd never become—just like our father. She shared this with me in confidence. I thought he was burying himself in work as a means of getting over Melissa...which he was, but I always knew he wanted more than just a career." He pauses.

I swallow hard as I reach into the cupboard and pull down two bowls, handing them to Aaron. He takes them from me and carefully spoons soup into the two bowls while continuing on with his story.

"Then he met you, Grace. You changed the narrative to his story. I could see he finally wanted something other than his career—he loves you. You know he loves you—I know he loves you...and I thought he was ready for more...but I think it just happened all too fast."

"He said he didn't want our baby," I say, barely above a whisper. "His words were full of contempt and..." I pause taking a deep breath. "I understand he was caught off guard, but so was I." My eyes sting with newly formed tears and I swallow hard against the growing lump in my throat. "But, I never, not even for one fraction of a second, didn't want our baby." I look up and meet Aaron's gaze. His eyes appearing misty.

"And I guarantee you, Drew feels the same. I think he used the wrong words to express what he was feeling—" he says with certainty.

I shake my head, disregarding his assumption. If only Aaron could have seen the look on his face. The way he looked at me, his eyes full of disgust. "Can I ask you a favor?" I ask Aaron as I carry the two bowls of soup over to the small bistro table that is my kitchen table.

"Anything." He follows me.

"I need you to make some calls for me."

He looks at me perplexed. "Calls for what?" He slides into the wooden chair across from me.

"I need you to help me get a job at another agency."

His eyes drop from mine to the bowl of soup in front of him. I sigh, feeling desperate. I need someone's help, and it's not going to be Drew. "I plan to do this alone, Aaron. Everything else in my life, I've done on my own." My voice breaks and I can feel my chin quiver as my emotions bubble to the surface once again. "I can do this too, but I can't see him every day. I'm not strong enough."

"Grace." He says my name softly.

"Please. It's the only thing I'll ever ask you to do for me." There is an edge of desperation in my voice.

He rests his elbows on the edge of the table and pinches his eyes closed, burying his face in his hands.

"Please."

We eat in silence as Aaron contemplates my question. When I press him again, he looks at me with sad eyes. "I'll do whatever you need me to, but, Grace," he pauses and swallows hard, "before I make any calls, you need to agree to meet with him."

I shake my head. "No. I can't—"

"Grace..." he scolds me.

"Not yet."

He nods his head in understanding. Aaron clears our bowls and I decide to take a shower. When I finish, I find Aaron on the love seat, pounding away on his phone.

"You can leave now," I say, knowing how rude it sounds, but I just want to be alone. I thought he would have left when I was in the shower.

"Jamie is asking about you." He looks up from his phone.

My jaw tightens. "Tell her I'm fine and I'll call her tomorrow."

He nods and pounds out a quick message. There's a knock on the door, and I narrow my eyes at Aaron in realization of his betrayal. It's Drew. No one comes to my door, ever.

He holds up his hands in surrender before standing up. "I

couldn't stop him," he swears, leaning in and pressing a quick kiss to my cheek. He holds my shoulders and looks me in the eyes. "Just hear him out." He releases my shoulders and shrugs on his jacket before opening the apartment door.

Drew, looking desperate and harried, pushes his way in past Aaron and stops in front of me. I'm a mess, dressed in dirty yoga pants and an oversized t-shirt left behind in my hamper, but Drew doesn't look much better. His eyes are rimmed red and his face is ashen.

He turns to Aaron, who's just stepping out of the apartment. "Tony will take you back."

Aaron nods in acknowledgement and winks at me, a silent vow of strength.

"What do you want, Drew?" I ask curtly. I'm done with his bullshit and I'm exhausted, not in the mood for a conversation at the moment.

"You," he answers sincerely. Tears shimmer in the corner of his eyes. "Our baby."

I huff out a breath of air and shake my head in disgust.

"Us. I want all of us," he continues.

"Twelve hours ago, you didn't want any of this," I remind him. "Aaron told me your fucked-up daddy issues. I don't give a shit, Drew. You think your life has been so bad...well newsflash, it hasn't been." Now I'm being a bitch. It's not my place to disregard his emotions or downplay his hurt, and I feel immediately guilty the moment those words roll off my tongue. But I'm angry and hurt and he needs to know that. "You promised me you loved me. You told me to trust you, and I did, and then you hurt me—"

"I know." His voice breaks. "I love you, Gracie. More than I love myself, and I fucked up. I fucked up so big." He shakes his head. "I panicked, I got scared...I hurt the one person who I'd die for...you."

I pace the small space, the wood floors creaking under my feet. "I need to get some rest—"

"I'm not done," he starts.

"I am." My expression is defiance. I don't have the energy to continue this conversation right now.

Now he stands before me looking broken, like the shell of the man he once was. Always so tall and strong, now he looks small and weak. I hate seeing him like this, but this is what he did. These are the repercussions of his actions.

"Good night, Drew. Lock the door when you leave."

As exhausted as I am, I fall asleep the second my head hits my pillow. I didn't hear Drew let himself out, but I'm not surprised because I don't think I even moved last night. Between yesterday's events and still fighting this sickness, exhaustion has taken its toll on me.

Since it's still dark, it's hard to see, but I see the lump curled up on the floor and I'd know that form anywhere. It's Drew. Curled up in a ball on the cold floor right outside of my bedroom. It's freezing in this apartment and here he is, not a blanket, not a pillow, just him on the floor. I slide out of bed and pad across the wood floor over to him.

"Drew," I whisper, not wanting to startle him. He doesn't budge. "Drew." He moves, grumbles, and finally sits up. "What are you doing here?"

"I'm not leaving, Gracie." He reaches for me and I let him take my hand in his.

"You can't sleep on the floor." I tug at him to help him up and he takes it. "It's four o'clock in the morning. Go home."

"It's not home without you there."

I sigh, too tired to argue with him. "Go lie down." I usher him to my full-sized bed with a too soft, worn-out mattress. He climbs in and holds up the quilt, wanting me to join him.

"Please," he says desperately as I stand there looking at him. "I need you, Gracie." His voice is tired and hoarse.

My shoulders droop with exhaustion, with reluctance, but ultimately with surrender. We can fight more tomorrow, but I don't have it in me tonight. Shuffling to the bed, I squeeze in next to him and he curls himself around me. His body trembles from the cold, but he makes sure I'm covered with the quilt. Then we lie in silence, both of us succumbing to sleep just as the sun begins to rise.

When I wake, I need to pee like I've never peed in my life. Only Drew's hand is placed firmly on my belly, holding me close to him. I wiggle out of the tight space and make a beeline for the bathroom. When I finish, he's sitting on the edge of my bed, waiting for me.

"Hey," I say quietly, shuffling from foot to foot.

"Thanks for letting me sleep here." He gestures to the bed.

"You should probably get going," I urge him, glancing at the clock to see it's almost eight o'clock. "The office needs you."

He shakes his head. "They need you. I'm not accepting your resignation, Gracie. You can hate me. You can never talk to me again, but I will not lose the best employee I have."

"I can't—" I pause, choosing my words carefully. "Drew, I can't work there. I can't see you every day, knowing I caused such a major disruption in your life—"

Drew runs a hand through his hair and clenches his jaw. "Goddammit, Gracie, did you hear a word that I said last night? I love you. I'm not going anywhere and you are not leaving me. I made the biggest mistake of my life, and I will spend every damn minute of every day making it right." He stands up and crosses the tiny room, standing in front of me. "I love you. I fucking love you more than I love myself. And I will love our baby and give both of you the life you deserve, if it's the last thing I do..." His voice breaks and he turns his head, averting my gaze.

"Aaron told me about your dad," I divulge. It's hard for me to watch him become emotional, but it doesn't excuse yesterday's behavior.

He nods and swallows hard. "I don't want to be him—" His voice breaks and he looks at me, his eyes full of remorse. "I promise I won't be him. Let me love you both. Please, Gracie." He reaches for my hand, but I resist.

My heart breaks for Drew, for our baby, for *us*. I don't know that I'm ready to forgive him so quickly. "I asked Aaron to help me find another job." My heart races when I tell him that. I know he's going to be upset, but I also want him to know that I can and will do this without him. "I can take care of myself and my baby—"

"*Our* baby," he corrects, so much regret and pain all over his face, "and you're not doing this alone. You're not leaving your job, and you can't leave me." His eyes mist over as we stand toe-to-toe. "I need you, Gracie. I never believed I needed anyone until you." The most vulnerable versions of ourselves are laid out in front of each other; all of our insecurities no longer hidden, stripped bare before each other.

"Please forgive me," he whispers. "Don't leave me, Gracie." My throat tightens when I think about losing him.

"I promise to be everything you need—"

"You already were. All I ever needed from you was...you. Just your love, but more importantly, our baby needs that from you." He nods and closes his eyes. "I'm scared."

"So am I," I admit. "So fucking scared."

With that admission, he takes a deep breath, pulling me into his arms. "We will do this together, Gracie. You and me forever. All the ups and downs, all the unknowns, but we're going to do this life together. Promise me."

I'm still hurting and I know it will take time to work through this, but I can't imagine my life without Drew. Our baby needs him, but so do I.

Relief washes through me with his words. I need Drew as much as he needs me, and our baby needs both of us. "Promise," I whisper.

EPILOGUE

SIX MONTHS LATER

"What is this?" Grace exclaims in surprise when she enters the conference room at AM Global.

"Surprise!" everyone yells as blue and pink balloons are scattered about the room, and a giant cake sits in the center of the conference room table.

I convinced Gracie, with the help of Aaron, to rescind her resignation from AM Global and stay on. She was promoted to a senior account manager, which, lucky for her, came with a hefty raise. Regardless of whatever happens with us, she is too good of an employee to lose, and I refuse to let personal issues hinder her professional career.

Fortunately, she accepted my apology and, after endless discussions, agreed to move back into the Chelsea condo with me —*our* home. She gave up her Red Hook apartment when the lease expired. It took me potentially losing Grace, and our baby, to realize I want—*need*—both of them. They are my family now, and I'll do anything to protect them.

I grin at Grace and her fucking adorable seven-month baby bump. Sue wanted to plan a baby shower at the office, and being the boss and baby's father, I shamelessly let her. It wasn't much of a surprise when we did announce to the office that we were dating. Worst kept secret ever, but our professionalism at work has proven that we don't let our relationship get in the way of our careers. Thankfully, everyone here supports us.

With Grace living in the condo and without her lease at her apartment in Red Hook, she's paying down her debt quickly. She refinanced her loan through a legitimate bank and is actively paying it down every month. Of course, she argues that her salary should go to more than her debt, and she tries to give me money for household expenses, but I told her it's her job to pay off her debt, then we'll renegotiate what she can contribute once that's done. However, she'll contribute nothing. It's my job to take care of her and our baby. What she does with her money after her loan is paid off is up to her.

Jamie sidles up next to me, bumping her shoulder against mine. I smile softly at her. Gracie was easy to win back, Jamie not so much. She's coming around slowly but surely, and truly, I believe she knows I love Gracie and our baby and would never do anything to intentionally hurt them.

"She looks happy," Jamie comments as we watch Gracie hug everyone who has come to the baby shower.

I turn and look at Jamie. "I hope she is."

Jamie sighs and leans against the wall. "I know she is, but it's the first time I've seen her look content, peaceful."

I smile, realizing she's right. There's a peace that surrounds her.

"You look happy too," I remark. We've tiptoed for months around the topic of her and Aaron. The night they left our condo, Aaron didn't return until the next day and they've been inseparable ever since.

She rolls her eyes and shrugs. "I'm all right." She's so full of it. She and Aaron are very much on the expedited relationship path

Gracie and I were on, minus the surprise pregnancy. He bought a condo in SoHo and she moved right in. She still has her place on the East Side, but I've heard Aaron mention her possibly selling it. No sense in maintaining a property that isn't being used. I chuckle, knowing that my brother is happy and has someone like Jamie to keep him in line.

"I have another surprise for her," I whisper to Jamie.

Jamie groans. "You better not propose to her here," she mumbles under her breath. "Way too cheesy."

I huff out a laugh. "I'm not going to propose to her here." However, I am going to propose to her, and soon. I have the ring, I'm just waiting for the right time. I don't want elaborate and over the top, though, because that's not Gracie. I want intimate and simple, like her.

"Aaron is at JFK, picking up Gracie's mom and should be here in the next few minutes." I glance at my watch. "The plane should have landed over an hour ago, so I expect them soon."

"What?" Jamie snaps her head and looks at me, her eyes wide in surprise. "You got her mom to come visit her?"

I was surprised as hell too. After Gracie called her mom and told her our baby news, she wanted to take a trip back to Montana. Only with the weather turning from fall to winter and the unpredictability of flights due to bad weather, she thought it'd be better to wait until summer to visit Montana.

Jennifer is very much like Gracie with her travel anxiety and was hesitant to travel to New York City. I convinced her we'd have someone guide her every step of the way and that Aaron would be waiting for her after she got off the plane. For anyone, New York City is intimidating. For someone who's never left small-town Montana, New York City is downright daunting. When I told her about the baby shower, and promised her a first-class ticket, she agreed to the visit—and we decided to keep it a secret from Gracie.

In lieu of gifts, because I know Gracie would have thought it was "too much" to expect from her co-workers, everyone chipped in for a diaper delivery service. I, of course, had never heard of this, but apparently, this is something that's a godsend for new parents. Diapers are delivered on the regular; you just pick the size and they show up at your door. Sounds fucking brilliant and seems reasonable and hard to argue with, because all I hear about is how much babies eat, sleep, and shit. yet, I couldn't be more excited for it all.

"They're here," I whisper when my phone buzzes with Aaron's text message telling me they're on their way up. I nod at Sue, who's been in on the surprise and helping me with all the details.

"Can I have everyone's attention?" Sue says loudly, getting the room to quiet down. "Gracie," she reaches for Gracie's hand, "we couldn't be more excited for you and Andrew, and we cannot wait to meet your baby. We've taken a poll to see what everyone thinks you're having, and overwhelmingly, we think it's a girl." Sue points to a poster board on the wall with a stork that's covered in blue or pink stickers. Only two of them are blue.

Of course, Gracie didn't want to find out the sex of the baby early. She said it's the only real surprise in life. So we're waiting. All we want is a healthy, happy baby.

Rubbing her belly, Gracie smiles before saying, "A girl, huh?" She's fucking beautiful with her round belly carrying our baby.

"Do you have names picked out?" Eddie asks.

"We have a few. Nothing has been agreed upon yet." She glances at me pointedly, and I roll my eyes. We've gone in circles discussing names and haven't narrowed it down just yet.

Aaron enters the conference room and winks at Jamie before nodding at me.

"Grace," I call her name and she turns her attention to me. "I have a surprise for you."

She grumbles and twists her lips into a smirk. "You know I hate surprises."

"I think you're going to like this one." I grin widely, and she walks over to me. I place my hands on her shoulders while Aaron guides her mom into the conference room. He positions her behind Gracie so she can't see her yet. "You know there are very few things more important than family, right?"

"Of course," she answers quietly.

"Turn around."

She turns slowly, her eyes scanning the room. When they land on Jennifer, everyone in the room can hear her gasp.

"Mom?" she says, getting emotional. It's been years since she's seen her mom, and I knew this would be the only meaningful gift I could give her.

"Gracie," her mom says, tears rolling down her cheeks. Gracie definitely gets her looks from her mom. Jennifer stands a few inches shorter than Gracie, but they share the same hair and eye color.

Gracie lunges as gracefully as she can into her mom's arms, where the two women embrace for what seems like hours. The room is buzzing with excitement and the look on Grace's face tells me there was no better gift she could have received.

"I can't believe you have a driver," Jennifer says as we slide into the back of Tony's Town Car that sits in the same spot it has every day since I bought Williams Global. I know having a driver is a luxury most don't have, so I appreciate Jennifer's exuberance.

"We don't have him full-time," Gracie explains.

We did, until Gracie told me we need to be more like "normal" people and take cabs and trains and walk. Of course, Tony is always available to us. I know we'll use him more once the baby comes, but to appease Gracie, we cab it places from time to time.

Gracie reaches out for her mom's hand. "Do you feel like going out for dinner or staying in?"

"In, if that's okay. I'm tired tonight." You can see the exhaustion on Jennifer's face. I'm sure the anxiety of traveling on a plane for the first time and the overwhelming atmosphere of New York City has her beat. We'll take her out another night since she's staying with us for a week.

Of course, Jennifer is staying with us at the condo. There is no way I could put her up in a hotel in New York City. Tony delivered all of Jennifer's luggage to the condo while we celebrated at the office. I can tell all of this is overwhelming to Jennifer as I'm sure it was to Gracie when she first moved here.

Gracie smiles understandingly. "I'm always tired. Drew has a list of restaurants on speed dial. Pick your poison: Italian, pizza, Thai, Indian, Mexican—"

"New York pizza," Jennifer says quickly, and we all laugh.

"New York pizza it is," I tell her. She reminds me so much of Grace, easy to please.

Tony delivers us to the condo and Gracie gets her mom set up in one of the guest rooms before showing her around the place. She's as overwhelmed by the condo as Gracie was at first, but I can tell she's happy that Gracie is comfortable here. So am I.

I order pizza and salads and get the table set. The women join me in the kitchen and Jennifer pulls me into a hug. "Thank you for taking such good care of her." Her eyes are misty and her cheeks are flushed.

"I always will," I tell her and release her. She's smiles knowingly.

Our pizza arrives and we eat and laugh and I can't help but smile as the two of them share stories and reconnect. Visiting in person is always better than over the phone, and I can't help but admire the striking resemblance between Jennifer and Gracie. The dark hair, the hazel eyes, the slightly crooked smile. My heart is content knowing how happy Gracie is having her mom here with us.

I clean up while Gracie gets her mom settled in the guest room for the night. She shows her how to work the shower and how to make coffee in the morning if she's up before us. Apparently, Jennifer is an early riser.

Just as I finish loading the dishes in the dishwasher and putting the leftover pizza in the refrigerator, I feel two arms wrap around my waist from behind.

"Thank you." She sighs, her cheek pressed to my back. "Best surprise ever."

I twist in her arms so I'm facing her and press a kiss to her soft lips. "You're welcome." Reaching over, I shut off the kitchen lights and guide Gracie down the hallway to our bedroom.

She changes and disappears into the bathroom to brush her teeth and wash her face. When she finally emerges from behind the door, she looks more beautiful than I've ever seen her. Her dark hair is all twisted on top on top of her head and her satin nightie hugging all of her curves. This is when she's most beautiful.

"Come here." I reach for her hand and pull her out the French doors onto the terrace. Under the stars, hidden by the city lights of New York City, I pull Gracie into my arms.

"What are we doing? It's freezing out here." She laughs, wrapping her arms around my neck.

My stomach twists in anticipation and my heart races in excitement. "Gracie Lynn Morgan," I pause, my throat tightening up. From the day I saw Gracie sitting in that bar, I knew I had to have her. Our love story isn't typical, but it's ours and I wouldn't change a thing.

As we move into the next chapter of our lives, I can't wait to show her what kind of father I'm going to be. The best kind, the kind that will do anything for his family. "There is nothing in this world that I love more than you and that little peanut you're growing in your belly." I reach for her arms and unwrap them from my neck. Pulling the little velvet box from my pocket, I drop to one knee before her and look up into the most beautiful hazel eyes I've ever seen. "Marry me? Love me for the rest of your life."

Her hands shake as she covers her mouth in surprise and nods frantically. "Yes! Yes!" she cries and laughs, dropping to her knees in front of me.

I open the ring box and pull out a two-carat princess-cut diamond wrapped in a vintage white gold band. I pull the ring from the box and slide it onto her ring finger. This is how I want our life to be: happy, peaceful, and simple. Just like Grace.

ALSO BY REBECCA SHEA

Unbreakable Series

Unbreakable

Undone

Unforgiven

Bound & Broken Series

Broken by Lies

Bound by Lies

Betrayed by Lies

Standalone Titles

Dare Me

Fault Lines

Hollywood Chronicles

co-written with A.L. Jackson

One Wild Night

One Wild Ride

CONNECT WITH REBECCA SHEA

Website
www.rebeccasheaauthor.com

Sign up for Rebecca Shea's newsletter
http://tinyurl.com/h8mfya2

Sign up for Rebecca Shea's new release and sale alerts
http://www.subscribepage.com/j1m3c5

Follow Rebecca Shea on Facebook:
www.facebook.com/rebeccasheaauthor

Follow Rebecca Shea on Twitter:
@beccasheaauthor

Follow Rebecca Shea on Instagram:
https://www.instagram.com/rebeccasheaauthor/

Join Rebecca Shea's Reader Group on Facebook:
https://www.facebook.com/groups/527432567356595/

Email: rebeccasheaauthor@gmail.com